"Keep your distance," Marguerite hissed, "or I warn you, I shall scream."

Jack lunged for her, pulling her close against his body so that she could not strike him, and clamped his large hand across her mouth.

"You waited too long, ma'am. Don't be afraid. I will let you go, but only if you promise not to scream. And if you tell me what you have done to Herr Benn."

She responded by sinking her teeth into the fleshy part of his thumb.

"Argh!" he gasped, instinctively pulling his hand away. She was still pressed firmly to his chest, but she was opening her mouth to scream at the top of her lungs.

There was no help for it. He kissed her.

* * *

His Forbidden Liaison
Harlequin® Historical #944—May 2009

The Aikenhead Honors
Three gentlemen spies: bound by duty, undone by women!

Introducing three of England's most eligible bachelors:
Dominic, Leo and Jack
code-named Ace, King, Knave

Together they are

The Aikenhead Honors
A government-sponsored spying ring, they risk their lives, and
hearts, to keep Regency England safe!

Follow these three brothers on a dazzling journey through
Europe and beyond as they serve their country and meet their
brides, in often very surprising circumstances!

Meet the "Ace," Dominic Aikenhead, Duke of Calder, in

HIS CAVALRY LADY

Meet the "King" and renowned rake, Lord Leo Aikenhead, in

HIS RELUCTANT MISTRESS

Meet the "Knave" and incorrigible playboy,
Lord Jack Aikenhead, in

HIS FORBIDDEN LIAISON

**Look for Ben's eBook story in
Harlequin Historical Undone!
Coming soon.**

Joanna Maitland

His Forbidden Liaison

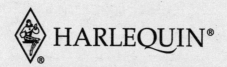

HARLEQUIN®

TORONTO • NEW YORK • LONDON
AMSTERDAM • PARIS • SYDNEY • HAMBURG
STOCKHOLM • ATHENS • TOKYO • MILAN • MADRID
PRAGUE • WARSAW • BUDAPEST • AUCKLAND

Recycling programs
for this product may
not exist in your area.

ISBN-13: 978-0-373-29544-9
ISBN-10:   0-373-29544-8

HIS FORBIDDEN LIAISON

First North American Publication 2009

www.eHarlequin.com

Printed in U.S.A.

Dear Reader,

I'm delighted to be able to introduce this third story in THE AIKENHEAD HONORS trilogy. It was a joy to write these stories, not only because I fell in love with every hero in my band of spies, but also because I could show you some of my favorite places, such as St. Petersburg and Vienna and medieval Marseilles and Lyons. Each city is so full of history and romance that it almost oozes from between the stones.

In Dominic's story—*His Cavalry Lady*—you see some of Russia, and meet a heroine who serves as a man in the tsar's cavalry. In Leo's story—*His Reluctant Mistress*—you see Vienna in the golden autumn of 1814 and meet a heroine with the most beautiful singing voice in Europe. In this story—*His Forbidden Liaison*—Jack is under cover, spying in France after Napoleon's return from exile in Elba, and relying on the help of a beautiful French silk weaver who has secrets of her own.

I originally intended to write only three books, but THE AIKENHEAD HONORS has four members, and Ben is insisting on having his own story. So this is now to be a trilogy in *four* parts! Ben's story—*Her Silken Seduction*—will be appearing soon as an eBook, in Harlequin's UNDONE!

His Forbidden Liaison is a milestone for me—my tenth book for Harlequin Mills & Boon. But writing ten books pales into insignificance compared to Harlequin's sixty years in the publishing business. Harlequin has given so much pleasure to so many readers over all these years. Congratulations! And long may it continue!

Joanna

DON'T MISS THESE OTHER
NOVELS AVAILABLE NOW:

#943 THE DIAMONDS OF WELBOURNE MANOR—
Diane Gaston, Deb Marlowe, Amanda McCabe

Welcome to Welbourne Manor! In this lush family home a
Regency house party is in full swing. Join three beautiful sisters,
Justine, Annalise and Charlotte, as they each discover something
more precious than diamonds—husbands!

#945 THE CATTLEMAN'S UNSUITABLE WIFE—
Pam Crooks

Ruthless Montana rancher Trey Wells has never met a woman
who ignites his passion so much as exotic beauty Zurina Vasco.
Despite all that separates them, can Trey give Zurina the love,
respectability and true home she deserves?

#946 THE BORDER LORD—Sophia James

Laird Lachlan Kerr knows the safety of his home depends on his
betrothal to Grace Stanton, but their passionate embraces are an
unexpected pleasure! Lach is used to betrayal at every turn, but
Grace's faith in him is powerfully seductive....

Chapter One

'You still look a bit groggy,' Ben murmured.

Jack shook his head. Now that he was safely on dry land again, he would soon recover from his confounded seasickness. More important was to stop Ben from betraying them, before their mission had even begun. Jack risked a quick glance over his shoulder. The port of Marseilles was crowded with people, but no one was close enough to have overheard Ben's unwary use of English.

Jack dropped an arm around Ben's shoulders, for all the world as if he needed his friend's support for his shaky legs. 'No English,' he hissed into Ben's ear. Then, switching to French, he began to bemoan the state of his health in a voice that was loud enough to be heard by anyone within twenty yards. Jack's French, learnt from his French mama, the Dowager Duchess of Calder, was flawless. He was able to pass for a Parisian without any trouble. Whereas Ben's French, though pretty fluent, had a definite foreign accent that might make him suspect. To avoid that, they had agreed, before leaving Vienna, that Ben would pretend to be a German.

It was still a hugely dangerous mission that the Duke of

Wellington had given to these two members of the Aikenhead Honours spying band. From Marseilles on the Mediterranean coast, Jack and Ben were to travel slowly north to Paris and thence to Calais, gathering information as they went about the extent of rebellious feeling in the country. Wellington was very concerned that the restored French King's harsh rule was provoking unrest, especially among ex-members of the army. He needed to know just how many Frenchmen would be ready to agitate for Bonaparte's return and where rebellion was most likely to occur. In Wellington's view, the strip of water dividing France from the island of Elba, Bonaparte's place of exile, was not nearly wide enough.

Jack slumped down on to a bollard by the water's edge. His legs really were wobbly. Why on earth was he, alone among the Aikenhead Honours, cursed with seasickness? Ben looked much frailer than Jack, but he had not had a moment's unease during their voyage. Jack—broader, heavier and much more robust in appearance—had collapsed almost before the ship had left Genoa harbour. It was shaming.

A barefoot sailor scampered nimbly down the gangplank with a valise in each hand. Spying the two young passengers who had been so generous to the crew during their voyage, he hurried along the quayside and deposited the bags at Jack's feet. Jack looked up. The sailor was waiting expectantly.

'Give the man some money, Benn,' Jack said, in French, using the *nom de guerre* they had been using since leaving Vienna. Ben, Baron Dexter, had become Herr Christian Benn and Lord Jack Aikenhead had become Mr Louis Jacques.

Ben dug into his pocket. 'I have no French francs,' he said, in French, staring down at the coins in his hand. 'But you might not want those anyway, I suppose.' He picked out a silver coin from Genoa and offered it to the sailor, who grinned and tested it with his few remaining teeth.

'Thank ye, sir,' the sailor said, and pocketed it before running back on board.

'Good,' Jack said in a low voice. 'I think we carried that off well enough. But now we must be doubly careful. All the crew on the ship were Italians. They had no way of knowing whether you were a Frenchman or not. But here, many ears will be listening. Take care.'

Ben nodded. 'If I think there is danger, I can always pretend to be mute.'

'Good idea,' Jack said, rising to his feet. His legs were feeling stronger now. He should be able to walk more or less normally. 'If needs must, you shall be my slow-witted travelling companion, who can barely speak and who needs me to look after him as we travel.' Jack grinned. 'Actually, that seems remarkably appropriate in the circumstances, don't you think?'

Ben grinned back and threw a mock punch at Jack's midriff, though they both knew that Jack was much too quick on his feet to be caught.

Jack sidestepped neatly. 'My dear Herr Benn,' he said, 'you will have to do better than that if you are to catch me. And now, as you are the junior partner in this enterprise, and also the one who is touched in the upper works, I suggest you pick up the bags and bring them.'

Ben spluttered a protest, but he was too late. Jack was already striding off past the Hôtel de Ville in the direction of one of the harbour inns. Ben had no choice but to pick up both their bags and follow.

After twenty yards, Jack stopped, turned and waited for his friend. Ben was not used to acting the servant. Back home in England, as heir to his grandfather, Viscount Hoarwithy, he was used to being waited on hand and foot. That would not be possible here in France, for they had both left their servants in Vienna. It was too dangerous to do otherwise. On the road to Genoa, they had relied on inn servants, but here in France, they might well have to shift for themselves. It would be only fair to break Ben in gently to the new routine.

Jack waited until Ben came level with him. He reached for his valise, but this time, Ben was too quick for him. He threw the valise at Jack, catching him on the shoulder. 'Servant, indeed!' Ben muttered. 'You, sir, are riding for a fall.'

With a wry smile, Jack hefted his valise under his injured arm and used his free hand to rub his shoulder. 'I can see that I shall have to be wary of you, my slow-witted friend. Come, then.' He turned to stare up at the harbour inn. 'What think you to this place? Good enough for one night?'

Marguerite Grolier stood in the middle of the floor while her groom and the hired servants stowed her remaining samples and the last of her purchases around the walls. She would barely have room to move, but these supplies were so valuable that she had to have them under her eye, for the future of the Grolier family weaving business depended on them. If any of this was lost or stolen, the whole family would suffer.

She smiled at Guillaume. He was groom, coachman and general factotum to her family, which he had served since before she was born. 'Have the coach ready to leave at first light, please, Guillaume,' she said. 'We will need to pack all this and leave as soon as we can. We must make the most of the daylight.'

Even this far south, darkness fell early in the first days of March. She would not normally have travelled from Lyons at this time of year, but the family could not afford to miss the opportunity of securing an export agent for their silks and velvets. He had been most impressed by the quality of Marguerite's wares and happy to take some to sell in Naples and Rome. Such sales might save their business, Marguerite knew, for the French market had become extremely difficult of late. Before the Revolution, Lyons had had thousands upon thousands of looms, and had provided silk to all the great houses of France, and beyond. But the continuing wars had taken almost all the men and, now that France had been defeated, the people who remained were more concerned about filling their bellies than putting fine clothes upon their backs.

The Grolier business could not afford to upset the few wealthy customers who remained in France. And one of the greatest of those—the Duchess of Courland—was waiting impatiently for the special silk for a court dress. Before this unexpected trip to Marseilles, Marguerite and her sister had been working day and night to finish it in time. As soon as she returned to Lyons, one of them would have to carry it to Paris for the Duchess's approval. The journey would be a huge expense, and Marguerite was only half-convinced that it was sensible, but her sister, Suzanne, maintained that it would be the making of their little business. Once the Duchess of Courland had approved Grolier silk, all the royalist ladies congregating around the restored King Louis XVIII would want to place orders. Marguerite and Suzanne would be able to employ more weavers, and to increase the number of their looms. They would no longer need to worry about having enough money to pay for bread and the medicines for their poor demented mama. They would be able to plan for the future at last.

It was not what they had been brought up to expect—it could never be that—but it might be tolerable.

Marguerite was finding it difficult to sleep, as she always did when she was away from her own bed. She would be very glad to be on the way home to Lyons in the morning. It was the first time that Suzanne had been left to run the household for more than just a day or two, and Marguerite was not sure how well she would have coped. She would have their maid, Berthe, to help her, of course, but Berthe spent much of her time watching over their sick mother, so Suzanne would be responsible for running the weaving shop as well as the house. There was a boy to help with the heavy work while Guillaume was away, but still…

Suzanne was younger and slighter than Marguerite, and she was also used to looking to Marguerite for decisions, and to give instructions to the servants. Would Suzanne be able to overcome her shyness enough to assert her authority when it was needed? Perhaps it would not have been necessary, Marguerite told herself. Suzanne would be able to continue her work at the silk looms unless there were problems with customers, or money. Or with their mother's increasingly unpredictable starts.

Marguerite worried constantly about their mother. She was barely forty-five years old and yet, since the accident, she behaved like an old woman. Sometimes she did not know who or where she was. Sometimes she did not even recognise her own daughters. And yet, at other times, she was almost as lucid and as loving as she had ever been. The problem was that her periods of lucidity were becoming shorter and the episodes of demented behaviour longer and more frequent. Soon, the family would need to watch over her night and day, but there was not enough money to pay another servant to help Berthe. Even with the export sales that might come through the new agent, there would be only just enough to keep the family. The Duchess of Courland's approval was vital. Would Suzanne have been able to finish the Duchess's silk during Marguerite's absence? It was such a slow and laborious business, because of the gold cord that had to be threaded through at intervals and the fineness of the other threads. Even a whole day's weaving seemed to produce only a few more inches of cloth.

Marguerite turned over in bed, trying to find a cool spot on the inn's lumpy pillow. If she had been rich, she would have travelled with her own pillows, and her own linen, as aristocratic ladies had done before the Revolution. As her own mother had done, once, before the family's fortunes had fallen so low. If only Papa—

The heavy silence of the night was broken by a tiny scrabbling sound. A mouse, perhaps? Marguerite pulled the blankets more closely around her shoulders and listened hard. There it was again! But it was not coming from floor level, surely? It seemed to be coming from somewhere near the door, and quite high up.

She concentrated all her senses on the door to her chamber, straining her eyes as if, by willpower alone, she could force them to see in the blackness. Yes, the noise was still there, and getting a little louder, too. Someone was trying to enter her chamber!

Oh, where was Guillaume? Why had she not insisted he remain on guard outside her door? *Because he needs to be rested enough to drive the coach in the morning,* her sensible self reminded her. Even on the edge of panic, with an intruder—perhaps even a rapist—at her door, her sensible inner voice would not allow itself to be overwhelmed.

If there is an intruder, he will almost certainly be a thief, come to steal the silks and velvets. Many people must have seen what we were carrying in the coach and how valuable it is. I should have expected this.

And I will deal with it!

Very quietly, Marguerite slipped out of bed and donned the wrapper she had left lying across the end of the bed. Now that she was fully awake, she could actually make out the shapes of the furniture in the room. She looked around for a weapon. Yes, there! She seized the tall brass candlestick from the dressing table. Its weight was comforting.

She crept across the floor to stand behind the door. If he forced his way in, she would fell him with the candlestick before he had gone even a yard.

The noise outside was getting louder and louder. Did the intruder assume, because Marguerite had not screamed, that she was cowering in the corner?

She gripped the candlestick even more tightly. She would not cower. If she had had a pistol, she would be ready to shoot him.

There was a loud click. Silence. Had he forced the lock? Marguerite dared to touch her left hand to the handle. She could not see it in the gloom, but she could feel it. It was turning.

Jack was awake and half out of bed before the sound had died away. A woman's scream. He was almost sure of it.

He was tempted to bang on the wall that separated his room from Ben's. But there was no sound of movement from next door. Too much of the landlord's heavy red wine had done its work.

Jack wasted no time. He had to find the woman, who must be in real trouble. But even for that, Jack could not leave his room in his naked state. Where on earth were his breeches?

He could not remember. And in the dark, he could not see them. In desperation, he ripped the sheet off the bed and tied it round his waist. Barefoot, and with no light, he groped for the door, unlocked it by touch alone and flung it open. A glimmer of light! Somewhere further along the narrow corridor.

Then another scream echoed round the wood panelling.

Jack launched himself along the corridor towards the light. Just round the corner of the passage, a bedchamber door stood open. A dark lantern had been set down on the floor just outside.

In the gloom, Jack saw a fair-haired young woman struggling with a dark-clad man. The man was about to overpower her.

'Let her go, you blackguard!'

The man turned his head just enough to see the new danger. Then he swivelled on the spot, dragging the woman with him, and putting her body between himself and Jack.

Jack did not waste any more words. A man who was prepared to use a woman as a shield deserved no quarter. Jack seized the man's nearest arm, and with a degree of sheer brute strength that he had not known he possessed, hauled it off the woman. Then he whipped the arm round and up the man's back, forcing it hard against the shoulder joint. The man screamed with pain. If he continued to resist, his shoulder might be dislocated.

Jack pushed the arm a little higher. That did the trick. The assailant dropped his hold on the woman and tried to use his free arm to fight Jack off.

'Save yourself!' Jack ordered in French. He needed her out of the way, so that he could ensure this man was truly disabled.

She ducked under their flailing arms and scrambled back into the bedchamber. But she did not bar the door. What on earth was the matter with her? Jack could not protect her and deal with the intruder at the same time.

The man was shorter than Jack, but much heavier. He was trying to use his free arm to fight. But Jack was behind him and he still had the man's arm locked against his back. He pushed it even higher. A loud gasp of pain. The villain must yield now, surely?

Jack tried to push the man face-first into the wall, but he continued to struggle. And then he kicked over the lantern. Everything went dark.

Jack swore. Fighting this man in the dark was no easy task, especially as he seemed to be able to ignore the pain of the armlock. He tried to trip Jack's feet from under him, but Jack was wise to that. He had wrestled too often with his brothers. Then suddenly the man used his free hand as leverage to propel his weight backwards into Jack's body. Taken by surprise, Jack staggered, letting go of the armlock. Now he had lost his advantage, and he could see nothing. He heard, though. There was a low growl and a filthy curse. 'I'll have 'ee now,' the voice said.

At that moment, a light flared. The woman appeared in the open doorway, holding a tiny candle high with her left hand.

Jack saw the scene like a *tableau vivant*, his attacker crouching, ready to spring, and now with a small, wicked knife in one hand. Behind him, in the doorway, stood the woman in a pale wrapper, the light held high in one hand and a brass candlestick in the other, her bare feet planted firmly on the wooden boards.

Jack took a defensive stance, waiting. In the flickering light, his assailant's advantage was lessened, but he still had that knife.

The man risked a quick glance over his shoulder towards the light. He saw the woman, the light and the candlestick, and for a moment, his attention wavered. Now was Jack's chance. He launched himself at the man, determined to wrest the knife from his grasp. He grabbed the man's wrist with one hand, and his neck with the other, trying to half-throttle him to make him drop the knife.

It took only a second. The man groaned and collapsed in a heap on the floor. The knife clattered against the wall and was still.

Jack gasped in relief. 'Thank God!' He had never known any man to succumb so quickly. He threw himself to his knees and pinioned both the man's arms behind his back.

The woman's bare feet edged a step nearer. Out of the corner of his eye, Jack registered that they were small and fine-boned. He looked up. Even in the half-light, she was very pretty, with a mass of fair curly hair and delicate features. Jack found himself trying to judge the colour of her eyes. Madness! This was no time for such idiocy.

The woman had put the candlestick on the floor and was undoing the belt of her wrapper. 'Perhaps you would tie him up?' She offered it to Jack.

He took it, suddenly conscious of the fact that she now had to hold her wrapper closed with her free hand. What glories was she concealing underneath? He remained stock still for a moment, his mind full of lustful imaginings.

'Sir?'

Her slightly testy tone brought him back to earth with a jolt. She had every reason to be cross. His behaviour was inexcusable. He hurriedly used the belt to tie the assailant's arms behind his back, making sure the knot was good and tight. The man would have severely bruised wrists, to add to his damaged shoulder, which was little enough by way of punishment for such a dastardly attack.

Jack had himself back under control by the time he stood up, though he was increasingly conscious of his half-naked state. It was no way to appear in front of a lady. And this fair-haired girl was definitely a lady.

'It is generally best, ma'am,' he said seriously, 'to keep your bedchamber door locked when travelling.' The implication was clear. She had put herself in danger, and unnecessarily.

'And I would do so, sir, but it is a little difficult at present.' She picked up the candlestick, took a step backwards into the room and gestured at the floor. There was another body lying there.

'You did that, ma'am?' he said in wonderment. She had taken on two assailants, at least one of them armed, and she with only a candlestick? This lady was an Amazon.

She nodded, weighing her candlestick in her hand. 'I hit him very hard. I hope I have not killed him.' There was a slight tremor in her voice. 'But I was alone, and afraid.'

Jack knelt by the second man and checked for a pulse. It was there, and surprisingly strong, considering what had been done to him. Jack rose to his feet. 'Have no fear, ma'am, he is alive.'

She smiled then, for the first time. Even in the relative gloom, he could see that it lit up her face and her eyes. But he still could not make out their colour.

'Do you have something else we can use to tie this one up? I have nothing, I'm afraid.' He gestured towards his makeshift attire.

She gave a low laugh. 'I should prefer if you did not remove your sheet for that purpose, sir.' She turned back into her chamber.

Jack took a step after her to find that the room was piled with packages. He watched as the woman ripped one open and took out some material. It shimmered as it caught the faint light from the candle. There was a ripping noise, loud in the sudden silence.

'Here.' She offered him the piece she had torn off. 'It's silk. Stronger than the best rope. It will certainly hold him.'

Jack took the delicate fabric and began to twist it. Yes, it was strong, but it also felt wonderful against his skin, slippery, soft, sensuous. It was the sort of fabric that should embrace a beautiful woman, not tie up a ruffian. But it was all they had, and he used it. Then he hauled the body over the threshold and dumped it in the corridor.

'Thank you, sir.' She was making to shut the door on him.

He held up a hand. 'A moment, ma'am. Would you be so good as to tell me what happened? I cannot understand why you would have opened your door to such villains.'

She frowned, possibly a little crossly. 'It would require a

complete ninny, sir, to do such a thing without cause. Those men were trying to break into my room, to steal my goods, I imagine.' She gestured to the piles of parcels. 'I had a choice. To lie in my bed and wait to be robbed, even murdered. Or to confront them on my terms.' She raised the candlestick. 'Would you have had me do otherwise?'

Jack was not absolutely sure, but he thought her eyes might have flashed with anger as she spoke. His Amazon was certainly challenging him. He had been wrong about her, and he would have to apologise. 'Your reactions were admirable, ma'am, and very courageous. If I have seemed to suggest anything else, I apologise.'

She softened a little then. Jack could see it in the slight relaxation of her shoulders. And she lowered the candlestick, too.

He peered past her into the room. 'You have no maid, ma'am?'

She shook her head. 'A manservant only. He sleeps in the carriage.'

'It might be safer to have him sleep outside your door.'

She seemed to consider that for a moment. 'You may be right, sir. I will remember your advice. And now, if I may impose on you a little more, I should be most grateful if you would arrange for these two would-be thieves to be taken to the authorities.'

He could not leave them as they were. Since only their hands were tied, there was a danger they might escape. 'Might I have two more pieces of your silk, ma'am? I think their legs need to be bound while I go for the constable.' He knelt once more by the two unconscious bodies.

At that moment, the knife man groaned. 'I should have hit him harder,' she said, before turning away to fetch more silk.

Jack sat back on his heels. So much for his choke-hold. He

owed his deliverance from the knife, not to his own quick wits and fighting skills, but to a brave Frenchwoman and a brass candlestick.

Chapter Two

Ben dropped his valise, groaned and put a hand to his head. Even the weak spring sunshine must be too strong for him, for he was trying to shade his eyes.

'Don't expect any sympathy from me, Ben,' Jack said. 'In this part of the world, the wine is remarkably strong and pure hangover juice. It's nothing like the fine champagnes we were served in Vienna.'

Ben groaned again. 'I'll know better next time.'

'And perhaps, next time, you'll be awake enough to help. If that Frenchwoman hadn't been so handy with her candlestick, I could have been sliced up like a prime ham.' He smiled softly to himself at the memory of his Amazon. A pity they'd had to leave the inn so early. He would have welcomed a chance to see her again, if only to ask after her well-being. And finally to see the colour of her eyes! 'That ruffian certainly meant business,' he added, forcing himself to put the fair Frenchwoman from his thoughts.

'Yes, I'm sorry. What will happen now? You don't have to stay to give evidence against those fellows, do you?'

Jack shook his head. 'No. The innkeeper is used to such

starts, it seems. He said he would deal with them. No need for me, or the lady, to remain. I must say I am glad of it. If I'd had to give evidence against those two, I might have been forced to say more than is wise. Indeed, I think it's best if we leave Marseilles immediately.' He bent to pick up Ben's valise as well as his own. He might not offer words of sympathy, but he could provide practical help for his friend's pounding head.

'But aren't we supposed to find out about the Bonapartists in Marseilles? Wellington suspected—'

'And he was right. I went out on to the quay earlier, while you were still snoring.' He grinned wickedly and started slowly along the harbour side. 'There's lots of talk about the Emperor and how he promised to return with the violets. Lots of treasonous muttering against King Louis, too. Must say I was surprised at how open it was. They knew I was near enough to overhear, but they didn't bother to lower their voices.'

'Sounds bad.'

'Yes. There are always troublemakers on any dockside, even at home, but Englishmen would have taken care not to be overheard. I had the impression that these Frenchmen are beyond caring, that they see Bonaparte as a last, desperate hope.'

Ben shook his head and made a noise in his throat.

Jack could not be sure if the moan was a result of Ben's hangover or his concern about the risks of rebellion. 'Best if we make our way to the coaching inn. There must be some kind of *diligence* to take us north, especially this early in the day. And if the coach is full of passengers, we may glean some useful information by listening to what they have to say. You'd be best to go back to being mute, I suppose.'

Ben nodded. They both knew it was safer that way.

'Never mind, old fellow.' Jack grinned suddenly. 'Shouldn't be for long, and then—'

'It doesn't matter.' Ben leant across to take his bag from Jack's hand. 'It's for the mission, remember?'

'Ah, good. You're feeling better.'

Ben nodded again. This time he smiled. 'Let's go.'

They quickened their pace along the side of the harbour. The ship that had brought them from Genoa was still lying at anchor, waiting for the tide. Her decks were swarming with Italian sailors. One or two of them shouted a greeting. Jack waved a hand, but did not pause. There was too much to do. 'We should be able to—'

A loud shout stopped them in their tracks. Jack spun on his heel. A group of burly men had appeared from the inn where they had lodged overnight. Two of them had dirty grey bandages round their heads, and they were pointing at Jack and Ben. Jack gasped. 'Those are the two ruffians from last night.'

Ben looked back. 'The men with them don't look anything like constables, either.'

As they watched, the group of Frenchmen split into two. The two bandaged men remained by the inn door, but their fellows were striding up the quayside towards Jack and Ben. A sudden shaft of watery sunlight caught the gleam of knife blades against dark clothing.

'Dear God! The landlord must have been in league with them, and now they're after us. I don't like the odds, with five of them and two of us.'

'We'd better run for it.' Valise in hand, Ben started for the end of the harbour.

'You go on. I'll follow.' Jack was digging into his pocket as Ben took to his heels. Then he yelled at the sailors on the Genoese ship. 'Hey, you fellows! This is for you, with our thanks.' He flung the handful of coins high in the air, right into the path of their pursuers. Without waiting to see the reaction from the ship, he turned and hared after Ben.

Behind him, Jack heard shouts in a mixture of languages. The sailors must be scrambling on to the quayside and fighting the Frenchmen for the coins. He and Ben had time to escape. They would—

Ahead of him, Ben had stopped and turned, foolishly waiting for Jack to catch up with him. A moment later, the sharp crack of a pistol echoed round the harbour. Ben cried out and fell to the ground. He had been shot!

In seconds, Jack had caught up with Ben and was hauling him back to his feet. He was conscious, though very pale. He had dropped his valise and was clutching at his shoulder. Jack put an arm round his waist. 'Come on. Let me take your weight. We can get away.'

Ben gritted his teeth and did his best to run.

'I will mind the horses, Guillaume, if you fetch the provisions.'

'But, mistress, it's not safe to leave you here alone with the coach and all the silk. You know what happened last night.'

Marguerite shook her head. 'It will not happen again. Look.' She took a step forward so that the folds of her skirt moved. They had been concealing her hand, and the pistol she had taken from the coach. 'No one will try anything. If anyone should accost me, I will shoot him. Now, fetch the provisions, Guillaume, and be as quick as you can. We will have precious little time to stop on the road, and even you cannot manage without food.'

He nodded and hurried across the Place du Cul de Boeuf to the baker's on the corner of the Canebière, the long, wide street leading up from the port to the main part of the city.

Marguerite sighed and buried the pistol more deeply among her skirts. She refused to be afraid, even though they were still all too close to the port and the ruffians who frequented it. Last night had been dangerous, terrifying even, but it had been her own fault for sleeping without a guard. She would not make such a mistake again. On another occasion, she might not be lucky enough to have a gentleman come to her aid. He had been most courageous, launching himself into the fray with no thought for his own safety. And covered by only a thin bed sheet, to boot! She should have been embarrassed, of course, but she had been too intent on dealing with the attackers.

Now she remembered that her rescuer's naked torso had seemed shapely and well muscled, like a classical statue. She fancied his hair had been dark. And he was tall, too. But what she remembered most clearly was his voice, its strong, rich tone inspiring confidence and helping her to overcome her terror. She would treasure the memory of that voice.

It was a pity she had not had a chance to thank him properly, or even to ask his name. Everything had happened so quickly. As soon as both men were securely bound, he had disappeared to arrange for them to be taken to gaol. Marguerite had been left alone to sleep, if she could. And she had, soothed by the memory of that remarkable voice.

This morning she had rid herself of such missish fancies. As a matter of courtesy, she would have liked to seek him out, but it had been much too early. She had not left a note. How could she, for a man with no name? But she now felt more than a little guilty. It was a breach of good manners to have failed to thank him. If she ever saw him again, she would remedy that, but the chances were extremely slim. She walked thoughtfully to the leader's head and raised her free hand to stroke his neck.

And then she heard the sound of running feet.

She tightened her hold on the butt of the pistol, and turned. Two men had rounded the corner from the Quai du Port. One, a fair-haired stranger, was leaning heavily on his darker fellow. Why, it was the gentleman who had come to her rescue just hours before! She stepped quickly away from the horses. What was happening? What should she do? The men looked to be in some distress. The fair-haired one seemed to be struggling to stay upright. Without the support of his friend, he would probably have fallen to the ground.

Marguerite knew she had to help her rescuer as he had helped her. It was a matter of honour. She owed him. She hurried forward, still gripping the pistol. 'Sir, what is the matter?'

'My friend has been shot,' the darker man gasped, 'by a gang of villains. They are just behind us.'

Marguerite did not hesitate. 'Quickly. Inside my coach.' She ran forward to fling open the door, scrambled inside and began throwing most of the parcels of silk to one side. 'Lay him here.' She pointed to the floor where the seat had been removed to make room for her stores.

The two men did not speak. They simply acted. The dark man threw his valise into the corner of the coach, then half-pushed, half-lifted his injured fellow into the space Marguerite had cleared. In seconds, he was lying on a bed of packaged silk.

'You, too.' She gestured urgently. There was room for both of them.

The dark man nodded and lay alongside his fellow.

Marguerite quickly heaped all the remaining packages on top of them. It was a ramshackle pile, but there was nothing to betray what was hidden underneath it. She jumped quickly to the ground and closed the door at her back. She took a deep breath, looking round. There was no one, yet, but she could hear running feet again. And this time, there were more of them. She swallowed hard, pushed the pistol more deeply within her skirts and straightened her shoulders.

She was about to move back to the horses' heads when she noticed a bloodstain on the ground by her foot. Dear God, that would give them away! She moved to cover as much of the stain as possible with her boot, hoping the shadow of her long skirt would hide the rest. Provided she did not move—and she had no intention of doing so—the blood would not be seen. Guillaume would return soon, and then there would be two of them to outface whatever scoundrel was prepared to shoot an unarmed man in broad daylight.

She did not have long to wait. Barely seconds after she had hidden the bloodstain, five dirty and sinister-looking Frenchmen rounded the corner at a run and skittered to a stop, one of them slipping on the gravelly surface of the square. They were all looking about them suspiciously, clearly wondering where their quarry had gone. She heard disjointed words in the local thieves' cant. She did not understand them all, but enough to make clear that the two fugitives were in real danger. As was she, for hiding them!

She pulled herself up to her full height and stared proudly at them. But if she had hoped to frighten them off, she was mistaken. Two of them muttered in low voices and then came towards her. One was openly carrying a knife.

Marguerite continued to stare loftily at them. She did not dare to move from the bloodstained spot. And she would not show fear. She had learnt that only a few hours ago. 'Put that thing away,' she snapped.

The knifeman stopped dead and stared at her. Then, looking suddenly a little sheepish, he tucked the knife into his boot.

Marguerite waited. She had had one small victory, but there were still five of them, five men against one woman. The pistol, hard against her leg, provided some reassurance. If either of these two tried to assault her, she would shoot him.

'We be looking for two men. Fugitives,' the knifeman said,

forcing a false smile. 'They came this way, mistress. Did you see where they went?'

'Two men?' Marguerite raised her eyebrows.

'Aye,' said the second man. 'One dark, one fair. The fair one would be limping, and bleeding. He was shot.'

'Shot?' Marguerite put as much horror as she could into her voice.

'By the constable, mistress. They be wanted, by the law.'

'Aye,' agreed the knifeman. 'We be deputised, by the constable. He's too fat to run.' The second man laughed shortly.

'Ah. Yes, I did see two men, one helping the other. They went into the old town.' She pointed to the maze of squalid streets that opened off the tiny square and ran the entire length of the harbour. 'Over there.'

'Thank ye, mistress.'

'I doubt you'll be able to catch them,' Marguerite said earnestly. 'They were some way ahead of you, and running. And in that labyrinth…' She shrugged her shoulders.

'True, mistress, but we be able to follow the blood trail. The fair one, he was bleeding.' He began to scan the ground for signs.

Marguerite took half a step forward. The bloodstain was completely hidden by her shadow. 'Well, I hope you do, if they are fugitives. But I must tell you that they stopped at the corner, over there, and I think the dark man put a pad on the fair man's wound. So there may be no trail for you to follow.' She raised her hands in the universal gesture of helplessness. 'But if you're quick, you may succeed.'

'Aye,' said the knifeman. 'Come, Jean. We must go.' They both looked across to the narrow street Marguerite had indicated. Then, waving to their accomplices to join them, they trotted off.

Marguerite stood motionless until all five of them had disappeared into the dark and malodorous streets of the oldest quarter of Marseilles.

* * *

Ben was barely half-conscious now. Jack rather wished he would swoon completely, for he was starting to mutter and groan with the pain of his wound. Jack laid a hand gently over Ben's mouth, trying to muffle the sound. If that did not work, he was going to have to hit him, to knock him out. It would be a terrible thing to do to a friend who already had a bullet in him. But he would do it if he had to, to prevent Ben's English moans from betraying them.

Ben gave another long groan and went limp. Thank God, Jack thought. Let him stay that way until they were out of this dangerous coil.

He listened intently. He could hear the woman dealing most adroitly with their pursuers. She was sending them off into the warren of the old city. It was the place where any fugitive would choose to hide, of course, but she had even concocted a story as to why there would be no blood trail to follow. What a woman! Not only was she ready to confront robbers at the dead of night, she was also extremely quick-witted. Jack was not sure he would have done half as well.

He could hear the sound of the men rushing away in pursuit of their phantom quarry. The woman would come back now, and then Jack and Ben would need to find somewhere else to hide. It could not be among the harbour inns, that was for certain, for they had already been betrayed once by that route. Perhaps if—

The carriage door opened. It swayed as someone climbed in. 'Do not move an inch.' It was the lady's voice, soft but strong.

The coach swayed again as the lady took her place on the bench seat.

'Put the provisions on the floor, Guillaume,' she said, in a slightly louder voice, 'and then let us be off. I have had quite enough of this city, full of thieves and vagabonds. Let us show it a clean pair of heels.'

'Yes, miss.' It was a man's voice, an older voice, and it was followed by the sound of the door closing.

'Don't move yet,' she whispered. And then the carriage started forward. She was leaving Marseilles. And she was taking Jack and Ben with her.

Jack did as he was bid, though he worried very much for Ben. He might have lost his senses, but he would still be bleeding. There had not been time to staunch his wound, which needed to be tended. And yet the lady was right to bid them stay concealed, for those blackguards might easily catch up with the coach in the busy streets of Marseilles. And if they did, the consequences could be dire. Two able-bodied men, one of them old, against five armed ruffians.

After some minutes, he felt the coach make a sharp left turn. Peering cautiously out from among the packages, his gaze met the shifting, dappled light of a tree-lined avenue. They must be well away from the harbour now.

The coach picked up speed for a while and Jack breathed more easily. They were leaving the centre of the town. Perhaps now he could—? But then the coach slowed once more, almost to a stop. What now? He tensed, ready to defend Ben.

'Be easy,' she said softly. 'We must go through the Porte d'Aix. I do not expect to be stopped.'

But what if they were? Jack listened intently, trying to make himself as small as possible. He heard a muttered exchange outside. Guillaume must be talking to the guards on the gate. Would they—?

The coach was pulling away again. They were through! Jack continued to lie motionless, however, for he did not know how far they still had to go to leave the city altogether. He took a deep breath. Yes, surely that was the smell of trees, and good moist earth? But he did not stir. He would wait for her to give the word. Gratefully he breathed in the fresh country smells. And then he realised there was something more. It was the smell of the sea.

'Sir, I think it is safe now. We have reached the Aix road. There is nothing here but fields, and the sea beyond.' She was starting to remove the packages of silk that lay on top of them.

Jack sat up and quickly pushed the rest away. The coach was barely a hundred yards from the shore. White-crested waves were beating in to break on the rocks. He felt his stomach heave, but he forced himself to concentrate on their escape. He was in a coach, after all, not a ship. 'You put yourself in grave danger, ma'am.'

She dropped to her knees beside the two of them. 'No more danger than you were in last night, sir. Now, let us see to your friend.'

She was right. For several minutes, they worked together in silence, stripping off Ben's coat and pulling open his shirt to get at the wound. It was high in his shoulder. The shot seemed to have missed the vital organs, but there was no exit wound. It would be necessary to find a surgeon to remove the ball. She lifted her skirt and reached for her petticoat, as if about to tear off a bandage.

'No, ma'am. There is no need. For some reason, I kept hold of my bag.' He nodded towards the battered valise, which lay at a peculiar angle against the far door. He reached for it, pulled out his spare shirt and quickly made it into a pad to apply to Ben's wound. Then he tied the pad in place with a makeshift bandage of his stockings. 'Thank God he fainted.'

The lady nodded. 'Shall we put him on the seat?'

'I think he is probably better there on the floor, among the bales of silk,' Jack said after a moment. 'It would hurt him if we moved him. And, to be frank, it is easier to conceal him there.'

She thought for a moment, but then she nodded again. 'Yes, you are right.' She pushed herself back up on to the seat and took a handkerchief from her reticule to clean the blood from her fingers. Then she looked out of the window. The sea was no longer in sight. 'Guillaume has made good time, even though he does not know what dangerous cargo he carries.' She gave a small, nervous laugh. 'He will berate me when he discovers it, but never mind. I owe it to you, sir. After last night.'

Jack made Ben as comfortable as he could, adding extra parcels of silk to stop him rolling with the movement of the coach. Then he looked up at the lady.

'Pray sit.' She indicated the other half of the bench seat. 'There is no need for you to remain on the floor. Not now.'

'Thank you, ma'am.' Jack ran a nervy hand through his hair. Then he dived into his pocket for a handkerchief to mop his brow and clean his hands. 'I'd wager I look as much of a ruffian as those five.'

'I think not. You, sir, are clearly a gentleman, and they—' She shuddered. 'They were not.'

'No, I—' Jack stopped, thunderstruck, for she had taken a pistol from the seat under her skirts and was calmly returning it to the leather holster by the window. 'A pistol, ma'am?'

'After last night, I was prepared to use it, I may tell you. It was concealed in my skirts all the time I was dealing with those men. It gave me a degree of courage I might not otherwise have had,' she added simply.

'*Madame,*' Jack said, very seriously, trying to bow from his sitting position, 'you have as much courage as any woman I have ever met, and I salute you for it.'

'Thank you.' She would not meet his eyes. 'Thank you, *Mr…?*' She looked up then. Her eyes, he could see at last, were an unusual shade of blue-green, and very wide. As beautiful as the sea. And as easy to drown in. 'I am afraid I do not know your name,' she said quietly.

'Nor I yours, ma'am. My name is Louis Jacques, from Paris.

My poor wounded companion is a German, Christian Benn. I am escorting him to Paris, on behalf of a mutual friend.' Jack cursed inwardly. He had been paying too much attention to the fair Amazon's eyes, and hazarding his mission as a result. He really should have prepared their cover story with much more care. He had assumed, stupidly, that he would never have to go into detail. How wrong could he be! His brothers, Dominic and Leo, would never have been caught out in that way. They always had a plan B, and usually a plan C as well.

Jack resolved to be more prudent in future. And also to tell this lady nothing more. For all he knew, she might be a Bonapartist, in spite of the fact that she had saved them. Indeed, he should have thought of that before. Still, he had told her only his *nom de guerre*, and Ben's. The mention of Paris as their destination was harmless enough. He had given away nothing of importance. He and Ben would be safe, even if she did favour the enemy, but he must say nothing more. She was a remarkable woman, and he might admire her, but he must not trust her. He could not afford to jeopardise his mission for a pair of limpid blue-green eyes.

He plastered what he hoped was a charming smile on his face, and said, in his most confiding voice, 'We are much in your debt, ma'am, and I should be glad to know your name, if you would allow it.'

She seemed to have been taken in by that smile, for she returned it. And hers was genuine. 'My name, sir, is Marguerite Grolier, and I am a weaver from Lyons. Which is where this coach is now going.' She twinkled. 'If you and your companion are bound for Paris, you will have no objection to our route, I take it?'

Chapter Three

The injured German was still lying unconscious on the bales of silk. From time to time, he moaned, but he had not yet opened his eyes. It was probably a mercy, for his pain must be intense.

'I think we should stop soon, Mr Jacques,' Marguerite said, breaking the silence that had held for nearly an hour. After those first few exchanges, when her companion's rich voice had filled her senses, her attempts to converse with him had been politely but firmly rebuffed. He had been unwilling to talk about himself or his companion. It seemed that Mr Jacques's attention was all still on escaping from the danger behind them, even though they had covered quite a distance. However, they had more pressing matters to deal with. The injured man needed a surgeon. 'Marseilles is well behind us, sir, and you are both out of danger now. Those men cannot follow us.' She was trying to sound reassuring.

Mr Jacques frowned in response. But after several moments, he shrugged his shoulders and relaxed just a little. 'No, you are probably right.'

Thank goodness he was seeing reason, and talking to her

at last, though his voice was somehow harsher than before. 'Forgive me, but why were they chasing you in the first place? I am sure they were not what they said. Not constable's men.'

He laughed mirthlessly. 'Of course, you did not see them all on the quayside. I am pretty sure that they were accomplices of the two men who attacked you last night. I am afraid that you and I were more than gullible, ma'am, in taking the landlord's word that your two attackers would be handed over to the authorities. I saw them both standing, free as air, outside the inn. No doubt they were in league with that scurvy landlord. And the other five were their accomplices, waiting for their share of the spoils.'

Marguerite exclaimed in disgust.

'Quite so, ma'am. They all came out of the inn just in time to spot Benn and me, making our way to the *diligence*. Your assailants were too weak to pursue us themselves—I must say you did a good job there, for both their heads were still bandaged—but they pointed me out to their accomplices and set them on to attack us. And then one of them shot Benn.'

'Oh, heavens! So it was all because of me that poor Herr Benn was shot? How dreadful.' She clasped her hands together in an attempt to control her racing pulse. Suddenly, another thought struck her. 'I suppose I should be grateful that the two injured men remained behind, for if they had recognised me, they would surely have suspected that I was hiding you.'

'Aye. And they might have assaulted you again. You and I had the luck of it, this morning. Unfortunately, poor Benn—' he glanced across at the motionless body on the floor '—has suffered grievously, even though he was snoring innocently throughout last night's attack.'

'He has paid for that now, poor man.' Marguerite dropped quickly to her knees and put a gentle hand to Herr Benn's brow. It was damp and hot. She looked back at Mr Jacques.

'We must get a surgeon to him. He has the beginnings of a fever. If the ball is not removed…' Her voice tailed off. They both knew that such a fever could be fatal.

'You are right, ma'am. If it will not inconvenience you too much,' he continued politely, as if he were conversing in some lady's salon, 'we could stop a moment when you change horses so that Benn and I could get down. The post-house landlord might be able to direct me to a surgeon.'

'Let us hope so. It is a blessing that he remains insensible.'

'Aye.' He nodded.

'I…I would be able to keep him so, if you think it wise. I have…I always carry some laudanum in my bag.'

'Do you indeed, ma'am? You astonish me. First a candle-stick, then a pistol, and now a phial of laudanum. You are full of surprises.'

Marguerite felt herself blushing. 'I…I have an invalid mother. I know the value of laudanum. And also its dangers. But sometimes…well, sometimes, it is the only solution.'

'Forgive me, ma'am, I did not mean to suggest—I am sure your phial may well be very useful if we have a need to keep him insensible. I certainly would not wish him to wake while the surgeon is ministering to him.'

'No, of course not. Ah, look.' She pointed out of the window to a bend in the road ahead of them. 'There is Rognac. We should arrive in less than another quarter of an hour. I recall the posting house there was more than adequate when we were travelling south to Marseilles. Let us hope the landlord can direct you to a surgeon.'

'Hmm. The place does look a mite small. But I trust you are right.' He reached down to help her back on to the seat. 'I am sure it would be best if you were not kneeling on the floor when we arrive at Rognac, ma'am, though I do thank you for your care of my companion. And I hope we have not delayed your journey too much. You have been a true Samaritan to us.' He smiled at her then, with real generosity of spirit. It wiped the lines of care from his face and made him look years younger.

His voice might still be hard, but Marguerite felt her heart lift. And without his hand under her arm, she would have staggered as she resumed her seat, for she had suddenly begun to feel strangely dizzy.

Marguerite had refused to leave Rognac. How could she possibly travel on to Lyons before poor Herr Benn had seen a surgeon? He had groaned horribly as he was carried from the coach and into the posting house. Even now, when he was lying on clean sheets in the best bedchamber of the inn, he was still moaning.

Oh, when would Mr Jacques return with the surgeon? Herr Benn's need was becoming ever more desperate. Marguerite soaked her cloth in the bowl of cool water once more. She was just about to lay it across the injured man's forehead when he stirred and half-opened his eyes.

He said something incomprehensible. Not French. German, perhaps? She leant across him and bathed his brow again. His gaze was fixed on a point somewhere beyond her shoulder. She knew he was not seeing her.

He spoke again. 'Mission.' It was very low, but audible enough. *Mission?* Then, 'Wellington. Mission.'

Marguerite stopped dead, the cloth hanging limply from her fingers. Dear God, he was an Englishman and, by the sound of it, a spy! What was she to do?

She forced herself to think. Mr Jacques was a Frenchman, and quite possibly a Bonapartist, as so many were. He had said he was conducting Herr Benn, a German, to Paris. But Herr Benn spoke English, and must surely be a spy. Did Mr Jacques know of it? It was impossible to say. They might be

accomplices, of course, but equally, Herr Benn might be
acting alone. If so, there was a real risk that Mr Jacques
might betray this poor man. And there were certainly Bonapartists a-plenty who would take pleasure in executing an
English spy, especially now that there were so many
rumours, and so many hopes, for the promised return of
their so-called emperor.

She could not take the chance. Mr Jacques's voice and his
touch might have made her senses reel, but her practical self
knew better than to yield to such missish fancies. She might be
wrong—she fervently hoped she was—but she had to work on
the assumption that Mr Jacques and the pretend German were
not fellow-conspirators. She must protect the wounded man.

She looked round wildly. Yes, her valise was here. Guillaume had deposited it in the bedchamber, all the while muttering about the dangers of taking strangers into their carriage.
And he would still have been here, berating her, if he had not
had to return to the yard to see to the safe disposal of the silk.

Marguerite grabbed her valise and scrabbled around in it
until she lighted on the little bottle, wrapped in raw silk to keep
it safe. She mixed a dose of laudanum in the glass from the
night stand. Then she slid an arm under Herr Benn's shoulders and lifted his head. 'Forgive me, sir,' she said softly, 'but
I must do this, for your own safety.'

She put the glass to his lips, but they were stubbornly closed.
Confound it! He must take it. It was the only way to save him.

In that instant, she heard footsteps on the stairs. Mr Jacques
might be returning, or Guillaume. Desperately, she seized
another pillow and pushed it roughly behind the man's head.
She pulled her arm free and pinched his nostrils closed with
her fingers. One second, two seconds, yes! His mouth opened
to take a breath. With a single, swift movement, she tossed
the contents of the glass down his throat, holding his nose until

he swallowed. He gasped for breath, and groaned. But it did go down. It was done.

She settled him back more gently on the pillows, and quickly rinsed out the glass. She was just about to return the bottle to her valise when the door opened. 'Mr Jacques!' she exclaimed. She hid the bottle among her skirts, as she had done the pistol, seemingly hours before. Was she blushing? It seemed it did not matter, for neither Mr Jacques, nor the man who followed him, was looking at her. The new arrival was a surgeon, to judge by his clothing, and by the bag he carried.

'Here is your patient, sir,' Mr Jacques said, gesturing towards the bed. 'And still insensible, thank God. You will be able to do your work without concern about the pain you may cause him.'

The surgeon crossed to the bed, took a cursory look at Herr Benn's wound, and began to unpack the instruments from his bag. 'This will not take long, sir,' he said briskly. 'I shall need a basin, and some bandages, if you would be so good.'

'Yes, of course. Miss Grolier, would you be so kind as to ask the landlord for a clean sheet, or some other cloth that we may use for bandages?'

Marguerite nodded. It sounded as though Mr Jacques was trying to prevent her from witnessing the operation. It was thoughtful of him, though unnecessary, for she was not afraid of the sight of blood. She had assisted at the bleeding of her mother, oftentimes. It had rarely made much difference, though on occasion it had calmed the poor demented lady's ravings.

Marguerite cast a last, cautious glance at Herr Benn. The laudanum seemed to have worked remarkably quickly. His eyes were closed, and he was no longer making any sound. She breathed a sigh of relief.

She hurried out of the room and down the staircase to the entrance hall, where she soon obtained what they needed.

She was determined that she would not be out of that chamber
for a moment longer than she could help. If Herr Benn spoke
again, she needed to be there to hear whatever he might say.
For now there were two potential betrayers: Mr Jacques and
the surgeon. It might fall to her, and her alone, to defend the
English spy.

The surgeon continued to probe into Ben's wound. 'The
ball lies deep.' He grunted as he worked. 'Ah, I have it now.'
A moment later, the ball rattled into the tin basin that Jack was
holding. It was followed by a gush of bright blood. The
surgeon calmly replaced the bloody pad of Jack's shirt and
pressed hard. 'We need those fresh bandages now.'

'Aye.' Jack glanced over his shoulder to the open door.
There had not yet been time. It was but a few minutes since
Miss Grolier had gone downstairs to fetch the bandages. He
looked back at the bed where Ben lay, very still, and almost
as pale as the linen surrounding him. Jack was grateful that
his friend had not come round during the operation, and yet
it worried him that Ben had shown no sign of regaining his
wits since they had left Marseilles. Perhaps Jack had been
wrong in assuming that the wound had damaged no vital
organs? 'He will recover now, sir?' Jack was unable to keep
the anxiety from his voice.

'Yes, with careful nursing. There is a deal of damage to his
shoulder, for I had to dig deep to remove the ball. 'Twill be a
long time before he wields a sword with that arm.'

Jack was instantly on the alert. Why should a surgeon
speak of swords and fighting? But he replied only, 'It is not
his fighting arm. He is left-handed.'

'Ah. Then he has been lucky, for his shoulder will take
some time to heal. How came he by this wound, sir?'

'We were set upon by a group of footpads, in Marseilles.

We were outnumbered, and running from them. When they saw that we were about to escape, one of them shot him.'

'Wicked,' the surgeon muttered. 'And cowardly, too, especially now, when we are like to need every Frenchman we have.'

'Especially now?' Jack echoed. 'Forgive me, sir, but I—'

The surgeon's eyes widened and he stared at Jack. 'Have you not heard?'

'Heard what?'

'The Emperor has returned. God save him!'

Jack felt as though he had been winded by a blow to the gut. 'Returned?' For a moment, he could not manage more than that single word. Then his common sense took hold and he breathed again. The surgeon was yet another of the many Bonapartists waiting all over France. Jack must take care. He must not allow the surgeon's suspicions to be aroused. 'Are you sure, sir?' he asked breezily. 'We heard nothing of that at Marseilles. Just that he *would* return.'

The surgeon paused. 'Be so good as to keep the pressure on the wound.' As soon as Jack had taken over, the man turned away. He began to clean his hands with a cloth and then to put his instruments back into his case. 'Well, I suppose the rumours could be mistaken,' he said thoughtfully. 'But the way it was told to me, I tell you, sir, it was not that the Emperor *might* return, but that he *had* returned. I pray it is so, for with fat Louis on the throne, France will always be under the heel of her enemies.' He spun round to face Jack. '*Vive l'Empereur!*'

It was a test. Jack swallowed. He had no choice. '*Vive l'Empereur!*' he echoed, trying to sound as though he meant it.

A sound from the doorway made him turn. Marguerite Grolier stood there, transfixed, with a bundle of white cloth clasped to her bosom.

Jack swore silently. If the lady was a Bonapartist, he might have improved his standing with her. But if she was not, he could have made himself an enemy. He wanted neither of those. He wanted her to trust him, without question. But she was standing as if stunned, her glorious eyes very wide. Was that from pleasure? Or dismay? He could not tell. He desired her as an ally, but he dare not risk treating her as anything but an enemy.

'At last!' the surgeon cried. 'Bring them here, ma'am. This man is bleeding.'

The surgeon's words spurred her into action. She started violently and hurried across to the bed. Between them, she and the surgeon tore bandages and had soon bound a clean pad on to Ben's wounded shoulder.

'He'll do now, sir,' the surgeon said.

'Thank you. How soon will he be well enough to travel, do you think? We should not remain here, especially if the news you bring is true.'

The surgeon grinned. 'Pray God it is, eh, sir? He promised to return with the violets. He would not break such a promise. Not a promise to France.' The surgeon had a rather faraway look in his eyes, which sat strangely with his burly figure and bloodstained fingernails. But many Frenchmen had revered Bonaparte as a hero. Just as this man clearly did.

'I need to know, sir. How soon?' Jack repeated. 'How long must my companion remain here before he is fit to travel?'

'Oh, that. A day or two only. Much will depend upon whether he develops a fever. That ball should have been removed hours since, you know.'

Jack nodded guiltily. 'I…I know it.' He straightened. 'May I escort you downstairs, sir? Perhaps you will take a glass with me before you leave?'

The surgeon beamed. 'That is kind, sir. I accept, gladly.'

Jack glanced towards the lady, who nodded. Since Ben was unconscious, she could safely be left alone to take care of him for a space, while Jack took the surgeon below and paid him for his services. There would still be plenty of light for her to continue her journey later. He would thank her properly then, and try to allay her suspicions, somehow. He wanted her to think well of him when they parted, just as he did of her, whatever her allegiance. In truth, she deserved more gratitude than he would ever be able to express, since she must never learn of their mission.

For now, that mission came first. He must stop thinking about Marguerite Grolier. His immediate task was to extract as much information as possible about Bonaparte. He would start with the surgeon. Over a glass of brandy, the man might disclose a great deal about the exiled Emperor. Was it possible? Could he really have landed in France again? Was the whole of Europe about to be engulfed in flames once more?

Now what was she to do? Herr Benn was an English spy. And Mr Jacques was all too clearly a Bonapartist. She swallowed hard, trying to control the nausea that had engulfed her when she heard those fateful words on his lips. He was a brave and generous man, he had rescued her with no thought for his own safety, but he was a Bonapartist. They were enemies, but she must not let him suspect that. She must keep him always at a distance and treat him with the utmost care. She had thought, for that fleeting moment when he touched her, that he might be a friend. Nothing of the sort. He was an enemy, to her and to everything her family believed in. She must beware of him.

Marguerite's hands were automatically clearing away the mess the surgeon had left. Herr Benn was deeply insensible and pale as a ghost. She fancied that the surgeon was a butcher as well as a Bonapartist. He had removed the bullet, but what else had he done? She dropped the last of the bloody cloths into the basin and turned to the dressing table to wash her hands. The water there was clean. Neither the surgeon nor Mr Jacques had washed off the blood.

She shuddered. Blood! If Bonaparte had indeed returned, there would be a great deal of blood.

She glanced around for a towel. There was none. She shook the drops of water back into the bowl and turned to her valise for her own towel. In a moment, she found it, tucked alongside the raw silk cocoon which normally held her phial of laudanum. She dried her hands, extracted the phial from her pocket and restored it to its place beside the basilicum powder. It would be best to give Herr Benn no more laudanum. But did she dare to let him alone? What if he began raving? Mr Jacques was surely not to be trusted. On the other hand, Herr Benn might not recover if Marguerite kept him dosed with laudanum. It was a wicked dilemma.

Reluctantly, she retrieved the phial in its soft wrapping and stowed it deep in her pocket. She would keep it to hand, just in case.

Was that a sound on the stairs? She looked round, guiltily, to see the door opening. Quickly, she grabbed the tin of basilicum powder and whirled to meet this new challenge.

'Mistress?'

Marguerite let out the breath she had been holding. It was only Guillaume.

'I have ordered food. It will be served directly, in the coffee room downstairs. Will you come?'

'No, Guillaume.' She glanced towards the bed. 'I cannot leave him.'

'But, mistress—'

She waved the tin at him. 'His wound needs to be redressed.'

'That is not for you to do, surely? The surgeon has seen to him, and he has his companion, also. You have been more than generous to them both, but it is none of our concern. We should be on our way home.'

Without a moment's pause for reflection, Marguerite shook her head.

'Mistress, your sister needs you more than these men. And there is the Duchess of Courland's silk. It has to be taken to Paris.'

He was right, of course. The family's future might depend on the Duchess's approval. And yet Marguerite was the only person who could save the English spy from the Bonapartists. She owed a debt of gratitude, perhaps even her life, to Mr Jacques, but she could not trust him with the English spy's life. He was the enemy. She repeated it yet again, forcing herself to ignore the tiny voice that urged her to trust him, to value his kindness.

She straightened her back and tried to look sternly at her old retainer. 'We cannot leave so soon,' she said firmly. 'Herr Benn has the beginnings of a fever. That butcher may have extracted the ball, but heavens knows what damage he did in the process. And Mr Jacques, for all his bravery in defending me last evening, is no nurse.'

'No, but—'

'Guillaume, I cannot leave this man. Not until he is out of danger. I am sure that it will take only a day, or two at most.'

Guillaume was shaking his grizzled head.

Marguerite would not permit him to voice the protest he so clearly wished to make. 'No, Guillaume, we are staying, at least for a day. We must take care, though, for Rognac seems to be a nest of Bonapartists.' She ignored Guillaume's worried frown. 'Do bespeak a bedchamber and make sure all our supplies are safely stowed there. I want no repetition of last night's trouble. Take the pistols from the coach and remain with our goods. It is your responsibility to ensure they are well guarded.'

He stood there, looking her up and down. She thought she

detected a new respect in his gaze. 'And tell the landlord to send up some food. I shall not be able to leave Herr Benn.'

'As you wish, mistress,' Guillaume said quietly. 'Shall I bespeak a separate bedchamber for you? Or shall you sleep with the silk?'

'Neither. I shall sleep here,' she said flatly. She pointed to the *chaise longue* under the window. 'Herr Benn will need constant nursing, and I do not imagine that Mr Jacques possesses the necessary skill. Ask the landlord to find me some extra pillows and a coverlet. I shall be comfortable enough there.'

Guillaume hesitated for a moment, but then, perhaps seeing the determination on Marguerite's face, he nodded and left the room. A second later, she heard the sound of his boots clattering down the stairs.

Her decisions were made. She crossed to the bed and began to untie the bandages so that she could apply her basilicum powder to the unconscious man's open wound.

She would save him at all costs, even if she had to shoot Mr Jacques in order to do so.

Chapter Four

'Come in.' Marguerite did not look up from her task of bathing Herr Benn's forehead. It did not matter who the visitor was. Herr Benn was still safely unconscious, while she was behaving like the perfect nurse, for anyone to see.

'I beg your pardon, ma'am.'

That unmistakable voice sent strange vibrations down her spine all over again, in spite of her resolutions. The earlier hard edge was almost gone, replaced by thick, velvet richness. She clenched her fists and dug her nails into her palms. By the time she rose and turned to face him, she was back in control of her wayward senses.

Mr Jacques was standing just inside the door, staring across at the motionless figure on the bed.

'It is too soon to expect any change, sir.' Marguerite was pleased that her voice was steady, though she found it easier not to look directly into his face. His deep blue eyes, so much more intense than Herr Benn's, were definitely best avoided.

He waved a hand dismissively. 'I apologise for disturbing you. I am going to the village. I wondered if there was anything you needed?'

Marguerite gestured towards the window. The sky was very dark. 'Is that wise? I'd say there's a storm brewing.'

He shook his head impatiently. 'I have no choice, ma'am. Herr Benn's valise was lost in Marseilles, and I do not have enough linen for two. If I can find a haberdasher's here, I might be able to purchase new cravats and so on, for us both.'

Cravats? His companion could be at death's door and he wanted cravats? His casual attitude to Herr Benn's condition caught her on the raw. Worse, he was taking it for granted that she would continue to nurse Herr Benn, without even a single word of thanks. She was too well schooled to rail at him, but she fanned the flames of her righteous indignation. Better to appear peevish than to succumb to the strange feelings this man was able to arouse in her. 'I have everything I require, thank you, sir. And I do not think Herr Benn has need of cravats, just at present,' she added, with relish.

That barb struck home. His eyes narrowed. For a second, she thought he would respond in kind, but he did not, though his throat was working as if he were swallowing his ire. Eventually, he sketched a bow and turned for the door, murmuring something inaudible. She supposed it was some kind of farewell.

Insufferable man! Was he really going to buy cravats? Or was that simply a pretext to go drinking with his new-found Bonapartist cronies? Either way, it should not matter to Marguerite. She was not going to allow herself to think about Mr Jacques. Not in any way. Not his voice, nor his astonishingly deep blue eyes, nor the half-naked torso he had paraded in front of her in that harbour inn.

That last image was much too vivid. She could feel her skin heating in the most unladylike way. She rushed across to the door and shut it quickly, leaning her back against it and closing her eyes. She should be glad that Mr Jacques had left the inn, for his very presence was dangerous. She would *not* think about him. She would concentrate on caring for Herr Benn.

The sound of muttering jerked Marguerite out of her light doze. She leapt up from the *chaise longue*. Herr Benn was thrashing around on the bed, clearly in pain. She hurried across to the dressing table to fetch her cooling cloth once more.

Herr Benn had thrown off most of the bedclothes so that he was naked to the waist, apart from the bandages around his shoulder and upper chest. Marguerite laid her fingers gently on his brow. He was getting hotter. She touched the skin of his torso. That was hot, too. At least he was still insensible. He might be in pain, but he was not aware enough to know it. She began to bathe his face, his neck and the exposed skin of his chest. It seemed to help, for he settled back into his pillows, and the frown disappeared from his brow.

'Sleep now,' she said in halting English, trying to reach more deeply into his troubled mind. Most of the English she had learned as a small child was long forgotten. Would Herr Benn understand her? 'You are safe here, I promise.' It seemed to help, for he gave a long sigh and his body relaxed a little more.

Marguerite bathed his skin again and then dried him with her own soft towel. For a moment, she stood gazing down at him. She had never before touched a man in such an intimate way. Herr Benn's body was beautifully formed, his skin white and his features finely sculpted, yet strong. He was a remarkably handsome young man, with the kind of fair good looks that might make ladies swoon. But she felt no tug of attraction at all. Why was that?

She busied herself with gently smoothing the sheets over his body and making him comfortable. She did not want to answer her own question. Indeed, she had not wanted to ask it, for she already knew the answer. For some unfathomable reason, the man who drew her was broader, darker and not nearly as handsome as her invalid. Mr Jacques's rich voice had twined itself around her thoughts, just as the image of him, half-naked in the gloom, had etched itself into her memory, like acid dripping on to a copper plate. She realised she had even been dreaming about him, which provoked a groan of frustration. Would she never be able to erase him? She refused to let him beguile her. He was a Bonapartist, the enemy, and a real danger to her invalid. She would oppose him with every ounce of strength and cunning she possessed. Even at the risk of failing her own family.

She swallowed hard. When faced with a choice between her duty to her family and her duty to her king, she had not hesitated, and she knew that every member of her family would have made the same choice. But it did not remove her worries, or her sense of guilt.

Marguerite shook her head at her own folly. There was no sense in worrying. She was duty-bound to care for Herr Benn, and to protect him from his companion, until he was able to mind his tongue. With constant nursing, that might be soon, perhaps only a day or two more. Suzanne would have to cope for a little longer. And meanwhile, Marguerite would focus all her wits on keeping Herr Benn safe, and strengthening her defences against Mr Jacques's unsettling charms.

Jack trudged back across the inn yard in the sheeting rain, cursing the sudden turn in the weather. His testy lady had been right about that. And about cravats, too, but what other excuse could he have offered her? Inexplicably, he found himself focusing on her reactions to him. Would she still be cross? Or would she give that delightful throaty laugh when she saw the state of him?

His simple greatcoat was almost sodden now, and he was

well-nigh frozen. Worse, it had all been for nothing. He had visited all the shops in the village, bought drinks for the local men in all the bars, and had even gone to the church to talk to the curé, but no one had been able to give him any definite news. The Bonapartists were all certain, on the basis of no evidence at all, that their beloved Emperor was among them once more. The royalists, who in Rognac numbered only the curé and a couple of old men, were equally sure that such a landing was impossible. The forces at Toulon would have prevented it, they said, even if it meant blowing Bonaparte's ship out of the water. Which side was right?

Jack shrugged his shoulders and then cursed aloud as the rain from his collar ran down the back of his neck. He raced the last few steps to the shelter of the inn doorway. Paris, and even little Rognac, would soon know everything there was to know, for news travelled very swiftly across France, relayed between tall telegraph towers with movable arms. Jack would have to be patient. He would soon learn whether these were simply wild rumours started by old soldiers in their cups.

The landlord came bustling forward as soon as Jack entered the taproom. 'You're soaked, sir. Let me help you off with that coat. You'll be needing to sit by the fire to get dry.'

Jack muttered his thanks, but did not attempt to make conversation. He had already tried humouring the landlord, a couple of hours earlier, while he and the surgeon were sharing a glass of brandy by the bar. The landlord, an old soldier, was loud in his praises of the returning Emperor, but totally lacking in real information. And so, as it had turned out, was the surgeon.

'I'll have another large measure of your best brandy, landlord.' Cupping the glass in his freezing fingers, Jack threw himself into the rough wooden chair nearest the fire. It had been well fed with logs and was roaring nicely, throwing out a huge amount of heat. Once his fingers were warmer, Jack leaned back in his chair, took a large swallow of his drink and stretched out his booted feet. He could allow himself just a few minutes by the fire before he went upstairs to check on Ben.

Poor Ben. At least he had remained safely inside, in the warm, but he had had the rough end of this mission, so far. Not only had he been shot, but he had lost all his possessions. They were no great loss, of course. Both Jack and Ben had brought only very ordinary clothes on this mission, since they could not afford to draw attention to themselves. But now Jack would have to face the delectable Miss Grolier, who would see at a glance that he had failed to buy any new linen. If questioned, he would have to admit that Rognac did not boast a haberdasher's. What would she imagine he had been doing all this time? Would she be furious that he had taken advantage of her generosity by leaving her to nurse Ben for so long? He realised with a jolt that he needed to concoct a plausible story. Such a needle-witted woman would not be easily gulled.

Jack gulped down the last of his brandy and stood up, turning for a moment to warm his back at the flames. Let her smell the alcohol on his breath and assume he had simply made a feeble excuse to spend the time in the local bars, well away from the labours of the sick-room. Let her assume he was a selfish wastrel. That would merely serve to confirm the low opinion she had formed of him earlier. That did not matter, surely?

It did matter. For some reason, part of him wanted her good opinion. He spent several fruitless minutes cudgelling his brain for a story that would show him in a better light. He failed. Ben would have been able to dream up some unlikely tale in a trice, but Jack could think of nothing.

The mission must come first, he told himself sternly. He was the leader. He had left Ben upstairs for over two hours, alone with Marguerite Grolier. That had been foolhardy. What if he started raving as a result of his pain? What would she do? She had saved Ben's life in Marseilles. Would she now betray him? Jack's instincts told him she would not, but he did not trust his instincts where she was concerned. She was a beautiful and extraordinary woman, admirable in every way—except that she might be a Bonapartist.

He told himself that she had not joined in with the surgeon's *'Vive l'Empereur'*. Then again, she had not objected to it, either. For Ben's safety, and his own, and for the success of their mission, Jack had to find out the truth about Marguerite Grolier. Whatever the cost. His childish instincts could go hang.

Jack ran up the stairs, pausing to listen for a moment outside Ben's door. He could hear no sound at all. Good. With luck, Ben had not regained his senses, or spoken. As soon as Jack was presentable again, he could go in to ask after Herr Benn's health and to probe, as subtly as he could, for where the silk weaver's true sympathies lay.

The fire in his chamber had not been lit and, without a change of clothes, all Jack could do was to towel his hair and rub his exposed skin until it glowed. The shirt was thin. It would soon dry from the heat of his body.

His quiet knock on Ben's door was followed by what sounded like a gasp. As if she were shocked to be disturbed? As if she were hiding something?

Jack had no way of knowing, and he could not enter the bedchamber without her permission. She was a lady, and he must continue to treat her as a lady, unless she gave him cause to do otherwise. Somehow, he did not think that would happen. She was not a lady in the usual sense of the word, of course, for she was a mere artisan, a silk weaver, but her speech and manners were impeccable. Many women in London called themselves ladies, but could not hold a candle to Marguerite Grolier. She was altogether remarkable. If only she were not also a Bonapartist…

'Mr Jacques! My goodness, how wet you look. Come in and warm yourself. There is a good fire here.' Marguerite stood back to allow him to enter. Since he had abandoned her for hours without so much as a by-your-leave, she had every right to be furious with him, but how could she rage at such a woebegone figure? He must have been totally drenched by the storm. His boots were dripping muddy water as he crossed the floor. His hair was wet, too, and tousled like a boy's. He had stripped off everything but shirt, breeches and boots, and his shirt was so damp that she could see his skin through it. He might as well have been wrapped in nothing but a bed sheet again! Marguerite tried to put that thought out of her mind. She told herself sternly not to look at his torso. It was just one more male body, like Herr Benn's. A lady should be able to ignore it.

Mr Jacques bent to the fire, spreading his fingers to the warmth. 'I am very much in your debt, ma'am, for tending to Herr Benn in my absence. I…I feel I have taken advantage of your good nature.'

A little gratitude at last. Marguerite automatically responded in kind. 'After what you did for me, sir, it was the least I could do.'

He straightened and turned to face her. It was only then that she smelled the alcohol on his breath. She tensed. Clearly, he had not been searching very hard for replacement cravats. He had been making the rounds of Rognac's bars. That was disgusting behaviour from a so-called gentleman. If she were not a lady, she would tell him so. Instead, she lifted her chin and drew back her skirts so they were no longer touching his contaminated boots.

He did not appear to notice. 'How is he now? Has he come to himself at all during my absence?' There was a hint of anxiety in his voice. Or was it shame over his own appalling behaviour?

Marguerite resolved to keep her anger under control. It was beneath her to lose her temper with such a man. 'He was hot and restless an hour or so ago, but he is improving now. He is still insensible, but he may come round soon.'

He crossed to the bed and stood gazing down at the invalid, who looked very peaceful now, his breathing slow, but not in any way laboured. 'He looks as if he is healing well, ma'am. And when he wakes, he will thank you for your care, I am sure. Unless, perhaps, you plan to continue towards Lyons today?'

He must know she did not. He must have heard when Guillaume made the arrangements for them to stay. She frowned at him, but said only, 'Travelling in such weather would be madness.' She nodded towards the window. The storm was still raging.

He ran his fingers through his unkempt hair and attempted a roguish smile. Yet again, he looked absurdly young.

'Carriage accidents happen all too easily, especially in conditions like these, when—' She stopped herself just in time. She was gabbling uncontrollably. She had been about to refer to her mother's accident, and its terrible consequences. It must be the fault of that clinging shirt. It had melted her common sense.

Shocked at her own weakness, she took refuge in attack. 'I take it you managed to acquire the linen you were seeking? Did the haberdasher keep you waiting while some of it was stitched for you?'

He had the grace to blush a little. 'I…er…I spent far too much time enquiring for a haberdasher's. Some of the locals sent me off on a wild goose chase, I fear, for there is no such establishment in Rognac. No doubt it amused them to roast a stranger so. I was gullible and got thoroughly soaked as a result. If you choose to call me a fool, ma'am, I will readily accept it.'

What a ridiculous story! She hurried across to the fire, holding out her hands to it as if she were cold. 'It would be the height of impoliteness for me to say any such thing, sir,' she said, addressing the blackened fire surround. 'I have no basis for making any judgement about you.' Oh, that was a lie. For all his faults, she knew he was a gentleman, and brave, with a body fit to grace a statue. Just as she knew that she must not trust him with Herr Benn's secret.

'You are very generous, ma'am. I can but apologise for having left you alone for so long,' he said gently. And then he was silent. Waiting.

His frank apology disarmed her. She gripped her hands together, feeling the tension in her neck and shoulders and arms. This man was such an extraordinary mixture of boyish charm and mature decision. He seemed to revert from man to boy in the blink of an eye. It was thoroughly disconcerting. But undeniably attractive. She did not know how to deal with it.

The noise that broke the silence was not made by Mr Jacques. It was a very definite groan, followed by a mumble that could have been words.

Marguerite raced back to the bed. Her mind was flooded with dire warnings. She must find a way of getting Mr Jacques away from here. Before he heard words he must not hear!

She almost pushed Mr Jacques out of the way in her haste to protect the invalid. She stretched across the bed, putting her own body between Herr Benn and his so-called friend in hopes of muffling any words Benn might utter. She bent low to his head, laid her hand on his cheek and then, keeping her back to Mr Jacques, she slid her fingers down until they covered Herr Benn's mouth. 'Oh, I think he may come round soon. Is that not wonderful?' she gushed. 'Pray, sir, be so good as to ask the landlord if the kitchen can prepare some barley water. Herr Benn will be so very thirsty when he wakes.'

Behind her, Mr Jacques neither spoke nor moved.

Marguerite bit her lip. He was making this very difficult, but she would not allow him to win. She smiled sweetly up at him over her shoulder. 'If you please, sir. I do not think I should leave Herr Benn at the moment. And the barley water would be so very good for him. Why my old nurse swears by it. She—'

He grimaced with the sort of pain she had often seen on her late father's face when confronted with gabbling women. 'Very well, ma'am. If you insist.'

Marguerite fancied that his good manners had won out over his real intentions. She held her breath, listening for the squelch of his boots across the floor and the sound of the door closing. At the click of the latch, she raised her body and removed her hand from Herr Benn's mouth. He was trying to shake his head, as if to free himself. He was going to come to his senses very soon.

With a muttered but heartfelt apology, Marguerite whipped the bottle of laudanum from her pocket and deftly forced the invalid to take another dose. 'It is done to save you,' she whispered as she hastened to hide all traces of what she had done. 'When you are well again, I will truly beg your pardon, I promise.'

Herr Benn was already slipping deeper into oblivion.

'I have done as you asked, ma'am.'

Shocked, Marguerite whirled round, her hand to her throat. She knew she must be blushing. 'Sir. You took me by surprise. You did not knock.' She was trying to suggest he had committed an outrage, but her ploy was not succeeding. He was not at all abashed. He looked large and powerful, framed in the dark wood of the open door. He was all mature, dangerous male.

'The barley water will be delivered as soon as it has boiled and cooled.' He shut the door and crossed to the bed once more. 'Has Benn come round?'

'Alas, no. I am afraid your friend has sunk back into insensibility. It may be some hours yet before he truly awakes.'

'Then I will tend to him.'

No! He must not! 'I…er… There is no need, sir. Since the weather prevents my travelling onwards, I am more than happy to nurse Herr Benn. I fancy—' she smiled at him, trying to assume the image of a simple, well-meaning female of the kind who could never be dissuaded when she knew she was doing her duty '—that I have rather more experience of such things than you do.' She raised an eyebrow at him and was rewarded with a long sigh of resignation. 'While you were out earlier, I had Guillaume bring up my things,' she continued quickly, giving him no chance to change his mind. 'I shall sleep here on the *chaise longue* where I can tend to Herr Benn if he needs me. I must tell you that I am used to such duties. I often nurse my invalid mother. And—'

'Spare me the details, ma'am,' he said gruffly. He took a step back from the bed and made her a tiny bow. 'It is not the sort of service that I would ever have expected a stranger— even one as well trained as yourself—to provide, but since you offer so generously, I shall accept. On behalf of Herr Benn.'

'It will be my pleasure to tend him,' she said simply. For it was true.

'But is there nothing I can do? Have you eaten? I could watch over him while you went down to the coffee room for a meal.'

'Oh, no, you—'

'I may be only a mere male, ma'am, but I am quite capable of bathing a man's brow, or calling for help if his case should be beyond my powers.'

He was baiting her now. She must be careful not to go too

far. 'Guillaume brought up some food while you were out. He will do so again later. I shall do very well, I assure you.'

He was trying not to smile. They both knew good manners prevented him from contradicting her. 'I imagine that you do very well in everything you undertake, ma'am,' he said at last.

'Oh. Oh, thank you.' She had a feeling that his compliment was sincere, even if it was double-edged. What mattered here was that she had won. Soon he would leave, and she could relax, alone to defend Herr Benn.

He started for the door, but stopped midway, as if remembering something. He spun round. 'But I have not had a chance to tell you what I learned in Rognac. It is not yet totally certain, but it seems that the Emperor has indeed kept his word to France, and is returning to liberate us. Wonderful news, do you not agree?'

Marguerite was caught like a bird in lime. What was she to do, to say? He was challenging her directly now. He was openly admitting that he was a supporter of Bonaparte and challenging her to do the same, to make common cause with him. 'Are you sure, sir?' Her voice cracked a little on the words. When he nodded, she swallowed hard and forced herself to speak in a bright, enthusiastic voice. 'Why, that is the most wonderful news. I had dreamed… All France had dreamed, but we never dared to hope that the day would come. The Emperor! The Emperor himself is to return to us! There will be rejoicing indeed.'

'*Vive l'Empereur!*' His voice was flat, but strong.

What choice did she have? She had to protect Herr Benn. '*Vive l'Empereur!*' she echoed.

Chapter Five

'Mr Jacques!' The hammering on the door grew louder. 'Mr Jacques!' It sounded like the landlord's voice. It must be something important, for it was only just beginning to get light.

Jack threw himself out of bed and dragged on his shirt. It had hung all night by the dying fire and was dry at last. He did not dare to risk appearing naked, in case Miss Grolier were outside in the corridor. He flung open the door. 'What on earth is the matter?'

'Great news, sir! It *is* true. The Emperor landed three days since and is already on his way north.'

'By Jove, that is wonderful news.' The lie came out without a moment's pause. 'But are you sure, landlord? Might it not be just another rumour?'

'No, sir. Not this time. I had it from the telegraph man himself. It's certain, sir.' The landlord's grin was so wide that it was almost splitting his face.

Jack beamed back. 'Every able man will flock to his standard, I am sure. But do we know where he is? Is he taking the coast road from Toulon?'

The landlord tapped the side of his nose and winked. 'Not

he. Far too wily to be caught in that trap. He landed well away from Toulon. And he's taken his men inland, across the mountains, where fat Louis's army would never think to look for him. He's outfoxed them all.'

Jack could readily believe that. 'So he's already moving north?'

'Aye. And fast. Paris will send troops against him, of course, but by the time he reaches Grenoble, he'll have thousands more besides the Imperial Guard. Fat Louis won't stop him now.' The landlord nodded in satisfaction. Then he narrowed his eyes and said, 'You'll be wanting to join him yourself, sir?'

'Yes, of course,' Jack replied at once, his mind whirling, 'but I must see my friend safely bestowed first.' He paused and scratched his head, trying to look as if he were wrestling with a knotty problem. 'Grenoble, you say? With a sick companion, I don't think I can— No, Lyons. That's the answer. The Emperor is bound to make for Lyons after Grenoble. I'll join him there.'

'Well said, sir. I've a mind to travel with you and do the same.'

Jack gave him a friendly pat on the shoulder. 'You are a brave soldier, landlord, but I suggest you leave it to the younger men. You are needed here.'

The landlord frowned. There was a look of yearning in his eyes, but it soon faded. 'Aye, you're right, sir. I'm too old to be chasing after glory now.'

Jack hoped he did not appear too relieved. 'Send up some hot water, would you? If my friend is well enough, we'll be able to make a start within the hour.'

'But you'll make much better time without an invalid to slow you down,' the landlord protested. He was now investing all his enthusiasm in ensuring that Jack joined the colours as quickly as possible.

'I cannot do that,' Jack said flatly. 'I must deliver Herr Benn to Lyons. But fear not, landlord. We shall travel with all speed. Every second counts now. My shaving water, if you please, and be so good as to order breakfast at once.'

The landlord hesitated for a moment, but then the good sense of Jack's words seemed to get through to him.

Jack stood in his doorway until the man had disappeared down the staircase. Then he took a deep breath, closed the bedroom door and leant against it, trying to force his riotous thoughts into order. Bonaparte was on his way to Paris. He might even be near Grenoble already, though that was unlikely, given the difficult terrain he had chosen to cross. He would get there soon enough, though. And then, from Grenoble, it was an open road to Lyons and Paris. But King Louis would send his army, surely? Even if Bonaparte managed to reach Lyons, he was bound to be stopped there. In spite of all the landlord's fervent hopes, Bonaparte's troops would be poorly equipped and would certainly be outnumbered by the royalists. No, he would be stopped, though perhaps not before Lyons.

That made it all the more important for Jack and Ben to travel there by the quickest possible route. Luckily, the road north from Rognac, through Avignon and Valence, was a good one. With reasonable horses, a coach could cover it in three days, or even less. He and Ben had intended to remain as inconspicuous as possible, and to travel to Paris by *diligence*, but that would be too slow now. A chaise would not do, either, for it would not provide enough space for Ben to lie flat. Jack would have to hire a carriage and a team. That would raise eyebrows. The landlord would be surprised to learn that a man who was planning to enlist as an common soldier was wealthy enough to travel in such luxury.

Jack pondered a little more. This time, he needed to have

his story prepared down to the last detail. The landlord must have no grounds for suspecting that Jack was anything other than an ardent Bonapartist. Yes! He would say that Herr Benn had a wealthy patron, in Lyons, who had sent money for their journey. They had travelled in the Grolier carriage as a result of a chance meeting with a lady who was skilled in tending wounds. But now they would travel on alone, funded by Benn's patron. Without the lady. Jack refused to let himself think about Marguerite Grolier. She was the enemy. It was much too dangerous to allow her any part in this from now on. He must put her out of his mind.

Would his plan work? Perhaps he should say that he was really looking forward to travelling in such luxury, that he had never been able to afford it before? That should do the trick. Had he forgotten anything? He was beginning to realise that planning a mission was like setting out a field at cricket. The captain had to work out precisely where his opponent was likely to hit the ball, so that he could have a defender in place to stop the runs. Jack could find no more undefended points on his cricket pitch. It was a good plan. Time to put it into action.

Marguerite managed to keep control of her features until the door closed behind Guillaume. Then she slumped down on to the *chaise longue* and dropped her head into her hands. It was true! That monster was back in France and would soon be at the head of another army of hotheads, all ready to die for him. And die they would, of that she had no doubt.

What on earth was she to do? She raised her head and glanced across at the bed. Herr Benn was still sleeping peacefully. He had passed the crisis in the night. There was no longer any sign of fever, and his wound seemed to be healing well. She could leave him here and hurry back to Lyons to protect her family. Without Guillaume, Suzanne and their mother were undefended. Although the Groliers had never talked about their royalist allegiance, even after Bonaparte's defeat, there were those in Lyons who might suspect them. A silk-weaving business, even a struggling one, was worth taking over, and the turmoil surrounding Bonaparte's return could provide just the opportunity their rivals needed.

Marguerite groaned. She could not stay in Rognac. She *must* return to her family. But what about Herr Benn? If she abandoned him, would it not be a sentence of death? She rose and began to pace.

'Where am I?' The words were in English, and the voice barely a thread.

Oh, no! Marguerite rushed to the bedside. 'Herr Benn, you are at an inn on the road to Avignon,' she said, in slow, careful French. She put her hands flat on his cheeks and gently turned his head so that he was looking directly into her face. His eyes were unfocused and barely half-open. 'Herr Benn, listen! Bonaparte is back in France. You are in great danger. You must speak only French. No English. Not a word of English. Do you understand me, Herr Benn?'

'No English,' he repeated, in English. 'No English.' His eyelids drifted closed. He had fallen asleep again.

Marguerite exclaimed in frustration. But there was nothing she could do. She could not abandon him to the mercies of Bonaparte's executioners. She must travel home to Lyons, and quickly, but she must find a way to take Herr Benn with her. If she promised to nurse him on the way, and take him to the Hôtel Dieu in Lyons to be cared for, surely Mr Jacques could not object?

He almost certainly would, she decided. Indeed, he would probably insist on accompanying them. In truth, the only sure way of getting rid of Mr Jacques would be to leave Herr Benn behind, and she knew she could not do that. So there was every likelihood that she would be travelling all the way to Lyons with Mr Jacques's perceptive eyes on her, and on the invalid. She felt her stomach turn over at the thought. He saw far too much, that one. Besides, the effects he had on her were uncomfortable. And dangerous. He could be so kind and so charming. It would be all too easy to let down her guard and then—*boum!*—she could find herself arrested, and handed over to that monster's guards, to be shot as a traitor.

No, she would not allow that to happen. She would not succumb to Mr Jacques's undoubted charm. She would treat him with perfect propriety, as a chance-met acquaintance, even if they were travelling together all the way to Lyons in the confined space of her carriage. She was a strong woman. She could do it.

Her inner voice reminded her that, when they first met, he had admired her for her strength and courage. His words then had beguiled her. Was she so very sure that she could be proof against his wiles?

Jack fastened his valise and straightened his back. He had paid his shot, and Ben's. It only remained now to prepare the hired carriage for the invalid. He crossed to the window. No sign of his carriage yet. The only vehicle in the yard belonged to Marguerite Grolier.

Marguerite Grolier. She kept intruding when he least expected it. And just when he had been telling himself he had banished all thoughts of her. It was lust, of course. What else could it be? Even when he was surrounded by real danger, his confounded body refused to see beyond one beautiful, and very desirable, woman. He was becoming as bad as brother Leo!

No, he was worse. Leo might be a womaniser, but in the grim business of spying, Leo was always able to concentrate on his role in the Honours. He had spent months in Vienna without thought of a mistress. So why couldn't Jack do the same? After all, Jack's vice had always been gambling, not women.

It had to be something about Marguerite Grolier. But why should he lust after her, when he had been able to ignore so many other women?

He began to pace his empty room, pondering. She was quick-witted and courageous. She was a skilled weaver, and a practical businesswoman, which was quite a combination. She was resourceful, too, and she was certainly compassionate. Poor Ben probably owed his life to those qualities.

Jack stopped by the window and rested his elbows on the sill to look out. Marguerite Grolier was an extraordinary woman. He had never met her like. But he knew he was not lusting after her because she was admirable—though she was. She was also beautiful and unconsciously alluring. Lately, when she touched his hand or her breath caressed his skin, his body had responded instantly.

He told himself it could only be because she was innocent. And forbidden. They had been thrown together by unavoidable circumstance. As in the Garden of Eden, temptation was all the stronger because the fruit was forbidden. And the serpent of lust was twining itself around him, hissing its message of betrayal. He would not heed it. He would not betray Marguerite to satisfy a moment's craving.

In a few minutes, once he had his body under control again, he would bid her farewell and thank her sincerely for what she had done. Then he would leave her without a single backward glance. He was the leader of this mission. Like a true leader, he would not allow himself to be diverted from his task.

They seemed to have reached an impasse. The charming boy she had glimpsed so often had been replaced by a grim, implacable man.

'I shall hire a carriage for myself and Herr Benn, ma'am,' he said again. 'It would be the height of bad manners to inflict ourselves on you when we must travel so fast. Such a journey will be too uncomfortable for a lady.'

Marguerite refused to be beaten. She tried another tack. 'I do understand your desire to join the Emperor as soon as possible,' she said, smiling admiringly up at him. 'I, too, long to see him. But there are grave risks along the way, especially for Herr Benn. If royalist troops should come upon your carriage and find a wounded man, what then? Would you be able to convince them that you were not the enemy?'

'I would tell them the truth, ma'am. That he was shot by footpads.'

She opened her eyes wide in disbelief. 'And you are both racing north to Lyons, *ventre à terre*? I think not, sir. A wounded man does not travel so. The only plausible reason for such haste is that you are going to join the Emperor. They will know it. And so do you.'

He drew himself up to his full height and looked down his nose at her. 'I suppose you have a better plan?'

Marguerite almost wanted to laugh. He was such an unpredictable mixture of frustrated schoolboy and decisive man. 'Yes, I do,' she said flatly. 'I have barely had a chance to say a word since you entered the room, but I do have a much better plan. Better for all of us.'

He quirked an eyebrow and stared down at her in a way that was all adult male, and all dangerous.

'My mother and sister are in Lyons. Guillaume is needed there to protect them while my father is away. The Emperor will be victorious, of course, but there may well be fighting first. We must get home with all speed.'

'I do not see that—'

'If we travel together, there will be much less danger. We

can give out that Herr Benn is…er…my brother and that he has a fever. We are taking him home to be nursed. Royalist soldiers will not enquire too closely if we tell them that his fever is highly infectious.'

Mr Jacques looked thoughtful for a moment. 'That is all very well, ma'am, but Herr Benn will need to agree to pretend to be your brother. Even if he comes to himself soon, which looks unlikely, we cannot be sure that he will be lucid enough to understand the part he is to play.' He shook his head. 'No, I'm afraid that your clever plan will not do. Benn and I will travel alone. You may do as you wish.'

Marguerite felt a real urge to slap him. She was glad she had been brought up without brothers. Men were always so sure they were right. 'Herr Benn will not be lucid enough to carry off your plan either, sir,' she said sweetly. 'What if he should start rambling just when the royalist soldiers open your carriage door?'

He paled noticeably.

She forced herself not to smile. 'There is a solution. *My* plan can be made to work. Unfortunately, yours cannot.'

He raised that infernal eyebrow and waited.

'Whether in my carriage or yours, Herr Benn will have a very uncomfortable journey. And if he begins to thrash around in pain, there is a danger that his wound may reopen. I have a remedy for both these problems. I shall dose him with laudanum. Then he will say nothing, and feel none of the discomfort. Indeed, it may even help him to heal. Well, sir? What do you say?'

He frowned and looked back towards the bed. For several moments, he was silent and pensive. At length, he said, 'You can keep him insensible without doing him any lasting harm?'

She warmed to him then. He was thinking, not of himself, but of Herr Benn. 'I have considerable experience of the drug, sir. My mother— Suffice it to say that I shall give him just enough to keep him from waking, but not enough to do him harm. Trust me. I promise that, once we have him safe in Lyons, he will wake again without any memory of his sufferings. Or any ill effects.'

'Very well,' he said gravely. 'I will trust to your skill, ma'am. I accept.'

'Excellent.' She wanted to shout in triumph. She would be able to administer the doses, in all innocence, while her Bonapartist companion watched complacently. And when they finally reached Lyons, she would find some way of taking Herr Benn into the Grolier household where he would could mend in safety, though she was not sure quite how she would persuade Mr Jacques to allow it. Perhaps he would be so keen to be off to join his idol that he would not argue?

No, that was unfair. Mr Jacques might be a hated Bonapartist, but he was a man of honour and of compassion. He would insist on ensuring that Herr Benn came to no harm.

'I have one more question.'

That brought her back to earth. 'A question, sir?'

'Yes. If Herr Benn is to be your brother, what, pray, is to be my role?'

She had not thought of that. She looked Jacques up and down assessingly. 'Herr Benn may be able to pass for my brother, but not both of you at once. You are too unlike. It would raise questions.'

'It would not be proper for an unmarried woman to be travelling all the way to Lyons with a man who was not a relative.'

'Nonsense,' she retorted. 'I will be travelling with my brother.'

'A brother who will be totally incapable of opening an eye, far less defending his sister's honour. No, ma'am, we must have a plausible tale to tell. You have two choices: would you prefer to travel as my betrothed, or as my wife?'

'As your w—?' How dare he suggest such a thing? Mar-

guerite instinctively stepped back from him. She bumped into
the bed and sat down very suddenly, trying to overcome her
shock. When she had recovered enough to look up at him once
more, she saw that he had not moved an inch. His features
were totally composed, but underneath, she was certain he
was laughing at her.

'Perhaps you should apply your skills now, ma'am?' he
said innocently.

'I beg your pardon?' She leapt to her feet in indignation.

'Herr Benn will need to be carried downstairs and laid in the
carriage. It will be a painful process, for the stairs are narrow and
twisting. It would be best if he were insensible while we do it.'

She refused to give him the satisfaction of besting her.
'That is very thoughtful of you, sir,' she said calmly. 'And you
are right, of course. I will do it now. In the meantime, perhaps
you would be so good as to check that Guillaume has made
room in the carriage for our invalid? I instructed him to place
as much as possible of the silk in the boot or on the roof. The
packages will come to no harm—they are well wrapped in
oiled paper. And the rain stopped hours ago.'

Now he was looking at her in disbelief. He still had not
moved.

'Is something wrong, sir?' she asked mischievously.

'You had already told him—?' He broke off and frowned,
looking down at her through narrowed eyes. 'I see that I have
underestimated you, ma'am. I shall not do so again.' Without
another word, he turned and strode out of the room, closing
the door behind him with a decisive click.

Marguerite held her breath for fully twenty seconds. And
then her triumphant laughter burst forth.

By the time Jack had made his way downstairs and out into
the inn yard, he was biting his lip to stop himself from

laughing out loud. What a woman! She knew precisely what she wanted, and she made straight for it. Definitely a managing female. She reminded him of Cousin Harriet, the formidable old spinster who acted as companion to his mother and who had terrified him since he was in short coats. But Marguerite Grolier did not terrify him. Far from it. She made him want to seize her and kiss her until they were both mindless with passion.

It was impossible, of course. She was not of his class, and she was a virtuous female. It would be dishonourable to take advantage of her. Besides, even though she was prepared to travel alone with Jack and Ben, her motives were of the highest. She had saved Jack and Ben once, and now she was proposing to do so again. She deserved to be treated like a princess.

Guillaume sprang down from the carriage and hurried across the yard. 'Some of the silk will still have to be carried inside the coach, sir. There ain't room anywhere else. But I've made up a bed on the floor for Herr Benn, with plenty of padding. He should be comfortable enough. Would you like to see?'

So much for Jack's belief that he had planned for every eventuality. He had forgotten one key factor: Marguerite Grolier. She was only a woman, but she had shown him his error. And his arrogance. She was the one who had had everything worked out in advance.

Everything except a role for Jack, of course. He smiled at the memory of her shocked response to his ultimatum. She would travel as his betrothed, not as his wife, he decided, relenting a little. If they were to be on the road for two or three days, they could not travel as man and wife without risking her reputation. As man and wife, they might be expected to share a bedchamber. As a betrothed couple, they would sleep apart, and be expected to behave with circumspection. Her reputation would be safe.

And so, he vowed, ignoring the urgings of his body, would her virtue.

Chapter Six

The city of Lyons was very fine. Approaching it from the south, Jack had seen splendid and imposing buildings and magnificent churches, their spires and towers straining up towards heaven, but now that the coach was actually driving through the streets, he was struck by how tall the houses were, and how richly embellished. Lyons was clearly a very wealthy city, at least partly built on centuries of silk.

'Remarkable.' He smiled across at her. 'Lyons seems to have almost as many bridges as Paris.'

'We need them more than Paris does,' Marguerite replied, returning his smile so warmly that it lit up her features. 'Lyons has two rivers to contend with. The city is grown so big now that it covers the banks of both. Wait and see.'

They had agreed during the journey that they must become much less formal in their use of names, as befitted a betrothed couple. She was to call him 'Jacques'—the name 'Louis' was best avoided—and he would call her 'Marguerite', at least in public. Jack no longer thought of her as 'Miss Grolier'. In his mind, she was now simply 'Marguerite', though he had not yet used her given name while they were alone. He was sorely tempted to try it, if only to see her bristle, for she bristled delightfully, raising her hackles like a small pet dog confronted by a large and intimidating newcomer.

Teasing her was the most he dared to do now, and even that was dangerous. Touching her, however innocently, was out of the question. It produced a physical response that was all too visible, for his lust for his lovely Amazon was growing more uncontrollable with every passing day. Still, his torture must end soon. They would part here in Lyons.

They had just left the Rhone bridge and were driving straight across the peninsula that lay between the two rivers. Narrowing his eyes, Jack could see another bridge some hundreds of yards ahead of them, presumably across the Saône. While he was focusing on that distant vista, the carriage entered a huge open space, and he gasped in surprise. It was enormous, big enough to muster an army, and surrounded by tall buildings with grandiose façades. Very few of them matched, but the effect was harmonious, softened by the bare but feathery branches of dozens of ancient trees.

'They say this is one of the finest squares in Europe,' Marguerite said with a note of pride in her voice. 'It is, or rather was, the Place Napoleon. They changed the name last year, of course, but perhaps they will change it back again, now that the Emperor has returned.' She had talked admiringly of Bonaparte throughout their journey together. Clearly she felt she could speak frankly to a fellow supporter. At first, Jack had had to watch his every word, but after three days on the road, he now spoke as if he, too, were an ardent Bonapartist.

He stuck his head out of the window to admire the square, so that he could respond to her sunny mood. 'That statue is not of the Emperor.' It was a huge sculpture of a man on horseback.

'No. It is King Louis XIV. He deserves his place there. Like the Emperor, he gave France glory, and a place in the sun.'

'True,' Jack said quietly. The sound of Bonaparte's name on her lips was profoundly depressing. He tried to concentrate on the city instead. The carriage was leaving the square and the bridge was only a hundred yards or so further on. He could clearly see the oldest part of the city on the far bank of the Saône. The houses were tall, and narrow, and seemed to be piled up on one another like a child's bricks, to fill the narrow strip of flat land between the river and the steep slope behind. Almost directly ahead of them, on the right of the bridge, was a huge, ancient cathedral, with two towers.

'Not much further now,' Marguerite said, leaning forward eagerly.

Jack could hear the impatience in her voice. It was understandable that she should want to get home to her family in such uncertain times. Unlike Jack, she had not suffered agonies of frustration during all those hours in the coach. She was too virtuous to be at the mercy of the demon lust.

In an attempt to divert his thoughts, he had tried to draw her out about her family during the tedious hours on the road, but he had not learned very much. There was a definite reticence there. Her father travelled a great deal, apparently, in order to find markets for their silk. Marguerite and her younger sister, Suzanne, ran the business during his absence, for their mother was some kind of invalid. With an absent father, and no brothers, it was no wonder that Marguerite had become a managing sort of female. He had no doubt that she ran the business extremely well. She did everything well. Including innocently tempting Jack.

'The area round the cathedral, St Jean, has been the home of silk weaving for generations. Or, at least, it was. Now the jobbing weavers are setting up on the hill at the north end of the peninsula, where the houses have the high ceilings they need for their looms.' Seeing Jack's puzzled look, she continued, with a shake of her head, 'I can see that you know nothing about silk, sir. The new Jacquard looms are immensely tall. They do not fit in our old workshops.'

'I see,' Jack said, though he was not sure that he did. Did that mean that the Grolier business was not involved in these new looms? From some of the things that Marguerite had not said, he suspected that their business was struggling to survive. He knew for a fact that both sisters took their turn at the looms. Perhaps they could not afford to employ the jobbing weavers at all? He was just about to probe a little further, when the carriage turned right into the square behind the cathedral and slowed almost to a stop. The square was full of colourful market stalls, selling everything a family might need, from live chickens to baling twine. There was barely room for a carriage to edge through, especially as the press of shoppers seemed to have no intention of making way for them.

'Don't concern yourself, sir. Guillaume knows the width of this coach to a hair.' She sat quite relaxed in her corner. Clearly there was no point in worrying.

A few minutes later, the coach drew up in front of a fine house of many storeys in a narrow, gloomy street. From inside the coach, it was impossible to see the sky. The street was deserted, which was as well, for the coach was blocking the full width of it. Jack jumped out and let down the steps for Marguerite to alight, but she was bent over Ben, yet again checking his brow for fever. She was unlikely to find any signs to concern her, for he was mending well. Mercifully, he was still insensible. Her laudanum strategy for the journey had worked wonderfully well. At each night stop, Ben had been carried into the inn and laid in a bedchamber shared with Guillaume, who tended to his bodily needs. Nursing was not necessary, and so Marguerite had been able to sleep undisturbed. And alone.

Jack wanted to curse aloud. Why on earth had his mind returned to that? Again? He had been trying so hard not to think about her in that way, though the image of Marguerite asleep, with her fair curls spread across a white linen pillow, had been haunting him. Especially at night. There was no doubt that her sleep had been longer and more restful than his.

He started for the horses' heads so that Guillaume could climb down from the box. He had been driving for hours, only occasionally permitting Jack to take over, and then only for short spells. The poor man must be very stiff and cold.

'Marguerite! Oh, Marguerite, we were so worried about you!' A small whirlwind had emerged from the house and thrown itself into the carriage. Jack turned, but caught only the briefest glimpse of a very slim figure in a plain brown dress with a mass of fair curly hair. This must be Suzanne, the younger sister. Her hair was lighter that Marguerite's, but otherwise they were probably very like.

Jack strolled back to the open carriage door and peered into the gloom. He had expected to see the two women embracing, but they were not, though Marguerite's arm had been thrown across her sister's shoulders. Suzanne was not even looking at her sister. Her worries appeared to have vanished. She was staring down at Ben's inert form with wide glowing eyes, and tightly clasped hands, as if she had never seen such a beautiful sight in all her life.

He was gone at last! Thank goodness! Now she must act.

Marguerite seized her sister's hand and pulled her away from the sofa where Herr Benn lay motionless. 'Suzanne, you must listen to me. Mr Jacques may return at any moment. Suzanne!' She was almost screaming the word into her sister's ear.

It had no effect. Suzanne was still gazing, rapt, at Herr Benn's face. 'What is his name?' she asked dreamily.

Oh, heavens! As if there were not enough dangers surrounding them! Marguerite grasped her sister by the shoulders and forced her to turn away from the blond vision on the sofa. 'His name is Benn, and he—' She broke off. It would be best to tell no one, not even Suzanne, that Herr Benn was an English spy. What they did not know, they could not betray. 'He is a German. I do not know his given name.'

'Mr Benn.' Suzanne rolled the sound caressingly round her tongue. She sounded nothing at all like her normal, retiring self.

'Suzanne, pay attention! We are in real danger. Have you not heard that Bonaparte is on his way? That he will soon be in Lyons with an army at his back?'

'Oh, yes. But the King's brother is here to defend us, and the army has already marched out to meet the monster. I imagine he will be stopped long before he reaches Lyons.'

Marguerite was nothing like so certain, but she would not frighten her sister by voicing her doubts. 'You may well be right. What matters now is that there are many here in Lyons who will support the usurper. As royalists, we will be in danger if anyone suspects where our sympathies lie. We have always been careful in the past, but now it matters more than ever. So no one in the household must say a word, either for or against Bonaparte. Not a word to anyone. Anywhere.'

'But surely we are safe enough inside our own house? Guillaume and Berthe believe in the cause, just as we do.'

Marguerite nodded towards the still figure on the sofa. 'We are not alone here. Herr Benn may come to his senses at any moment. And Mr Jacques has very sharp ears.'

'You think they are Bonapartists?' Suzanne gasped. 'Then why did you bring them here?'

'I cannot be certain where their sympathies lie, Suzanne.' Marguerite knew the truth all too well, though it would do nothing but harm to say so. In the last hours of their journey, she had extracted a promise from Jacques that he would not talk about their beloved Emperor in the house, for fear, she had said, of royalist neighbours and eavesdropping servants. Now she must secure a similar promise from her sister. 'Promise me that you will not talk about the King, or about Bonaparte, until this is over. Promise me, Suzanne!'

'Oh, very well. I promise, though I don't see why it should be necessary.'

'It is necessary because men love to fight. Royalists will attack Bonapartists who will attack Royalists. If we appear to have no sympathies either way, they will have no grounds to molest us.' She put a comforting arm round Suzanne's shoulders. 'You know how vulnerable we are, my dear, with so many other houses ready to pounce on Grolier's. If they even suspected the truth about Papa, we would have been swallowed long since.'

Suzanne nodded. She had begun to look a little scared. 'Yes, I'm sorry. You are right. I promise.'

Marguerite smiled in relief. 'Now, you must talk to Berthe and ensure that she promises, too. Don't bother about Guillaume. He is already well aware of what needs to be done. And he has always been close-mouthed.'

'But what about Mama? She would never give you such a promise. And even if she did, she would forget to keep it. You know how it is with her.'

Marguerite had been considering that problem for hours. 'You must tell Berthe to keep Mama as close as possible. She rarely ventures out of the house, which is a blessing, but it would be best if she were not to meet any visitors.'

'But we cannot treat her like a prisoner!'

'No, of course not,' Marguerite agreed at once. 'If she should chance to meet any visitors, you and I must try to ensure that she does not start talking about the monarchy and the importance of the aristocracy.' Suzanne was shaking her head sadly. They both knew that, once their mother started on her favourite subject, she was not to be diverted. 'And if we cannot stop her, we will have to make it clear that she is raving.' Marguerite sighed. 'That should not be too difficult to do. No one will believe anything she says once they realise how ill she is in her mind.'

At that moment, Marguerite heard booted feet in the passageway outside. It was probably Jacques, returning from helping Guillaume with the unloading. Her heart began to race. She put a warning finger to her lips. 'How has the silk been progressing while I have been away?' she asked brightly, just as the door opened.

'Forgive me, ladies. I was looking for— Ah, there he is.' Jacques strode across the room to the sofa and stood looking down at Herr Benn.

'Suzanne, you must allow me to present Mr Jacques, who travelled with us from Marseilles.' Suzanne smiled and curtsied. Jacques bowed, but his eyes remained on Marguerite. 'I think I may owe him my life, sister,' Marguerite continued, 'for he saved me from a knife attack in Marseilles.'

Suzanne gasped. 'You did not tell me that.'

Jacques was smiling warmly down at Marguerite. 'I am sure she also did not tell you, Miss Suzanne, that she saved both myself and my companion when we were attacked by ruffians on the quayside. If your sister had not taken us into her carriage and whipped up the horses, we would have been at their mercy. And they did not look the merciful kind.' He reached for Marguerite's hand and raised it to his lips, keeping his gaze locked with hers all the while. 'We are very much in your debt, ma'am.' His voice was suddenly much deeper than usual.

Marguerite could feel herself blushing. Her throat was so tight that she could not say a word. And the skin of her hand was burning, even from that tiny touch of his lips. It took several seconds for her brain to register that he was still holding her hand. Why? He had been deliberately avoiding her touch since their departure from Rognac. Yet now he was not only touching her skin, he was kissing her hand! It made no sense at all.

'You exaggerate, sir,' she managed at last, in a rather shaky voice, forcing herself to pull her fingers out of his grasp before her legs gave way beneath her.

He shook his head, but he did not argue. She was relieved, and grateful for yet another example of his impeccable manners. He was most certainly a gentleman. A strange question struck her then. Why would a gentleman wish to enlist as a common soldier in Bonaparte's army? She should have thought of that before, but Jacques had created such turmoil in her mind that she had rarely been able to think at all.

'Is something wrong, ma'am?' he asked gently, still gazing down into her face. 'For a moment, you looked quite worried.'

'Oh, it was nothing. I was…' She swallowed hard. 'I was thinking about Herr Benn. We need to arrange a bedchamber for him.'

'You are most kind, ma'am. But it will not be necessary. Benn is in no danger now, so if Guillaume can lend a hand, we will carry him to the inn. The Croix d'Or further along the street looks respectable enough.'

'No!' Both sisters gasped out the same word in the same instant.

'No, sir,' Marguerite repeated firmly. 'You cannot take him to a public inn. For who would look after him? He still needs careful nursing. You would not trust him to the mercies of the tavern wenches, would you?'

'Actually, I was planning to look after him myself.'

'Twenty-four hours a day? The innkeeper certainly wouldn't

let his servants help you. He would probably insist you had
Herr Benn taken to the Hôtel Dieu so that the nuns could nurse
him.'

'There can be no question of it,' Suzanne said flatly, in a
voice more determined that Marguerite had ever heard her use
before. 'We owe you a debt, and we shall repay it by nursing
your companion. Here, in this house. Say no more about
moving him to an inn, I beg of you, or to the Hôtel Dieu. Such
a thing would shame us. You must both remain here with us
until Herr Benn is quite recovered.'

'Your offer is more than generous, ma'am, but I— It is bad
enough that your sister has nursed Herr Benn all through the
journey from Marseilles. I could not possibly impose on her
to continue.'

'There is no need,' Suzanne said quickly. The skin of her
cheeks had turned a delicate rose, but her gaze was intent. 'I
shall nurse him myself.'

'You should not be here, Miss Suzanne. This is a man's
bedchamber.' Guillaume sounded more than a little concerned.

Suzanne gazed down at the invalid. He was sleeping peacefully now, and the smooth white skin of his bandaged chest
was rising and falling slowly with each long breath. With her
to nurse him, he would soon recover.

'Miss Suzanne!'

'Oh, Guillaume, do not fuss so. What risk can there be to
me when he is so ill? He needs a nurse, not a…a paramour.'

'It is not right for you to be doing this. You should—'

She laid a caressing hand on his arm. 'If it will content you,
dear Guillaume, I will confine myself to dressing his wound,
and feeding him. You may tend to his other bodily needs
yourself. Though I fail to see how you will find the time.'

'I will make the time,' he growled.

She twinkled up at him. 'If you have so much time to spare, you can come and chaperon us, too. Would that satisfy you?'

He grunted. They both knew it was impossible. Guillaume, as the only man in the house, had far too many chores to do. He could not watch over Suzanne, even though she was the apple of his eye. 'If I had the time to chaperon you, missy, I'd have the time to change his bandages myself.'

She seized one of his callused, work-worn hands and rubbed it against her cheek. 'I know you mean well, Guillaume, but just imagine how your rough hands would feel against tender, wounded flesh.' She used her own soft hand to stroke his stubbled cheek. 'My hands will hurt him less. He will heal more quickly with me to tend him. Just wait and see.'

He pushed her hand away. 'Enough of your wheedling ways, young lady. You always did know how to get the better of me, but you won't do so this time. A lady's reputation is her most treasured possession, and, once it's lost, it can never be regained. You don't understand the risk you are taking.'

His concern was all for her, and she must not distress him any further, even though she was quite determined that she would have her own way in this. 'I will nurse him while he lies insensible, Guillaume. Once he comes to his senses again, I will consult Marguerite about what is proper. Will that content you?'

'Aye.' He smiled reluctantly. 'I suppose so. Now I'd best bring up some more coals for that fire, or your precious gentleman will end up dying of cold.'

The moment he left the room, Suzanne sat down by the bed and took Herr Benn's limp hand in both her own. He seemed so weak. Would he ever be well enough to sit up, to look at her, to speak to her? What would he think of her? Would his eyes warm and his lips smile?

She stroked his hand, just once, and then tucked it under

the sheet before pulling the coverlet up to his chin. He was her dear invalid, and she was determined that it would be her nursing, and her care, that would cure him.

Jack stood watching from the doorway of the tiny room, but she was totally unaware of his presence. She was a pretty little thing, but rather unworldly. Shy, probably, perhaps as the result of having a managing elder sister. She would not have had the opportunity to acquire the steel of Marguerite.

No, that was not quite right. Miss Suzanne had shown considerable determination when she insisted that she would be the one to look after Ben. And now, it seemed, she had achieved her aim, though Jack was at a loss to know why she should be such a passionate advocate of a man she had only just set eyes on. Perhaps such things happened in a house full of women? Having no sisters, Jack had always found it difficult to fathom the female mind. This time he was going to have to try, however, for he had to ensure that, when Ben finally came round, neither Marguerite nor Miss Suzanne was in the room.

He stepped forward and coughed loudly.

She jumped to her feet. She was blushing rosily.

'Forgive me, ma'am. I did not mean to startle you. How does my friend?'

'I…er…he is sleeping peacefully, sir.'

'Splendid.' Jack crossed to the bed and touched his fingers to Ben's forehead. 'Not a hint of fever. I imagine he'll be on his feet again in no time. I may tell you, ma'am, that he's as strong as a horse, however delicate he may appear. It is more than generous of you and your sister to house us, but we will be gone as soon as Benn is well enough. A few days at most.'

Her blush had subsided. Without it, she seemed paler than when they had first met. She tried to smile in response to his hearty words, but it was far from convincing.

'Poor Benn. He is in a sad way. His hair hasn't seen a comb in days—'

'I can do that for him!' she exclaimed.

'—and he is much in need of a shave,' Jack continued, without a pause. 'If you would be good enough to order me some hot water, ma'am, I could make him presentable enough to entertain a lady.' He grinned at her, and waited.

'I… Certainly, if you will excuse me for a moment.' She cast a long look at the figure on the bed and then made for the door.

'Do not be concerned, ma'am,' Jack called after her. 'I will sit with him. Our invalid shall not be left alone.'

The moment she was out of sight, he took the two steps to reach the door and closed it silently. Then he turned back to the bed and shook Ben by his good shoulder. 'Ben. Ben! For God's sake, man, wake up!' His whisper was low, penetrating, and in English.

To Jack's relief, Ben gave an answering groan and half-opened one eye. 'Jack?' His voice cracked. 'What on earth—?'

Jack clamped his hand over Ben's mouth. Ben's eyes widened a little, but it seemed he was able to focus, so Jack risked removing his hand. Ben did not attempt to speak again.

'We have very little time. Listen,' Jack hissed. 'We are in Lyons, in the house of Bonapartists. They are good people, but if they suspect what we are, they are bound to have us arrested. You must speak only French, and give nothing away. Do you understand me, Ben? Ben?'

Ben let his head roll sideways on the pillow. His eyes drifted shut. 'I could do with a drink,' he croaked. In French.

Chapter Seven

Jack stood in the doorway of the office with his hand on the latch. 'May we have a private word, Marguerite?'

She appeared to be working on accounts. She looked up, frowning.

Jack realised his mistake. 'I beg your pardon. Miss Grolier, I should have said.'

She inclined her head graciously.

'May I close the door?'

She looked up again. This time she seemed intrigued, but she nodded.

Jack shut the door and crossed to the desk. 'I have kept my promise to you. I have said nothing about the Emperor within these walls. But much is being said outside, as I am sure you know. The Emperor will reach Grenoble soon, if he has not done so already, and the King's brother has sent a detachment of the army against him. I must ride south. I cannot remain here in such a crisis.'

'You are going to enlist?' She sounded worried. Was it possible that she was concerned for his safety? 'But what of Herr Benn?' she continued, dashing Jack's rising hopes. 'You said you would do nothing until he was recovered.'

'I am not going to enlist, ma'am. I will fulfil my trust to Herr Benn first, as I promised. But, equally, I cannot sit idle in Lyons while the Emperor is in danger. I have to—' He stopped. It was such a lame excuse, but what other could he offer her? He had to see, with his own eyes, what was going on, so that he could report to London. Somehow. 'I have to be there, when the Emperor meets the King's army, even if I do not actually fight.'

He tried to assess her reactions from her changing expression. Surely she would never swallow such tosh?

She pursed her lips thoughtfully. 'I see,' she said slowly, nodding to herself. 'And if you do not return, what is to become of Herr Benn?'

'You have no need to be concerned, ma'am,' he said, relieved. Clearly she had concluded that he was simply a young hothead who was determined to join in the fighting on behalf of his idol, but was not honest enough to admit it. Since a real Bonapartist might act in exactly that way, he would say nothing to suggest she was wrong. 'I do intend to return to Lyons, and with a whole skin, though possibly not for two or three days.' Seeing her returning frown, he added, placatingly, 'Herr Benn is himself again this morning. He is still very weak and in a lot of pain, but he appears to have suffered no ill effects of the laudanum. It is just as you said, ma'am.' He smiled down at her. He hoped she would take that as the compliment he meant it to be. 'I no longer have any concern for his survival. It is simply a matter of time, and good nursing, which I know your sister is determined to provide. And you, too, of course,' he added hastily.

She rose from her chair and came round to his side of the desk. She was not returning his smile. 'Mr Jacques, I can promise you that we will take good care of Herr Benn in your absence. As to your mission—'

Jack started in shock. Surely she could not know?

'As to your mission,' she said again, 'it is not for me to

restrain a man who is going to the aid of our beloved Emperor. I wish you God speed, sir, and a safe return.' She looked up into his face then. Her glorious sea-witch's eyes were so clear that he fancied they offered an opening on to her innermost thoughts. She was certainly afire for someone but, sadly, the man of her dreams was Napoleon Bonaparte, usurping Emperor, rather than Jack Aikenhead, English spy.

He swallowed his disappointment and bowed, resisting the temptation to kiss her hand once more. That earlier kiss had been most unwise and must not be repeated. He had intended it to be a kiss of farewell, before he removed Ben to the local inn. He had told himself that one simple kiss on the hand would not be an assault on her virtue. But it had rendered her speechless, and the effects on his own body had been even worse than when they were cooped up together in the carriage. Only his greatcoat had saved him from real embarrassment.

And yet he was not sorry that the sisters had insisted they stay in the Grolier house. Jack was going to find it very hard to part from Marguerite, even though being close to her was a sore trial.

She was standing with her back against the desk and no longer meeting his eye. Both hands were behind her back. The message was clear. She wanted him to leave. And she did not want him to touch her.

He bowed again and left without a word. It was only when the cold draught in the corridor hit his neck that he remembered what he was about to do. He must concentrate on his mission, his real mission, and banish all thoughts of his beautiful, fair-haired Amazon. He was riding south into real danger. If he did not keep his wits about him, he might well fail to return.

Marguerite stood totally rigid, clutching the worn edge of the old wooden desk behind her, until she heard the sound of his horse's hooves disappearing up the street towards the cathedral. He had gone. He was going to throw himself into the battle to save his damnable hero, Bonaparte. How ridiculous! She had not been wrong when she judged Jacques to be part-man and part-schoolboy. The callow youth, filled with impossible heroic dreams, had been very much in evidence this morning. Did men never grow up?

She shook her head in an attempt to clear her thoughts. She must be practical. Jacques might return, in a few days. Or he might not return at all. She must not brood on that, for that way lay nothing but pain. Surely she had too much common sense to indulge her emotions in such a way? Whatever happened, Marguerite had to defend Herr Benn, for only she knew that he was an English spy. She had to ensure that he recovered enough, here in Lyons, to continue with his mission, whatever it might be.

She had slipped in to see him before anyone else was about and had found him much improved. He had greeted her lucidly, and thanked her for her kindness, in slightly accented French. Since he was no longer delirious, there should be no risk that he might babble in his native tongue, but to drive home the point, she had complimented him on his French, stressing how fluent it was, coming from a *German*. He had frowned a little at that, but she was fairly sure that the message had gone home. He would surely stick to French from now on. He would be safe.

There was a knock on the door. It was Guillaume, come to build up the fire. He looked searchingly at Marguerite, but said only, 'I am glad he is gone. He asks too many questions, that one. I even caught him asking Berthe about where your father might be.'

The muscles of Marguerite's belly clenched to the point of pain.

'You need have no fear there, miss,' Guillaume went on, kneeling down in front of the fireplace next to the desk. 'Berthe knows better than to betray this family's secrets. But it is dangerous to have these men in the house. What if they were to start asking the neighbours about when your father was last at home? Even the neighbours might become suspicious then, if they thought about it for long enough. You should have sent them both to the Hôtel Dieu, as I said at the time.'

Much as she trusted Guillaume, she could not tell him the truth about Herr Benn. It was not her secret to share. She muttered platitudes instead, about the debt she owed Jacques.

Guillaume was in full flood, now that there was no risk of being overheard by strangers. 'Your sister, too, is determined to throw away all claim to the reputation of a lady. I have warned her, but she refuses to heed me.'

'Suzanne—'

'I even asked Berthe to act as chaperon, but that did not last above ten minutes, of course. Your lady mother—may heaven bless her!—was soon in the bedchamber as well, enquiring after Berthe and talking to the invalid. When she began to say some…er…rather awkward things, Berthe had to take her back to her room. So Miss Suzanne is still alone with a half-naked man in his bedchamber. You should not permit it, Miss Marguerite. Truly you should not.'

She should not permit a servant to talk in such terms, either, but she could not berate this man who had served them, and cared for them, since before they could walk. His words simply proved his deep affection for the Grolier family, and especially for Suzanne. 'I have spoken to Suzanne,' she said gently. 'We are both agreed that once Herr Benn is able to rise from his bed, she will not enter his room again. If his wound needs dressing after that, she may do it downstairs. Or you may do it yourself, Guillaume, if you have time. For the moment, she is in no danger from him.' He was shaking his head vehemently, but Marguerite would not allow him to speak. 'The only risk to Suzanne's reputation would be if someone inside this household were to mention what is going on to an outsider.' She fixed him with a stern gaze. 'I am sure that no one would do such a thing, no matter how much they disapproved of Suzanne's behaviour.'

Guillaume looked hurt. He rose from his knees, dusting off his hands. 'You know that Berthe and I would never gossip,' he said tartly, 'and the boy is not permitted to go beyond the kitchen, so he has nothing to gossip about.'

Chastened, Marguerite reached out to put a hand on his arm. 'Thank you, Guillaume,' she said simply. 'You know we could not manage without you.'

He cleared his throat and swallowed hard. Then, without saying another word, he picked up his bucket and left the room.

Marguerite slumped against the desk. She had not intended to upset him, but she had so many burdens to carry that she had not thought before she spoke. If only Mama were able to share the load, or Suzanne. But it was not possible. Mama spent most of the day in a strange world of her own, and Suzanne appeared to have become besotted with Herr Benn as soon as she set eyes on him. If she were ever to discover the danger he was in, there was no saying what she might do to protect him. That was yet another reason not to tell her that he was an English spy. Marguerite was going to have to deal with her problems all by herself.

And the first, and worst, of those problems was Louis Jacques. She had betrayed her family's trust by bringing him here, even though her motives had been of the best. A nagging seed of guilt was growing in her mind over that. Had she really done it for the royalist cause? Or perhaps it was the aura of danger surrounding Jacques that drew her to him?

She tried to bring some sense to her tumbling thoughts. She had sworn to protect Herr Benn, whatever the risk. That had been a patriotic decision, nothing more, for she felt not a shred of attraction to the man. For Jacques, on the other hand… Oh dear, that was so very different. Unlike Suzanne, she had not fallen at first sight—indeed, she refused to admit that she had fallen at all—but theirs was not a normal relationship between chance-met acquaintances. At least, not on her side. Every time they were together, she found herself longing for the touch of his fingers on her skin. Or, better, of his lips. And his every word rippled through her like a warm breeze through pliant spring leaves. It did not matter that she had tried—oh, how she had tried!—to keep him at a safe distance and to remind herself that he was the enemy. For she had failed.

She began to pace, angrily. She ought to be able to control her feelings, especially when they were so badly directed. She would control them! She forced herself to think with cold calculation. Jacques was a continuing danger to Herr Benn. If he discovered that Herr Benn was an English spy, he would be bound to have him arrested. Then the Grolier family would be arrested, too, for harbouring a spy. And what would happen to Suzanne, and to poor Mama?

She shuddered. If Jacques had even the slightest inkling of the truth, she would have to find a way of stopping him. Permanently. But how? He was a wily man, good in a fight, and far stronger than she. In a confrontation, she would lose, for she could never bring herself to shoot him.

She began to consider all sorts of schemes, each more outrageous than the last. A knife thrust, perhaps, or poison in his coffee? But how would the deed be concealed? And could she ever steel herself to do it?

* * *

It was only when she heard the horse stop outside the house that Marguerite realised she had been listening for him almost since the moment he had left. He had been gone for more than two days, and she had been waiting and praying for his safe return, hour after hour, without once admitting it to herself. Until now. So much for her plans to make away with him. She was precious little use as a conspirator, and even less as an assassin.

She forced herself to remain at her desk in the little office off the front hall. She would not go out to meet him.

But what if he was hurt? What if he needed help?

She was already half out of her chair when she heard his voice at the street door. It was that same rich, strong voice that had first invaded her senses. And it proved that he was fully in control. 'Send the kitchen boy round to take my horse back to the livery stable, would you, Guillaume? He's covered a lot of ground today, and he deserves an extra ration of oats.'

She could not make out Guillaume's low-voiced reply, but she heard the clink of coins. There would be money for the livery stable, for the oats, and no doubt for the kitchen boy as well.

Whatever Jacques had discovered, it could not be good for the royalist cause. She had detected real satisfaction in his voice. Would he come in to her, to share the news of his hero? Would she be able to conceal her disgust if he did? A shiver ran down her spine. She had a fleeting vision of the Imperial Guard marching over bloody corpses, and shouting for their Emperor.

She could not face him. She ran to the door and opened it a crack so that she could peep out. She saw Jacques still silhouetted against the fading light in the open doorway, talking quietly to his horse. One look was quite enough. She slipped along the passage and ran up the stairs to her own room. There, with her door firmly closed, she sank on to her bed and stared at her grim reflection in the glass. It seemed that every last vestige of colour had drained from her face. Even her hair seemed to have faded, as if a film of grey had been laid over her.

Jacques had returned. He was safe. But his success had brought the death of all her hopes for her country.

Jack ran a hand through his filthy hair. What he really needed was a bath. His whole body was bathed in sweat, and his skin was tight with the clinging dust of the road. No doubt he smelt to high heaven, too.

He was glad that Marguerite had not come to meet him. He did not want her to see him—or smell him—like this. She would be overjoyed at his news, of course. What Bonapartist would not? Her eyes would widen and her skin would glow, as if he were telling her that her lover was on the way to her, rather than her beloved Emperor. What was is about that little man that inspired such adoration, in women and men alike?

He shrugged his shoulders and made for the stairs. He would look in on Ben, and then, since a bath was out of the question, he would strip and scrub himself clean, inch by inch. He wished, now, that he had not seen that encounter on the road. He would never be able to forget it. It had both impressed and astonished him. But it terrified him, too.

Marguerite's door flew open with a crash.

'Miss Marguerite! Oh, come quickly to your mama!' It was Berthe. She looked distraught.

Marguerite jumped to her feet. 'What has happened?'

'She is ripping her gown to shreds, mistress. And cursing like a trooper. I tried to stop her, but she is too strong for me.'

It had happened before, and there was only one solution. Marguerite seized the bottle of laudanum from her dressing table and rushed headlong for her mother's chamber.

She crashed straight into Louis Jacques.

He grabbed her by her upper arms to save her from falling. 'Why, Miss Grolier. Good evening. I had not expected you to be *quite* so eager to see me again.' He grinned impudently, his teeth very white in his dirty face. His eyes were gleaming, too, as he set her back on her feet and loosened his grip a little. But he did not quite let her go. His large hands still rested on her flesh, burning through the fabric of her sleeves, while his gaze was boring into hers, searching, as if for something hidden.

She could not move. She could not even begin to shake him off.

His eyes widened, and darkened. His mouth opened a fraction, and the tip of his tongue moistened his upper lip. Otherwise, he, too, stood motionless.

'Miss Marguerite! Please!'

Berthe's urgent summons broke the spell that held Marguerite. She saw that her hands were against his chest, one still clutching the laudanum bottle. She pushed hard and fled into her mother's chamber.

As the door closed, Marguerite heard his voice behind her. 'Happy to be of service, ma'am.' It was followed by a deep chuckle. 'Always.'

Jack held his smile until the door had closed on the two women. A shudder ran through his frame. What the devil had just happened?

He had no idea. But he could tell that it mattered. It certainly proved he had been right in his resolve to keep Marguerite Grolier at a distance. One touch, one innocent contact, and his exhausted body was almost fully aroused. Inexplicable, uncontrollable lust, all over again!

When her gaze had flickered to his lips, his mouth had dried instantly. With hot, blistering desire. For one mad moment, holding the soft warmth of her so tantalisingly close, he had been on the point of kissing her on the lips!

Shocked by his own weakness, he turned on his heel and ran up the stairs to his own bedchamber on the floor above. Ben could wait while Jack splashed cold water on his over-heated face. A few moments' delay could make no different to Ben, but it would make all the difference in the world to Jack's self-possession.

When Jack returned to the first-floor landing, it was empty and silent. He refused to think about where Marguerite might be. He must concentrate on Ben and on the next stage of their mission.

He tapped quietly on Ben's door. There was no response. He put an ear to the panel. Perhaps Ben was asleep? He would just peep in to check. Slowly and quietly, Jack raised the latch and pushed the door open.

'Oh!' Suzanne Grolier sprang up from the bed where she had been sitting. Her face was scarlet. Ben, too, looked distinctly uncomfortable, and there was just a hint of a blush on his neck. Well, well, well. So that was the way of it. How very interesting. And how very dangerous.

'Good evening, ma'am.' He bowed. 'I trust I see you well? I can see that I need not ask after my friend's health. He looks to have improved beyond measure in the time I have been away.'

She tried to reply, but no words came out. Defeated, she dropped him a sketchy curtsy and rushed out of the room.

'Oh, dear. I seem to have frightened her away.'

'Looking like that, you would frighten anyone. What on earth have you done to yourself, Jack?' Ben's embarrassment had vanished in a trice. His customary sharp-witted self was back, to Jack's relief.

Jack laid a finger along the side of his nose and crossed the room to check that the door was securely fastened, before returning to take Miss Suzanne's place on the bed. 'I have ridden more miles than I can count these last few days, hence my disreputable state. But, more important, I have watched the most astonishing sight of my life. If you are well enough, I will tell you about it.'

He raised an eyebrow at Ben, who nodded slightly and settled back on to his pillows with a satisfied sigh. 'In your whole life, eh? Now that I really do want to hear.'

Chapter Eight

The swish of Suzanne's skirts as she ran along the passage to her room was enough to rouse Marguerite's curiosity and take her to the door. What was the matter? She glanced back to check one last time that all was well. Mama was sleeping peacefully at last, with faithful Berthe by the side of her bed, holding her hand.

Marguerite opened the door just in time to see Herr Benn's door close. Yes, of course. Jacques had gone in to see his companion and had found him closeted with Suzanne. No wonder Suzanne had fled. She must have been mortified.

Marguerite looked up and down the passage and craned her neck to see down the staircase. There was no sign of Guillaume. Berthe would not stir from her mistress's side. Marguerite strained her ears. The only sound she could hear was the low murmur of men's voices in Herr Benn's tiny bedchamber. Encouraged, she swallowed her scruples, crept across the bare floorboards, and put her ear to the thinnest panel of the door.

She could hear Jacques remarkably clearly through the wood. There was excitement in his voice. Perhaps that was why he had not lowered it to a whisper?

'It was extraordinary. If I had not seen it with my own eyes, I would not have believed it.' That voice was unmistakable. Jacques was not excited; he was jubilant.

Marguerite began to listen more avidly, her heart pounding.

'Tell me all of it. From the beginning.' That was Herr Benn. He was bound to want as much detail as possible to pass on to his masters in England.

'As you wish. I reached Grenoble with no difficulty. There were plenty of soldiers on the road, all wearing the white cockade, but none of them challenged me.'

'I'm not surprised, Jacques. Even in those appalling clothes, you look and ride like a gentleman.'

Jacques laughed. 'Thank you for the compliment. I think.' The amusement in his voice prickled down Marguerite's spine. 'In Grenoble, I saw at least a regiment of soldiers spread all over the city. Obviously, I had to be careful not to arouse suspicions by asking questions, but it looked to me like a very neatly laid trap. Riding south to Gap, I found the road pretty well deserted. So much so, that I began to wonder if I would ever find them. And then, at the top of a narrow pass, there they all were, right in front of me.'

'All?'

'Yes. The King's soldiers were blockading the full width of the road, muskets at the ready. The Imperial Guard was drawn up facing them, just out of range. Their formation was immaculate. They didn't look in the least like men who had struggled over trackless mountain passes. And even I could tell they were spoiling for a fight. It's no wonder they strike terror into opposing armies. They look formidable. I found myself feeling rather sorry for the royalists who had to stand against them.'

'And Bonaparte was there?'

Marguerite caught her breath. Would Jacques notice that

Herr Benn had betrayed his true allegiance by referring to the usurper in such a disparaging way?

It seemed not. Jacques continued his tale, the excitement in his voice mounting all the time. 'At first, I almost missed him. I had expected more splendour, I must say. His horse didn't look particularly fine to me, and his dress certainly wasn't—a plain grey coat and the kind of broad black hat that any merchant might wear. He sat his horse at the front of the Guard while the two formations just stared at each other. The silence was uncanny. I thought the royalists might advance and fire, but they didn't move. The Guard didn't advance, either, but I suppose they'd have been shot to pieces if they had.'

'So what did he do?'

'He scrutinised the ranks of royalist troops as minutely as if he were the reviewing officer on a parade square. Then, once all their eyes were fixed on him, he walked his horse forward, cool as you like, until he was well within musket range. I expected them to fire on him, but no order came. Even the officers must have been transfixed, wondering what he would do.'

'And?'

'He dismounted—quite casually—and walked forward towards the muskets. You should have seen him, Ben. One small, vulnerable figure apparently advancing into certain death. Such supreme confidence. Such courage.' Jacques paused and swallowed audibly. 'By then, the silence was absolute. When he stopped, I even heard the thud as he planted his boots in the dust. He looked slowly along the front rank of faces, and I could have sworn I saw the hint of a smile, as if he had recognised them. He certainly addressed the regiment by name. And he made sure every one of them heard him.'

'What did he say, exactly?'

'He has a fine carrying voice. "Soldiers of the Fifth, don't you know me?" And then he put his bare hand over his heart and shouted, "If there is any man among you who would shoot his General—his Emperor—let him do it!" By God, it was magnificent. The two armies just held their breath. It felt like a lifetime before anyone moved. The shouts started in the front rank and soon the whole of the Fifth was yelling *"Vive l'Empereur!"* and surging forward to touch him. I tell you, Benn, the Emperor Napoleon has truly come into his own again.'

Marguerite could not bear to hear any more. This was not just hero-worship, it was blind adoration. How was it that a man like Jacques, a man of such sterling qualities, could fail to see what a monster Bonaparte was?

A bitter sob rose in her throat. She managed to swallow it, but she knew that the combination of nausea and fury was going to overwhelm her at any moment. Besides, she had heard enough. She crept back to her own room, barred the door behind her, and threw herself on to her pillows. Hot tears were coursing down her cheeks. She wiped them away impatiently with the back of her hand, berating herself for such childish weakness. She was a grown woman. She had known, almost from the first, that Louis Jacques was a Bonapartist and therefore an enemy. But somehow, until the moment when she heard that soaring jubilation in his voice, she had believed, in a tiny corner of her heart, that he might be redeemed. How ridiculous! There was not the least chance of redemption for such a man. She had been a fool to imagine it, even for a moment.

She rose and scrubbed at her eyes. They were red, but only a little swollen. She poured some cold water into the wash-basin and splashed her face vigorously. When she looked in the glass again, the result was much improved.

She would sit here alone for a little while, to recover completely. And then she would emerge as the woman she had been before that disastrous visit to Marseilles. She would be Marguerite Grolier, mistress of a Lyons silk business. And of herself.

* * *

'He may be only a puffed-up little Corsican, but I tell you in all honesty, Ben, I cannot fault his personal courage. Or his understanding of men. The old soldiers of the French Empire are clearly longing for the victories and the glory they achieved when he led them. When he faced them, and addressed them by name, they flocked to him like chicks to the mother hen. They love him. And everything he stands for. I have no doubt they are all ready to die for him.'

'That is a very potent mixture,' Ben said with a deep sigh. 'There is no Allied commander who inspires such selfless devotion. Wellington may be admired and even respected. But he is not loved.'

'I fear you're right. When I came back through Grenoble, the whole of the Seventh Regiment was stood to arms, waiting for him. Whatever their officers may intend, I doubt very much that the Seventh will shoot where the Fifth would not. Bonaparte will soon be marching into Grenoble with his Guard at his back, and now the Fifth as well. I would wager good money that the Seventh will join him. He is recreating his old legend. Grenoble will fall to it. And probably Lyons as well.'

Ben was beginning to look very tired now. It was time to leave him to rest. But before Jack did so, he had to find a way of broaching an even more difficult topic. He began breezily. 'Look, old man, I know you're not really fit to travel yet, but we've got to make sure this news gets back to England. They need to know that Bonaparte is on the loose again, and that there's not one of the French King's regiments will stand against him. They'll have to muster the Allied armies again. And quickly, too, or Bonaparte will have his armies halfway across Europe.'

Ben tried to raise himself from his pillows, but with only one good arm it was an awkward movement, and he fell back, cursing his own weakness. 'I'm not fit to go, Jack. We both know that. You must go on alone. The mission comes first, remember?'

'No! We'll manage somehow. We can—'

'Stubble it, Jack! You know we can't. You're the leader. It's your responsibility. I'm only a foot soldier, and a pretty poor one at that.' He grimaced down at the bandages that swathed his upper body.

Jack shook his head sadly. 'You're right,' he admitted after a moment. 'I shall have to go alone. I'll make the arrangements tonight and leave at first light tomorrow. Don't worry, I'll see you before I go and bring you up to date on everything. And I should have time to get you out of this nest of Bonapartists and into somewhere safer as well. If you stay here, you'll probably end up being shot. By a firing squad this time.'

Ben shook his head, smiling lazily. 'You know, my friend, I take leave to doubt that. Somehow I fancy that the Grolier household is the safest place in the world for me at present.'

'Oh?' Then the truth dawned. 'Oh. So that's the way the wind is blowing, is it? I had not imagined it had gone so far. Well, I wish you joy of her, Ben. Just make sure you don't end up in parson's mousetrap with a Frenchwoman you daren't present to your grandfather.' Jack stood up and grinned down at the helpless figure on the bed. 'And make sure you get home in one piece, too. I give you fair warning. The Honours need you back in England. If you don't appear, I shall be back to collect you, pretty French mistress or no.'

With that, he strode swiftly out of the room, totally ignoring the spluttered invective that was thrown at his back.

Marguerite examined her face in the glass once more. She looked quite normal, she decided. She could venture out now, without risking awkward questions from the servants. Or, worse, from a solicitous Jacques.

But just that passing thought of him had sent her heart racing all over again. She sat down with a bump on the edge of the bed and clasped her hands in her lap. What on earth was she going to do? He seemed to be haunting her, like a fierce, evil spirit. She needed to be rid of him. Oh, for those earlier fantasies of shooting him, or stabbing him, or lacing his cup with poison! Sadly, they *were* only fantasies. She could not kill any man, not even in order to defend her country. Not even to protect Herr Benn.

Goodness! She had almost forgotten Herr Benn. What on earth must he have thought while his companion was relating tales of Bonaparte's extraordinary personal courage? Herr Benn had said very little apart from a few neutral questions. He would know where Jacques's sympathies lay. Marguerite was quite sure Herr Benn would never be foolish enough to jeopardise his mission by slighting Bonaparte to such an ardent supporter.

It had been astonishing, to her, that Herr Benn was prepared to travel with such a man. But then again, what better cover could he find than a Bonapartist? No doubt, Jacques could talk them both out of any difficulty they might encounter.

Marguerite's respect for Herr Benn was growing by the moment, and so was her ambition to learn to detest Louis Jacques. Unfortunately, in spite of her best endeavours, she was failing there. Her rebellious body continued to respond every time he appeared. The closer he came, the more her heart raced and her skin burned. She could not understand what was happening to her. Even as a green girl, she had never reacted in such a way to any man.

In a flash of burning insight, she understood that it was useless to wonder why it was so. It simply was. And there was no help for it.

* * *

Guillaume drew Marguerite into the deserted kitchen. 'He's leaving tomorrow. Your Mr Jacques.'

'What? But surely not. Herr Benn is nowhere near well enough to leave his bed.'

'That's as may be, mistress. All I know is that he had me send the boy to the livery stables to arrange a horse for him. It's to be brought round at first light. He's in his room now, making ready.'

For a moment, Marguerite was speechless. She could not understand what the man was about. He had promised to fulfil his trust to Herr Benn. He couldn't leave, surely? Perhaps he was simply riding out for another glimpse of his idol? 'Is there any news of Bonaparte?' she asked, hoping that she sounded suitably innocent. 'He should have been arrested by now, surely?'

'The rumour is that he'll be arriving here soon, mistress.'

'Here, in Lyons? No, that's impossible. There's half an army between him and us. He's bound to be taken.'

'That's your heart speaking, and not your head, if you'll forgive my saying so,' Guillaume said bleakly. 'We had all those years of him before. You know, just as well as I do, how much the army loves him. They'll not touch so much as a hair of his head. You mark my words.'

Marguerite gulped. More than anything she had learned today, the old servant's words had brought home to her just how much danger surrounded her family. 'What can we do, Guillaume?' she whispered.

'We must keep our heads down, and our mouths shut,' he said bluntly. 'And, if you'll allow me to give you a word of advice, you'll get rid of those two men you brought from Marseilles. They're trouble.'

'But you said that Mr Jacques was going tomorrow, in any

case? Or did I misunderstand?' She was playing for time, now. She had to find out just how much Guillaume suspected. She needed to decide how far she could trust him, with another man's life. On one issue he was right, though—Louis Jacques was most certainly trouble.

Guillaume gave her a long, assessing look. When she returned his gaze unflinchingly, he nodded to himself and glanced over his shoulder to the kitchen door. It was firmly closed. The kitchen boy had not returned. 'I think you have suspicions, just like mine, Miss Marguerite. I reckon they're Bonapartists, those two, and that Mr Jacques will be off to join his Emperor tomorrow. What he said about looking after his friend—I reckon it was all lies, to enlist our sympathy. He's a deep one, and sly.'

'So what do you think we should do?'

'Let him go, and good riddance. And the moment he's out of the house, send t'other one to the Hôtel Dieù. We can't afford to have strangers in the house if Bonaparte does return. His informers won't be far behind.'

Sensible advice, if the situation were as simple as it seemed to Guillaume. But it was not. Marguerite took a deep breath and laid a confiding hand on the servant's arm. 'You are right, but only in part,' she said softly. 'Mr Jacques is a Bonapartist, just as you suspected. And Herr Benn pretends to share his companion's views. But he—' She swallowed. 'He is an English spy, Guillaume.'

'*What?*' Seeing Marguerite's sudden frown, he lowered his voice and said, 'A spy? No, you must be mistaken, mistress. He'll be a Bonapartist, just like his friend.'

Marguerite shook her head vehemently and quickly explained what she knew of Herr Benn. 'So you see, Guillaume,' she finished, 'we must protect Herr Benn until he is well enough to continue with his mission. And we must prevent Mr Jacques from discovering that he has been duped.'

'Best let him leave tomorrow then, as he plans.'

It was the obvious solution, but Marguerite felt sure, somehow, that it was the wrong solution. 'No, we dare not, however tempting it may be. We do not know what he plans to do, nor how much he may suspect about Herr Benn. He may be waiting for an opportunity to come back to arrest him. And us, too, if Bonaparte wins power again.' Her mind seemed to be filled with quarrelling voices, some arguing that Jacques would betray her, others that he would never do such a dishonourable thing. She was beginning to feel as if her head would burst asunder.

Guillaume stroked his chin. 'There are too many unanswered questions here. What we need is time. After all, Bonaparte may be captured, or even killed, long before he reaches Lyons.'

She had forgotten to tell him! She must be losing her wits. 'No, Guillaume, you were right about that,' she said quickly. 'When the usurper met the first of the troops sent to arrest him, they disobeyed their officers and changed sides. No doubt Bonaparte will be in Grenoble by now.'

'How do you know that, mistress? I've heard only rumours, nothing definite.'

'Mr Jacques was there. He saw. I overheard him telling Herr Benn. And he was jubilant. Guillaume, we must stop him from leaving. He may betray us all!'

Guillaume picked up the kitchen knife from the table and weighed it in his hand.

'No! There must be no killing!' It did not matter what Jacques was, or what he might do. Marguerite could never allow him to die. In his own way, and in spite of his misguided allegiance, he was a fine and honourable man.

'No?' He laid the knife down on the table once more. 'Well, perhaps you're right, mistress. It would be plaguey inconvenient to dispose of a body just at present, with all those soldiers in the city. So… Yes, I think I can see a way. But, for this, I will need your help.'

She would agree to anything as long as Jacques was allowed to live. 'You shall have it,' she said firmly. 'Whatever you need.'

Chapter Nine

Jack had barely slept. His body had been tired enough, after almost two solid days on horseback, but his mind would not be still. He was struggling with pangs of guilt at leaving Ben behind in a city which was like to welcome Bonaparte at any moment. Ben was cavalier about the risks; he was certain that he was safe in the Grolier house, because the younger sister was making sheep's eyes at him. Jack was not nearly so sure. The decisions in the Grolier family were made by Miss Marguerite, and she was a Bonapartist to the tips of her elegant little toes.

He rolled over and tried to ignore the image that word had conjured up. But he could not. It was so real that she could have been there beside him, standing in the doorway of her room in that mean little inn, her feet bare, her glorious hair spilling around her shoulders, and her wrapper loose, as if her body were beckoning him to reach behind the fabric and sample the exquisite body beneath.

He groaned into his pillow. His imagination was playing tricks, but his body continued to respond in the most inconvenient way, even though she had never made any deliberate move to entice him. If her wrapper was undone, it was because she had given him the belt to tie up a would-be robber, not because she wanted Jack's hands to explore the delights of her body. She would doubtless have made him another victim of her candlestick if he had tried! And every subsequent encounter had been just as innocent. On her part.

He must stop thinking about her. He must focus on his mission. He was the leader and responsible for its success, or failure, though he had made a pretty poor fist of it thus far. He had been much too unwary in Marseilles, blithely sauntering into the first harbour inn they came upon. Dominic and Leo never took such chances. He remembered it now, much too late, and he burned with shame at his own failings. His brothers always spent time in the taprooms of a town, listening and talking to the regular drinkers, before they decided on a new lodging. They usually checked on emergency escape routes, too. Why had Jack forgotten all those simple rules? It was at least partly because of his lack of care that Ben had been shot. And it was certainly Jack's fault that Ben was now dangerously lodged in a Bonapartist household where one unwary word could betray him. Dominic and Leo would never have allowed matters to come to such a pass.

Jack had to admit that both his brothers were a great deal more experienced, and a great deal wiser about this spying game than he was. Game? At the outset, back in Vienna, it had seemed to be just a jolly spree, a replacement for the thrill his reckless gambling had previously provided. There would be no more gambling now. Without Leo's generosity, Jack would have faced public dishonour, to add to his private guilt and shame. That was why this mission mattered. It was a chance for Jack to redeem himself with his brothers, and to serve his country into the bargain. He had been immensely proud that Wellington himself had selected him to lead the mission. He had laughed at any mention of danger, for he and

Ben had been in many scrapes in the past, and had always come through with a whole skin. In the event, he had behaved like an utter fool. He was bidding fair to be just as reckless over this French mission as at the gaming tables.

From now on, things would be very different. As soon as it was fully light, Jack would have to ride out from Lyons, and somehow make his way home to deliver his crucial burden of information, gathering more along the way. From now on, every inn would have to be carefully checked, every chance acquaintance viewed as suspect. That was what he should have done from the moment they set foot on French soil. But he had been too hot-headed, too puffed up with his own importance as mission leader, to bother with the most basic precautions. And, as a result, he would be leaving Ben behind, wounded, to face he knew not what.

He had been thoroughly irresponsible. He should never have allowed Marguerite Grolier to take them beyond the gates of Marseilles. The Aikenhead Honours always worked alone. He should have remembered. But he had been bewitched by a mass of fair curls and more cool courage than any woman should ever possess.

It would be best if he never set eyes on her again.

He continued to toss and turn for what seemed like hours. Eventually, he gave up and got out of bed. He would wash in cold water and dress by candlelight. He might even manage something approaching a shave. Then he would creep down to Ben's chamber to say his farewells. At least he had had the forethought to identify which creaking stairs to avoid. With luck, he would be able to leave the house undetected, before anyone else was stirring. He knew where the livery stable was. He would simply walk there and collect the horse himself.

If he did not see her again, he might one day be able to put her out of his mind.

* * *

By the time he was more or less presentable, it was definitely less dark outside. He peered out through the crack between the shutters, trying to get a glimpse of the sky, but even here, near the top of the house, it was very difficult to see beyond the windows of the house immediately opposite. If he opened the shutters, he would be able to stick his head out, but he doubted he could do so without making a great deal of noise. As far as he could tell, it was not raining, which was all that really mattered.

He turned back into the room, automatically checking that nothing had been left behind. Everything but his shaving gear had been packed away. He crossed to the dressing table where he carefully dried his razor and shaving brush, before returning them to their places and tying the leather roll. He was just about to tuck it down the side of his valise when he heard a tiny knock on the door.

He only just managed to bite back the curse that rose to his lips. It could not be Ben. He was improving, but not enough to manage a flight of stairs. It was probably Guillaume, up far too early, bringing him hot water.

Careful, Jack! This is just the kind of situation where you need to think before you act!

For a moment, he stood stock still, desperately trying to rework his plans. It would not matter if he was unable to creep out of the house unseen. His reason there had been nothing vital, simply a reflection of his own childish desire to avoid any further meeting with Marguerite. He could revert to the original plan. He would accept the hot water graciously—he might even take a few minutes to give himself a proper shave—and he would do everything else quite openly, leaving only when the livery horse was delivered to the door. At this early hour, Marguerite was bound to be still asleep.

He crossed to the door and pulled it open. 'Good mo— Oh!'

It was Marguerite. She was carrying a heavy wooden tray with a jug of steaming water, a cup of coffee, three slices of bread and a lighted candle. The single flame made a halo of her beautiful hair and cast strange upward shadows on to her face. She looked ethereal, he decided, though there was a cast of almost grim determination in her features.

He swallowed hard, and bowed to her. 'Miss Grolier. I had not looked for such an attention from you. I—'

'If you would allow me to lay down my burden, sir?' She smiled and took a pace forward, forcing Jack to make way for her. He reached for the tray, but she ignored him. Without the slightest sign of embarrassment, she walked straight across his bedchamber to put her tray on the dressing table. Then she took up her candle and turned back to him.

He saw that she was wearing a white cook's apron that covered her almost completely. She might seem as pale, as insubstantial as a ghost, but she was a working ghost. Who else was there to prepare coffee for him at this hour? The daily cook did not arrive until much later than this. Apart from Guillaume and the kitchen boy, who was biddable but simple, the household consisted of only the two sisters and the old female servant who cared for the invisible invalid mother. Besides doing their own weaving, and running their business, the two sisters must also do many of the household chores. Did they ever have time to sleep at all?

He should be ashamed that, by accepting her hospitality for himself and a wounded man, he had increased her already heavy workload. That had been arrogant of him, and selfish. Now he was contrite, even though it was too late to make practical amends. 'There was no need for you to take so much trouble over me, ma'am, though I do thank you for it,' he said, and meant it. 'I would—'

'You would do me a kindness, sir, if you were to drink my coffee while it is hot.' She picked up the cup and held it out to him. She was looking steadily up into his face. A brief flicker of her candle showed him eyes that seemed to have turned a deep, forest green. It would be how he would remember her.

He took the cup with a murmur of thanks and swallowed a mouthful. It was hot, bitter and delicious. He almost gasped aloud at the realisation that his feelings for Marguerite were all of those things. Embarrassed, and trying to avoid her gaze, he tossed back the rest of the coffee and held out the empty cup. The movement was a little awkward, for he had splayed his fingers round it, in hopes that her hand might touch his. Just for a second. One last touch. One last, searing memory.

She avoided his childish trap without the least difficulty. She was still staring up at him, but for some reason her face was becoming quite indistinct, as if a heavy veil had been drawn down between them. As if—

Marguerite almost tossed the cup back on to the tray, but even with both hands free she was unable to do more than break his fall a little. The drug had worked much more quickly than Guillaume had predicted, perhaps because Jacques had taken it on an empty stomach.

He had crumpled into an untidy heap on the floor. She tried to straighten his limbs, but his legs were too heavy, and awkwardly trapped beneath him. All she could do was to free his right arm and to fetch a pillow for his head. Guillaume would have to do the rest.

She knelt on the floor, staring down at his unconscious body. She must not feel in the least sorry for him. She had done only what she had to do to protect Herr Benn. If Jacques had to suffer a little, it was on his own head, his just reward for supporting a monster. Such was the way of war.

But nevertheless, she could not resist laying a hand gently on his cheek, savouring the contact with his warm, vibrant body. His cheek was smooth, with delicate shadowed skin just below his closed eyes, but his jaw line was a little rough. She peered more closely. He had certainly shaved, but he had not done it very well, with no hot water to soften the stubble. Poor Jacques. He was young, and brave, and committed to his cause. In many ways he was admirable, but he—

Her musings were interrupted by a creak on the stairs. She jerked her hand away and jumped to her feet. What on earth had she been doing, allowing free rein to such treacherous thoughts? She would not allow it to happen any more. She would keep herself under rigid control.

She reached the open door, just as Guillaume appeared. One look at the body on the floor was enough to produce a grunt of satisfaction, but it did not remove his worried frown. He pulled Marguerite further into the room and closed the door. 'The stable lad has just arrived with the horse. He brings bad news, and not mere rumour. The regiment was ordered to muster at first light, for review by the Comte d'Artois. It was a shambles. Instead of saluting the King's brother as they should have done, half of the regiment made faces at him. It was a rabble, not an army. Once they started shouting for their Emperor, the comte knew that it was all up with him. He's ridden off for Paris.'

'Oh, God help us!'

'Just so, mistress, for the regiment will not. They are waiting for their Emperor to enter Lyons in triumph. He is expected within hours.'

Marguerite realised that she had been wringing her hands throughout Guillaume's appalling story. She forced them apart and held them tight to her sides. This was a time for action, not hand-wringing. 'There is nothing we can do about that, Guillaume. If he comes, he comes. We must concentrate on dealing with *him*.' She nodded towards the body on the floor. 'Help me get him up.'

It took their combined strength to lift him on to the ladder-back chair. Marguerite propped him up and supported his poor head while Guillaume knelt to tie his ankles to the chair legs. Jacques's thick hair was falling softly over his face. He must have washed it. Without thinking, she stroked it back from his temples. It felt like strong silk under her fingers. It—

Guillaume rose again to bind Jacques's wrists and she stepped back quickly. The limp body slumped forward, held only by its bonds. 'That won't do. You must find something to tie around his chest, to anchor him to the chair.'

Guillaume's eyes lit upon the unconscious man's belt. Without hesitation, he pulled it free and tightened it round Jacques's chest and the back of the chair. 'Have you a handkerchief, mistress?' he said finally.

'What for?' She could guess. Jacques was already trussed like a chicken for the pot. Now he was to be gagged. It was the ultimate indignity.

'You know what for, Miss Marguerite. This may be the only occupied room on this floor, but his voice could still be heard below, or down in the street. We dare not take the risk.'

She nodded glumly and produced a clean handkerchief. Guillaume lifted the lolling head and gagged Jacques tightly. 'That will do for now,' he said, with satisfaction. 'Once the drug has worn off, I'll come back and unbuckle the belt so that he has a little freedom of movement. But the bindings on wrists and ankles must stay. As must the gag. You do see that, mistress?'

She nodded again. 'How long do you think we will need to hold him?' When they had made their plan, they had not expected Bonaparte to arrive so soon. They had hoped to have enough time to get Herr Benn on his feet, and on his way out of Lyons. Everything had changed with the stable lad's shocking news.

'I don't know. It will depend on how soon the usurper arrives, and how soon he moves on to Paris. We may end up having to keep both our *guests* hidden until after Bonaparte has left Lyons. Once Herr Benn is well enough, we can tell him what we have done. He will decide on the best tactics.'

'We could ask him now,' she said eagerly. 'He may be prepared to take Mr Jacques's parole. Then we would not need to keep him bound.'

'You are too soft-hearted by far, mistress,' Guillaume said with a wry smile. 'But it will not do. Herr Benn is still extremely weak. I thought I detected a hint of fever when I tended to him last night, so we must do nothing to cause him concern. Besides, you know we must keep his true identity from your sister. If we tell Herr Benn the truth now, he is bound to betray it to her.'

'But she—'

'She is normally the soul of discretion, and biddable to a fault, mistress, but she is in love with Herr Benn. Have you not seen the steely determination she has acquired where he is concerned? She would be like a tigress if she thought that Mr Jacques, or any of us, was like to harm her darling. She must learn nothing of this.'

Guillaume was probably right. Everyone else in the household must be given to understand that Jacques had ridden off, as intended, at first light. Then no one would enquire after him. Guillaume would see to his needs. There was no reason for anyone else to come up to this floor, or to enter the room, though it was a pity the door had no lock.

Then she saw the real flaw. 'What about the horse?'

'I thought of that,' Guillaume said rather smugly. 'I sent the stable lad about his business. Once he was gone, I told the kitchen boy to lead the horse out of the city and keep him hidden for a few hours. He's to let the animal loose a few streets away from the livery stable, so that it will return home of its own accord. Horses always do. Its owner will think only that there was some kind of accident. He won't care twopence provided his horse is unharmed. He was paid in advance.'

It was a good plan and would probably work. Jacques was fated to remain a prisoner, undetected, until Herr Benn should be well enough to decide his fate.

The body in the chair was stirring. Marguerite heard a muffled groan.

Guillaume pushed her roughly towards the door. 'He must not see you,' he hissed. 'Go quickly, and do not return until I tell you it is safe.'

When Jack finally managed to open his eyes, he was surprised to see Guillaume standing in front of him, with his feet firmly planted and an aggressive look on his face. Jack tried to move. It was only then that he discovered he was sitting down, and that he was bound and gagged, to boot. He began to struggle.

'I wouldn't waste your strength, sir,' Guillaume said equably.

Jack shook his head fiercely, straining against the gag. He would not yield. He had been drugged, and he was a helpless prisoner. With a pounding headache.

'You won't be harmed,' Guillaume said, 'unless you do something rash, like trying to escape.' He paused, scrutinising Jack's mutinous face. 'If you stop struggling, I'll remove that belt from round your chest, and fetch some lotion for that bump on your head. You did that yourself when you fell,' he added, as though it worried him that Jack might believe he had been struck from behind.

Jack ignored the pain. He saw that he was tied to the chair

with his own belt. So much for his careful planning! It was
the ultimate ignominy! The leader of the Aikenhead Honours
in France had been overcome by a grizzled old servant.

No, that was wrong. The guiding hand was not Guillaume's,
but Marguerite's. She had given him the coffee and encouraged him to drink it. She had smiled, too. If he ever got free
of this, he would wring her beautiful neck!

Jack's initial fury had abated a little. Guillaume had
removed the belt, though he had then passed it round Jack's
biceps and through the slats of the chair. He could not move
his arms, but he could breathe more easily. Guillaume had fed
him the bread from Marguerite's tray, washed down with
water from the shaving jug. Since it was almost cold by the
time he drank it, Jack knew he must have been unconscious
for a considerable time. It must be nearly noon.

Guillaume had said he would come to no harm, but Jack
did not believe that. If they freed him now, Jack would find a
way of taking his revenge on them. They must know that.
Somehow, they must have discovered that he was not the
Bonapartist he claimed to be. No doubt they would deliver
him to the usurper's forces at the first opportunity. At best, he
faced prison; if they discovered he was English, he would be
shot as a spy. His mission was a failure.

And what of Ben? Had they secured him, too? That would
require no elaborate trick with drugged coffee. They had only
to keep Ben in his room, for he was still too weak to fight back,
or to try to escape. Ben did not deserve to be shot. If he died
here, it would be Jack's doing. His mission was doubly a failure.

Marguerite Grolier had won, curse her!

She had brought the drugged coffee to him herself. Did she
suspect how his body reacted to her presence? Or was it simply
that he was bound to be surprised, and grateful, for such

kindness? If Guillaume had brought it, Jack might well have set it aside, impatient to be on his way. But it would have been the height of ill manners to do so to Marguerite. With her clear green gaze on him, he had drunk it down. And she, no doubt, had smiled while she watched him crumple to the floor.

Yet he could not hate her. Why? What was it about this fierce and formidable Frenchwoman that stopped him from hating her, for the enemy she was? He pondered that for a long time without arriving at any very clear answer. She was extraordinarily brave and resourceful, as she had just proved by besting him so efficiently. She was beautiful, hard-working and dedicated to her cause. She would make a wonderful mate for a man who shared her beliefs and matched her qualities, but he doubted she would ever find a man worthy of her among the artisans of Lyons. She was only a weaver's daughter, but she had the manners of a lady, and the clear-sighted virtues of a queen.

Chapter Ten

'**M**arguerite! Guillaume! Come quickly!' It was Suzanne's voice, from the floor above. She sounded to be in complete panic.

Marguerite raced out of the kitchen and up the stairs with Guillaume at her heels. The door to Herr Benn's little room stood open. Inside, Marguerite could see Suzanne kneeling on the floor near the end of the bed.

'Suzanne, what on earth is the matter?' And then she saw. 'Oh, goodness. Guillaume, fetch hot water and fresh bandages. Quickly.'

Marguerite flung herself down beside Herr Benn's motionless body. His head was bleeding copiously, and the bandages round his chest and shoulder were turning redder by the minute. Whatever had happened, it had reopened his wound. She felt for a pulse. It was there, and fairly strong, but irregular.

'When Guillaume returns, we will get him back on to the bed and dress his wounds. Do not look so concerned, Suzanne. Head wounds always bleed like this.' She mopped away the blood with her handkerchief so that she could gently spread the hair around the new injury. She examined it carefully. 'It is not so very deep. I expect Herr Benn has a hard head. I am sure he will soon mend.'

Suzanne was shivering. Her eyes were wide and staring from the stark whiteness of her face. Had she heard a single word? Marguerite took a blanket from the bed to wrap round her sister's shoulders. Herr Benn would not need it until his wounds had been dressed. By then, Suzanne would be herself again.

Guillaume rushed back into the room. He had been re-markably quick.

'Put the water down by the bed, Guillaume, and help me to lift him. Once we have dressed his hurts, we must not move him again.'

Guillaume took Herr Benn's shoulders and Marguerite his feet. Suzanne, still shivering and staring vacantly, did not move an inch or react in any way.

'Good. Now we'll start with this head wound.' Marguerite bathed it gently and bound a pad of linen over it. The bandage covered most of his left eye, too, though it had sustained no injury. 'He will have to use only one eye for a while. Heads are remarkably difficult to bandage,' she added, trying to sound light-hearted. She looked round to see whether Suzanne was responding to her feeble quip. But she still had not moved.

'Do you lift his shoulders, Guillaume, while I take off this bandage.' The wrappings round his upper body were gradu-ally unwound. Underneath, the pad was soaked with fresh blood. Marguerite said nothing. She simply cleaned the wound, applied a new and larger pad, and bound it in place. 'Now we must make him comfortable and keep him warm.' She rinsed her bloody fingers and rose. 'Suzanne, I shall need the blanket you have there. Herr Benn is becoming chilled.'

'What?' Suzanne turned to face the bed, ignoring the

blanket, which fell from her shoulders. She gazed wide-eyed at Herr Benn as if for the first time. 'He is dead!' Her face was more grey than white. Her eyes were filling with tears.

Marguerite helped her sister to her feet. 'He is not dead. Come and see for yourself,' she said in rallying tones. She picked up Herr Benn's wrist, checking the pulse. 'His heart beats strongly. He will soon recover.'

In a rush of emotion, Suzanne threw herself on her knees, clasped Herr Benn's hand in both her own, and carried it to her lips for a passionate kiss. Her tears were flowing strongly now, but the warm flesh seemed to reassure her a little. After a moment she looked up at her sister. 'You swear he will recover?' It was the hesitant voice of a child seeking certainty from an all-powerful parent.

'He was mending very well until now, my dear. I am certain that he will again.' When a little of Suzanne's colour began to return, Marguerite risked a question. 'Were you with him when it happened? How came he to be out of bed?'

'It was my fault.' Suzanne gulped and dug out a handkerchief to blow her nose. 'I was telling him about Bonaparte's arrival in Lyons and about how the Comte d'Artois rode off this morning with his tail between his legs. I thought no harm. Benn is a German, after all. What is it to him whether we have a king or an emperor to rule over us? But he became agitated. I tried to keep him in bed, but he pushed me away. He fell heavily and hit his head on the corner of the chest. He muttered something, and then he passed out. That is when I called for help.'

'Very wise, my dear. And by the sound of it, there was nothing you could have done to prevent this…um…unfortunate accident.' Marguerite put a comforting hand on her sister's shoulder and squeezed gently. 'You said he was muttering,' she added, airily. 'Could you make out any words?'

'No, not really. It sounded a little like "Jacques" but it was not that. He could barely speak, you see, for he was face down on the floor.'

Marguerite was in no doubt that Herr Benn had indeed referred to his travelling companion. He would know that, now Napoleon had entered Lyons in triumph, Jacques presented a very real danger. What had Herr Benn intended to do? There was no way of knowing. But it was certain that he would now be confined to bed for a considerable time. Marguerite sighed. She had hoped to be able to speed Herr Benn on his way as soon as Bonaparte left Lyons for Paris. There was no longer any chance of that. For all she knew, his whole mission might have been put in jeopardy by this new delay. Suzanne should have known better.

'Suzanne, why did you tell him about Bonaparte? I thought we had agreed to say nothing to anyone about either king or emperor?'

'I…I'm sorry, Marguerite. I'm afraid I didn't think about that. Herr Benn and I, we have become so comfortable together these last few days. He said he was bored, having to lie in bed all the time, and so I told him about the Comte d'Artois in hopes of making him laugh. The comte may be the King's brother, but he is a ridiculous little man, and deserves to be laughed at,' she added, with venom. 'Benn became agitated, and asked me whether Bonaparte had actually arrived in Lyons. I could not lie to him, Marguerite. And then he pushed himself out of bed, and—'

'Say no more, my love. You have had a shock. I suggest you return to your room and rest.'

'But I should stay to—'

'Do not concern yourself about Herr Benn. Guillaume and I will look after him, I promise.'

* * *

Jack swallowed the last of the stewed meat from the spoon. 'What was all that commotion I heard earlier? A woman's voice, screaming for help.'

Guillaume frowned but said nothing. He retrieved the gag from the dressing table. 'If you have finished, sir, I'm afraid I must put this on again.'

Jack shook his head. 'I need a drink. Surely you have some water, or some small ale?' He desperately wanted to avoid the gag for as long as possible.

Guillaume poured water into a glass and held it to Jack's lips so that he could drink. 'If you freed one of my hands, Guillaume, I could shift for myself. It would save you a great deal of trouble.'

Guillaume grinned briefly down at Jack. 'Now that, sir, is what I would call a plumper. You know, and I know, that if I freed even one of your hands, you'd have your fingers round my neck before I could say a word.'

Jack laughed. He was beginning to think that the old man did indeed mean him no harm. But if Jack was not to be handed over to Bonaparte's agents, what on earth did they intend to do with him? 'Perhaps you should experiment with releasing only a finger or two? I cannot strangle you without a thumb, you know.'

Guillaume raised an eyebrow. 'Don't think I'd put anything past you, sir. 'Fraid I have my instructions. Bound and gagged at all times.' He offered Jack more water but, when that was done, he made to replace the gag. He would do it with an apology, and a degree of gentleness, but he would ensure it was tight.

'A moment, Guillaume. I have a bargain to propose.'

Guillaume stood in front of the chair, the gag dangling threateningly from his fingers. 'Sir?'

'You do accept that I am a gentleman?' He waited for

Guillaume's nod before continuing. 'If I give you my word of honour that I will not cry out for as long as you hold me bound here, will you not agree to forgo the gag? It is suffocating, you know,' he added confidingly, 'besides undignified for any man.'

Jack could see that Guillaume was already half-persuaded. Guillaume himself had a certain dignity. Jack's words had struck home.

'You give me your parole that you will not shout, or call for help? You will not even call attention to the fact that you are in this room?'

Jack's mind was racing. He must respond without hesitation. 'I give you my parole that I will not use my voice to call attention to myself in any way, if you will agree not to restore the gag.'

Guillaume considered that, but seemed to detect no flaw. 'I cannot see that Miss Marguerite would object,' he said carefully.

That was the first time Guillaume had admitted, in terms, that Jack was imprisoned by Marguerite Grolier's command. Jack had known it, and yet the confirmation settled like a lead weight in his gut.

'I accept your parole, sir. I will leave aside the gag.' He bowed and left.

Jack listened for the sound of Guillaume's boots on the floorboards and then on the stairs. He needed to be absolutely sure there was no one within earshot before he embarked on his plan. It was the slimmest of chances, but he was not prepared to sit and wait for whatever fate Marguerite Grolier had decided to inflict on him. He wanted to meet her, face to face, and on equal terms. There would be no more lusting after her glorious body. It would be a battle. And only one of them would emerge victorious.

After almost an hour of rocking methodically back and forwards in his chair, and banging the legs down on to the bare floorboards, Jack was beginning to lose heart. He had been so sure that he was above the room where Marguerite's sick mother was nursed. It stood to reason that someone would come up to find out who, or what, was creating all the noise and disturbing the invalid.

Thus far, nothing. Jack had never set eyes on Marguerite's mother. Indeed, he had had only a few glimpses of old Berthe, the maid who looked after her. Berthe seemed to spend almost all her time on her nursing duties, though, just occasionally, Jack had seen her performing chores such as changing bed linen or sweeping floors. Obviously, the mother was a demanding patient who needed constant nursing. So, either Berthe was stone deaf, or she was out on some errand.

Should he stop? It was a useful way of moving round the room, and he was now close enough to the window to be able to peer out through the chink in the shutters. On the other hand, if the invalid mother was lying downstairs alone, and unable to rise from her bed or to call for help, the noise could well be driving her to distraction. But perhaps she was not even there?

Jack's conscience got the better of him then, and he stopped banging his chair. His plan was not working. Besides, even if the noise did bring someone upstairs to investigate, there was no certainty that it would help. Berthe might be part of the plot to hold Jack captive, just as Marguerite and Guillaume were.

And yet he wondered about that. Marguerite and Guillaume were very close-mouthed. Nothing had been said to suggest that even Miss Suzanne knew what was going on, far less Berthe and the invalid mother.

Jack sighed. He would have to think of something else. Or he might try again later, after dusk, when the mother was sure to be back in her bedchamber.

'I do think a gentleman should rise when a lady comes into the room.'

The voice came from behind him, by the door. It was a clipped, cultured voice that reminded Jack very forcibly of his French mother.

He twisted his head round, but he could not see her. He had to rock the chair backwards and forwards several times before he turned it round far enough to see. His jaw dropped. There, in the open doorway, stood a lady who was an older version of Marguerite—the same features, the same height and neat build, and the same hair. Apart from the colour, which was grey. Marguerite's mother.

This lady was no helpless invalid. She appeared well nourished and healthy. She was dressed in what Jack took to be a silk gown, though the style might be a little old-fashioned. Another sign that the Grolier silk business was less prosperous than it had been, Jack decided.

'Have you lost your tongue as well as your manners, young man?' she asked waspishly, taking a couple of paces into the room.

Jack craned his neck to see beyond her, to the door. It seemed she was quite alone. Berthe, for some reason, had abandoned her vigil.

'I beg your pardon, ma'am. Most humbly. It was not my intention to offend you in any way.' He sat absolutely still, waiting to see what she would do.

'Hmmph.' She came slowly across the room, and then walked round the chair, frowning down at Jack as if he were an exhibit in a museum. Jack could not help noticing that she had a remarkably elegant carriage, again very reminiscent of his mother. Most odd in the wife of a lowly silk weaver.

'It's a fine day,' she said suddenly. 'Spring has come at last. A young man should not be inside doing nothing when there's work to be done on the land. The peasants will be doing the ploughing. They need a master's supervision.'

Jack held his breath, waiting.

When he did not respond, her voice began to rise indignantly. 'Young men today. I don't understand them at all. Thoroughly work shy.' She cuffed Jack around the ear. 'Now, get along with you, do.'

'My lady,' he said humbly, judging it the best form of address to use with this strange female, 'it would be my pleasure to obey you but, unfortunately, I seem to have got myself caught in this chair. The fault of my own clumsiness, I readily admit. If your ladyship could perhaps help me to free my hands, I would be able to go out straight away. Heaven knows what kind of furrows the peasants may be ploughing without me there to supervise them.'

She seemed to be noticing his bonds for the first time. 'I'm not at all sure,' she said, beginning to untie his left hand, 'that a man who can tie himself in knots like this should be entrusted with any kind of supervision.'

Don't let her stop now! 'I am clumsy with my hands, as your ladyship has said, but I know what needs to be done in the fields. I can direct others, even if I do not have the manual skills to do the work myself. I came highly recommended.'

'An aristocrat does not need recommendations,' she said flatly. She had freed his left hand, but was making no move to start on the right. She frowned. 'I had taken you for a gentleman, not a mere steward. Clearly I was mistaken.'

Surreptitiously, Jack flexed the fingers of his left hand. He would be able to free himself now, but it would be so much quicker if she did it for him. He would have to humour her strange fancies. 'I am no steward, my lady.' He had injected the appropriate note of pride into his voice. 'I am the son of a duke.'

She nodded, as if it was all perfectly normal, and began to untie his right hand.

The moment both his hands were free, Jack bent to untie

his ankles. The lady had taken a step back and appeared to be watching him. She had not spoken again, however, and a rather vacant look had come into her eyes. Jack was not at all sure that she had the first idea of what was happening.

He resolved to continue this weird charade. As soon as he was able, he stood and made her his most elegant bow. Even a duchess could not have expected more. She did not seem at all surprised. She acknowledged it with a slight nod and an airy wave of the hand as she walked across to the shuttered window.

'If your ladyship will permit, I will be off about my duties at once.'

She did not turn. She was fiddling with the latch. 'You have been very remiss until now, young man. Do not repeat your failings. You may go.'

Hardly daring to believe his luck, Jack fled out into the passage and silently closed the door on that extraordinary encounter. He was free! But he still had to rescue Ben, and to get them both out of this house. He had very little time. Someone might come searching for Madame Grolier at any moment.

He slipped down the stairs, carefully avoiding the creaking treads. The passageway below was empty, and there was no sound from any of the bedchambers. He crept forward to put his ear against Ben's door. No voices. No movement. He must take the risk. He put his hand to the latch and began to raise it, a fraction at a time. Mercifully, it did not grate. In a trice, he was inside, the door was closed again, and he was leaning against it, letting out a long breath.

'You!'

Marguerite Grolier had sprung to her feet. On the bed, as motionless as a corpse in a coffin, lay Ben, his eyes closed and his head swathed in bandages.

'What have you done to him?' Jack cried, starting forward.

'Stand where you are!' she spat.

That stopped him in his tracks, but only for a second. 'And if I do not? You will shoot me, I suppose?' he asked sardonically. Her hands were empty, and he could see no sign of a weapon in the room.

Her response flashed back at him. 'I shall scream for Guillaume, and he will shoot you without hesitation.'

Jack moved quietly to the end of the bed, only a couple of paces from her.

'Keep your distance,' she hissed, 'or I warn you, I shall scream.'

He lunged for her, pulling her close against his body so that she could not strike him, and clamping his large hand across her mouth. 'You waited too long, ma'am. Don't be afraid. I will let you go, but only if you promise not to scream. And if you tell me what you have done to Herr Benn.'

She responded by sinking her teeth into the fleshy part of his thumb.

'Argh!' he gasped, instinctively pulling his hand away. She was still pressed firmly to his chest, but she was opening her mouth to scream at the top of her lungs.

There was no help for it. He kissed her.

In all her twenty-three years, Marguerite had never been kissed by a man. She had hardly ever had the time to wonder how it might be, except on those few occasions when she and Suzanne sat alone together, late at night, spinning stories before the dying fire. Suzanne had mused about a man who would carry her off to a life without hardship, or care. Marguerite had dreamed of a man who would simply love her, a man whose kisses would transport her to paradise.

This was not paradise.

Jacques was determined to silence her, and she was determined to fight him. She tried to bite him again, but this time he was ready for her. No matter how much she tried, he would not permit her to open her lips wide enough to bare her teeth. And she could hear him laughing, deep in his throat, though he never once lifted his lips from hers. He was enjoying this, damn him!

In desperation, she began to kick him, but he laughed all the more. With only soft house shoes on her feet, she was probably hurting herself more than him.

'Mmm.' It was a long moan of satisfaction. He slid one arm up her back until his fingers were on the nape of her neck, and then in her hair.

She shivered. It was a caress, and she did not dare to think about being caressed by this man.

He moved her head a little, so that he would have easier access to her mouth. He moaned again, never for a moment breaking the kiss. This time, it was a deeper, richer sound, the voice that could make her whole being vibrate like the strings of a violin. She found herself longing to return his kiss.

He must have sensed it, for he gentled the kiss and touched his tongue to her lips. She could have bared her teeth then, but she had lost all desire to attack him. Instead, she parted her lips in welcome. When the tip of his tongue flicked along the length of her upper lip, a shaft of pure molten gold lanced into her belly. She clung to him, and began to return his kiss with sudden, unstoppable fervour.

'Mistress, where are you? There is terrible news.' It was Guillaume's voice, from the top of the stairs. The door swung open with a crash. 'That monster Bonaparte has—' The old servant stopped dead, his mouth open.

Jacques drew Marguerite more tightly against him. Both her hands were still trapped between their bodies. 'And what, pray,' he began in an impudent, lazy drawl, 'has *that monster Bonaparte* done, exactly?'

Chapter Eleven

Behind his deliberately cool façade, Jack's mind was turning somersaults. And his body's reactions were under even less control than his mind. Kissing Marguerite Grolier had been a mistake, especially once she had begun to kiss him back. Though she was clearly untutored in the art of kissing, her innocent responses had set him ablaze, as if a lighted spill had been touched to dry tinder.

He was still holding her crushed against his body. They were so close that she must be perfectly aware of how he was reacting to her. Since he had been able to feel the pouting of her nipples through the combined layers of their clothing, she must surely have felt his equally physical response. Unless she was such an innocent that she understood nothing at all about men?

At that moment, she began to push against his chest with the flat of her hands. 'Let me go!' she muttered.

He looked down into her face. She had turned quite scarlet, but whether with passion, or with fury, he could not tell. 'I said I would let you go when you promised not to scream. And when you told me what had happened to Herr Benn. The first of those is of no moment now.' He glanced towards Guillaume, who was standing thunderstruck in the doorway. 'But I am still waiting for the second.'

'It is not Bonaparte who is a monster,' she cried angrily. 'It is you!' She pushed hard against him, and this time he let her go. It was so sudden that she stumbled backwards. He had to grasp her arm to stop her from falling.

'I—you—' She looked totally confused, and totally adorable, like a ruffled kitten. 'Oh, a plague on you, sir!' She dragged her arm free. For a moment, it seemed she was about to stamp her foot in vexation, but then she remembered her dignity and drew herself up, trying to look down her nose at Jack. It was more than a little difficult, of course, since he was so much taller than she.

Jack turned to the servant, deliberately giving Marguerite a moment to collect herself. 'Close the door, Guillaume. I want to talk to you,' he added. This was much more serious than kissing. He was quite sure he had not misheard. Guillaume had referred to Bonaparte as a monster. So had Marguerite. Had Jack been mistaken in thinking they were ardent Bonapartists? Surely not? Marguerite had spoken at length about her beloved Emperor. She had been utterly convincing.

Guillaume did not move. 'This has gone on long enough,' Jack snapped and marched round the bed to put himself between Guillaume and the open door. When Jack turned to close it, the servant retreated to stand protectively alongside his mistress. He was glaring at Jacques with acute dislike.

Poor Ben was still lying motionless, and he must be Jack's immediate concern. 'Now tell me, one of you, what happened to Herr Benn.'

'It's more important that *you* tell us—' Guillaume began hotly.

'He attempted to leave his bed.' Marguerite silenced Guillaume with a sharp gesture. 'He was far from well enough to do so. It seems that he swooned, and hit his head when he fell.'

'It *seems*?' Jack repeated, the question clear in his voice.

'Neither of us was here at the time,' Marguerite replied firmly. 'But Suzanne was. There can be no doubt of what happened.'

Jack nodded slowly. Miss Suzanne would have done nothing to harm Ben. It had probably been an accident, for why would they harm a man they had spent so long trying to heal?

'It was not a bad wound.' Marguerite was beginning to sound a little more confident. 'Unfortunately, the fall also wrenched his shoulder and his first wound reopened. It will take him much longer to recover than we had previously thought. But he will recover,' she added, with renewed steel in her voice. 'No one in this house has done *anything* to harm him.'

Jack was in no doubt that she was telling the truth. She was clearly concerned about poor Ben and truly sorry that he had come to further harm. One mystery was solved. But the other—much greater, and much more important in the complicated dance of European politics—remained to be unravelled.

'Now, tell me,' Jack said softly, directing his question at Guillaume, 'what was it that you were about to report? I think you mentioned "terrible news"?'

Guillaume's face was full of thwarted fury. Jack suspected he had been assessing the chance of fighting his way out of the room and had concluded that he would never succeed against a younger, stronger man.

'I am waiting,' Jack said silkily.

'And I am waiting to learn how you come to be standing here,' Guillaume retorted, his voice rasping, 'when I left you bound and helpless not two hours ago. I should have known better than to accept the parole of a Bonapartist.'

At Guillaume's side, Marguerite nodded vehemently. Jack fancied she was trying to force herself into an outburst of fury. But what on earth was going on? Marguerite Grolier had given him to understand that she supported Bonaparte. Why? He racked his brains, trying to remember precisely when she had first declared where her sympathies lay. There had been nothing said at the Marseilles harbour inn, he was sure. She had been much too busy with her candlestick. And in the coach? He could not remember anything there, either. No, it had been later, at the inn at Rognac. Was it only after she had heard Jack repeat the surgeon's heartfelt *'Vive l'Empereur!'* that she had spoken?

Was it possible that she had been lying to him, humouring him, because she believed him to be a Bonapartist? He shook his head, trying to clear his thoughts. Yet that one solution refused to be dismissed. It was the only one that fitted all the facts. She had claimed to support Bonaparte because she believed that Jack did. But now it was clear, from her own words, that she did not.

There was only one way to be absolutely certain. Ignoring Guillaume's angry question completely, Jack fixed his stern gaze on Marguerite's face. She paled a little, but continued to meet his eyes. 'You will tell me, pray, ma'am, where the sympathies of this house lie. You claimed to support, to love, the Emperor Napoleon. I take it that was a lie?'

She raised her chin proudly. 'Of course it was a lie. I could not put Guillaume or my family in jeopardy by telling you the truth. Though I might as well have done so, for you hold all the cards now. Your hero, your idol, has arrived in Lyons. Just yesterday, he established himself in the royal rooms vacated by no less a man than the King's brother. And he is surrounded by the cheering soldiers of the King's army, every one of them forsworn. Since you have broken your word, just as they have, I am sure it will not trouble your conscience to break the laws of hospitality as well. Are we to be delivered up to your little Corsican simply as foolish royal-ists? Or as spies?'

By God, she was magnificent! He cared not a whit that she was accusing him of breaking his word. That mistake could easily be remedied later. What mattered now was that, even when she was convinced she was about to be executed, she was holding steadfastly to the cause she believed in. King Louis did not deserve such loyalty.

'I must ask you, Marguerite,' Jack said, speaking very slowly and distinctly, 'to accept that I do not, and never will, support Bonaparte. I swore the oath to uphold my king, and that is what I continue to do.'

Her mouth opened, but the only sound she produced was a weak, strangled cry. For a second, all her limbs were shaking so much that she seemed on the point of collapse. When she eventually mastered herself enough to move, she picked up her skirts and fled, her hand extended in front of her to push Jack out of the way.

He did not attempt to stop her. She needed time alone. And so did he.

Jacques was not a Bonapartist. In spite of everything, he was not!

She could scarcely believe it. Was it possible that he was still playing a part? But why should he? Bonaparte was here in Lyons, and triumphant. There was nothing to stop Jacques from declaring himself, and bowing the knee to his Emperor. Except that Bonaparte was not his Emperor. Jacques had sworn his oath to the King and would hold to it.

It had all been a charade, a terrifying, dangerous, mis-guided charade!

She stopped pacing and sat down on the very edge of her bed, clasping her hands together in an attempt to stop them from shaking. Her body felt as though she was in the grip of the ague. Her bones ached, her every limb trembled, and her skin burned hot as fever. Could it really be true? It must be! There was no other explanation.

And she had drugged him, and imprisoned him, as if he were the enemy. She had even dreamt, however fleetingly, of what it would be like to shoot him. Even if he never learned of that, could he ever forgive her for what she *had* done? He had every right to feel revolted, just as she now did.

She dropped her head into her hands, but the bloody pictures that rose before her closed eyes were too much to bear. She raised her head again and stared unblinkingly at the blank partition between her chamber and the silk store.

Her thoughts became as clear, and as simple, as that flat, whitewashed wall. Louis Jacques was no longer her enemy. It was not wrong to be attracted to him, to value him. It would not be wrong to love him.

Her heart began to thump in an erratic rhythm, racing and missing beats by turns. Was that what she felt for him? Love?

The soaring joy that flooded her showed her where the truth lay. Yes, she loved Louis Jacques. Now that she knew the truth about him, she could at last allow her battered heart to feel. She had denied it to herself, and shrunk away from her own emotions, but she had loved him the very first time she saw him, wrapped in that ridiculous bed sheet.

She laughed at the memory. It was like being released from a dark dungeon to gaze in wonder at the sky. She loved him. Yes, he had looked ridiculous, but he was also brave and chivalrous. How many other men would have raced, unarmed, to the aid of a lady they had never met, to face an unknown danger?

Louis Jacques was certainly worthy of her love. But, after all she had done, what chance did she have? Would he ever forgive her enough to accept that she was worthy of him?

* * *

So Bonaparte had expelled *émigrés*, confiscated lands, and abolished all feudal titles. Guillaume had announced it as terrible news. Mama would agree, if she understood what it meant. But Marguerite did not care. A silk-weaver's family had no interest in such things.

What really mattered was that Guillaume refused to trust Mr Jacques. Jacques had given his word of honour not to escape, and had then broken it, according to Guillaume. No royalist supporter would do such a thing.

It had taken Marguerite some time to convince the old servant that Jacques could not be a Bonapartist. If he were, he would have joined Bonaparte long since. And given up the Grolier family, to boot. Jacques had to be a royalist. It was the only explanation that fitted the facts.

It was the only explanation that allowed her to love him without sacrificing her honour. It was the only explanation that gave her a chance to prove that she was worthy of him.

Marguerite's mind was in confusion. Her thoughts kept revolving round that one fixed point—she loved Jacques with her whole heart. She had to protect him, just as she had to protect Herr Benn. But she could not predict how Jacques would react if he learned Herr Benn was an English spy. Many Frenchmen, even ardent royalists, would be horrified at the thought of helping the country that had caused so many French deaths. Dare she trust Jacques with Herr Benn's secret?

After much painful thought, she decided that she must not. Herr Benn could decide who was to share his secret. It was his neck, after all. And he might regain his wits sooner that anyone expected.

She had sent Guillaume downstairs with orders to make sure she was not disturbed. Then she crept across to Herr Benn's door and put her ear against it. She had been right! She could hear men's voices, two of them. Herr Benn was conscious, and recovered enough to speak to Jacques.

She was tempted, for a moment, to march into the room and order Jacques to leave, to insist that Herr Benn needed his rest. But the opportunity to discover exactly what was going on between these two proved irresistible. She leaned even closer against the panelled wood and strained to hear every single sound.

'I've got the devil of a headache, Jacques.' That was Herr Benn's voice. 'Do we really have to keep speaking French? It would be so much easier on my poor wits if—'

'You must stick to French.' Jacques sounded very forceful. 'Please keep trying. Your…er…native tongue might be easier on your cracked pate, but it could be dangerous. Walls have ears, you know.'

Herr Benn mumbled something, but Marguerite was barely listening any more. Herr Benn's plea had started a wild train of thought in her brain. Did Herr Benn wish to revert to German, or to English? And if to English, did that mean that Jacques spoke English, too, and knew Herr Benn's identity? What if—?

This was all becoming so convoluted and confusing that she could not unravel it without time alone to think. Better she should concentrate on just listening. She bent back to the panel.

'—told me it was an accident. Is that true?'

'My own stupid clumsiness again. When you did not return, I suspected something was wrong. Then Suzanne told me that Bonaparte had arrived in Lyons, and I knew something must have happened to you. Must say I'm not totally sure what I intended to do once I got out of this room, but…' Herr Benn's voice trailed off ruefully.

'Thank you for trying. As it happens you were right. I was…er…unavoidably detained. But I am free now. Since we cannot go on together, I must complete the mission alone.'

Fear ripped through Marguerite. There could be no doubt. Jacques and Benn were collaborators. Jacques was a spy for England, too! He was intent on fulfilling their mission, whatever it was, by himself, in spite of the huge risks. If he were caught by Bonaparte's men, he would be sent to the guillotine, or shot. They might torture him, too. They would always be harder on a Frenchman than a foreigner, for betrayal cut deep.

It was too dangerous. He must not go alone.

She had just put her hand to the latch when she heard a soft laugh. It was Herr Benn. How could he?

'Why not enlist with Bonaparte, Jacques? No reason why you shouldn't pass for one of his supporters. You always were a plausible rogue. The army will certainly be accompanying their precious Emperor to Paris, so you would have plenty of opportunities to gather information. Once you reached Paris, you could melt away. It's a good plan, don't you think?'

'Another one of your hare-brained schemes. Still, it might work if—'

Marguerite flung open the door and marched into the room. Hands on hips, she glowered at the two men, 'No, it is not a good plan. It is a ridiculous plan. Have you no idea how the army operates? Soldiers who "melt away", as you call it, are shot as deserters.'

Herr Benn looked thunderstruck. Jacques rose lazily to his feet and bowed to her. He was laughing.

Still furious, Marguerite tried to frown him down, but he continued to laugh. Herr Benn, however, was looking exceedingly embarrassed. He gulped and made to speak.

Jacques lifted a hand to silence him. 'It seems I was right to say that walls have ears, Benn,' he said, fixing Marguerite with his fierce blue gaze.

She refused to be cowed. 'No, sir,' she retorted. 'Not walls. Doors.'

He really laughed then, though it had been a feeble sally.
The tiny sun-kissed creases at the corners of his eyes folded
together as crisply as the finest drapery. He was enjoying this.
And, whatever lay before him, he was not afraid.

Whereas Marguerite was terrified. Not for her family, not
for Herr Benn, but for Jacques. There must be a solution. It
was up to her to find a way of reducing the risk, for Jacques
would never be persuaded to abandon his mission. She knew
that as surely as she knew she loved him.

Perhaps it was her love that provided the inspiration. 'You
cannot join the army, Jacques, and you cannot travel to Paris
alone. It would be suicide. The roads are teeming with Bonapartists, all just waiting for a chance to curry favour with their
idol. Delivering you up as a spy could be extremely good for a
man's prospects.' She glared at him. 'Not for yours, of course.'

'No,' he agreed airily, 'I imagine my prospects would be
rather…er…limited.' He grinned at her. He seemed to be relishing this battle of wills. 'I am grateful for your concern,
Marguerite, but this is men's work.' When she bristled, he
added, 'Forgive me. I know I can trust your discretion, and I
know you will protect Benn, but I must do my duty. I will take
no unnecessary risks, I promise.'

It was not his reassuring words that soothed her heart, but
the way he was gazing at her. As if they were the only two
people in the whole world. As if their spirits had touched, and
lingered, and held. He reached out to her heart like a shaft of
sunlight reaching down to warm the cold earth after rain. And
her heart sang.

'If you are determined to go to Paris, Jacques, I shall go
with you.'

'No! You cannot! You—!'

It was the obvious solution. She could see it all so clearly.
She dared to reach out and silence him with a finger across

his lips. 'We shall travel to Paris together, as silk merchants. We shall be carrying the Duchess of Courland's silk.'

'The Duchess of Courland supports King Louis,' Jacques growled against her finger.

She smiled at him, shaking her head. 'We shall make clear, to anyone who enquires, that our only interest is in selling our wares. We make no distinction between royalists and Bonapartists, provided their coin is good. Believe me, there will be no difficulty. I have done this before.'

He took a step backwards, but not before he had placed a tiny parting kiss upon her skin. Or had she imagined it? No. It had been real. It tingled, still.

'The times are too dangerous. It is out of the question. I forbid it.'

Marguerite opened her mouth to demand by what right he sought to order her life, but Herr Benn forestalled her. In the most reasonable of tones, he said, 'I think you should listen to her, Jacques. Oh, don't turn your temper on me. I'm an invalid. And immune.' He grinned mischievously. 'The truth is that you are thinking about your own sense of chivalry, of obligation, to Miss Marguerite, when you should be thinking about our mission. It *has* to come first. If Miss Marguerite is prepared to help us, for the cause that we all believe in, we must consider, coolly and rationally, whether her plan is more likely to succeed than yours.'

'We cannot—'

'I have to tell you candidly, my friend, that I think she is right. You should travel to Paris together.'

The argument continued for some time. In the end, Jacques was persuaded to agree to Marguerite's plan. 'But, at the first hint of danger, you will place yourself under my orders. You will do as I say. Do I have your word on that, Marguerite?'

She bridled at the thought. No doubt he would decide there

was danger whenever he wanted her to do as she was told. 'Why should I agree to such a thing, when—?'

'One of the things I've learned, working with Jacques,' Herr Benn drawled, 'is that there are times when it is best not to argue with him. Just occasionally, he actually does know best. I think, Miss Marguerite, that this is one of those times.'

'Oh.' She glanced up from Herr Benn's bland countenance to see how Jacques would react. For a fleeting moment, she fancied she saw tenderness in his face. Then it was gone, and his expression became unreadable. 'Very well,' she said quietly, holding his gaze. 'On Herr Benn's advice, I agree to your terms.'

Chapter Twelve

It was decided. They would leave on the morrow, at first light. They would have to carry the fabric for the Duchess of Courland's gown, and enough samples of silks and velvets to give the appearance of silk merchants, but they would not carry enough to need the lumbering old coach. They would travel post. Jacques, it seemed, had plenty of ready money. Were spies always so well endowed?

The key to their success, Jacques had admitted once he had come down from the boughs and begun to confide in Marguerite, was to be out of Lyons before Bonaparte. By all accounts, the man was relishing his return to absolute power; he was certainly issuing decrees right and left. He would need to appear in Paris soon, of course, but he would remain in Lyons for a day or two yet. He was very sure of himself now. It was rumoured that he had summoned his wife and son to his side.

Marguerite had finished packing the samples in their protective oiled paper. They were waiting in the store room next to her bedchamber, ready to be carried downstairs in the morning. Now she must decide what to take for herself. How long was she likely to be from home? Where were they likely to go? She had no idea. The only certainty was that she would have to wait on the Duchess of Courland. For that, Marguerite would need to be dressed in her best. She took down her favourite evening gown from the clothes press and folded it carefully. It was more than a year since she had sewn it, but its cut was so simple that it would never look out of fashion. It was the fabric itself that drew every gaze, a figured silk in a deep vibrant blue that brought out the colour of her eyes. She knew it became her. Would Jacques admire her when she wore it?

There was no time for daydreaming, she reminded herself sternly. She must finish her packing and then she must talk to Suzanne. And her mother. Marguerite was not looking forward to that encounter. With Suzanne, it would be simply a question of ensuring she was content to take charge of the business during Marguerite's absence, and that she would protect Herr Benn. Marguerite had no more doubts on that score. The danger was that she would protect him too well, and lose her own virtue in the process. Marguerite ought to have stern words with Suzanne before she left.

But what would their mother say? Would she remember that Marguerite had planned to travel to Paris to deliver the Duchess of Courland's silk? Would she assume that Marguerite would travel with Guillaume, as she usually did? It would be best if Mama learned nothing at all of Jacques. Mama was the most passionate royalist of the whole family, and she would not willingly do anything to harm a man so closely linked to her cause, but her mind was increasingly fragile. Often, she hardly knew what she was saying.

Marguerite laid the last few items carefully into her valise and placed it on the floor by the bed. In the morning she would add the final things—her nightrail, her hairbrush, her tooth powder. There was no more to be done now.

She straightened and tried to ease the tension in her shoulders. The interview she dreaded would have to be faced tonight, whether Mama was lucid or not. But first, she would speak to Suzanne.

She went along the landing and knocked on Suzanne's door, but there was no reply. She should have known. There was only one place where Suzanne was likely to be.

With a slightly grim smile, Marguerite knocked on Herr Benn's door. As she had expected, her sister was there. For once, she was not sitting on the bed, but Marguerite was almost sure that something improper had been going on, since Suzanne was blushing. Perhaps they had been holding hands? Marguerite doubted it could have been anything more, for Herr Benn was still unable to sit up, and much too weak to indulge in anything at all strenuous, like kissing.

Jacques, on the other hand, was certainly strong enough to indulge in kissing. But would he wish to? The two of them would be closeted together for hours at a time in a small post-chaise. The thought of being close to him, being near enough to touch, sent shivers down her spine. It was a chance, however slim, for her to win his regard, perhaps even his love. She would take it, for she would never have another opportunity. He had kissed her before and, if she encouraged him enough, he might do so again. Oh, she fervently hoped that he would, for it had been glorious. She knew there were risks attached, of course. She was not a complete innocent. Berthe had explained exactly what happened between man and wife, and Marguerite had seen for herself that men could be driven by their passions. Was Jacques such a man? She found that she was hoping, rather daringly, that he was.

'What is it, Marguerite?' Suzanne's blush was fading.

'If you will excuse us, Herr Benn, I need a private word with my sister.'

He smiled up at Marguerite. She sensed that he had said

nothing to Suzanne of their plans. He would understand that Marguerite needed to tell her sister herself.

Suzanne nodded and came round the bed. 'Shall we go to my bedchamber?'

'No. It's too cold in there. Let us go downstairs and sit in front of the fire.' Marguerite smiled at a sudden memory. 'It will be just the two of us, as it was in the old days.'

Suzanne smiled, too, but it was directed back at Herr Benn.

Marguerite's explanation did not take long, for Suzanne barely spoke. Her eyes widened, and gleamed with pride, when she learned Herr Benn's true identity and that she was to have the responsibility for his care, but she was not in the least disconcerted at the thought of taking charge of the weaving business.

'Are you sure, my dear?' Marguerite asked. 'Guillaume will be here to advise you, of course, and there are unlikely to be many new customers while the times are so uncertain.'

'If they should come, I shall deal with them,' Suzanne said firmly. 'I have taken charge before. I can do it again.'

'But that was for a few days only. This time, I might be gone for—' She stopped. In truth, she had no idea how long she would be away. And what was the point of saying things that could undermine Suzanne's new-found confidence? 'I am sure you will cope extremely well. I know you to be very capable.'

'Thank you.' It seemed that Suzanne had accepted the compliment as no less than her due. Marguerite's shy little sister was coming out of her shell.

'About Herr Benn.' Marguerite sucked in a deep breath before continuing. 'It is not appropriate for an unmarried girl to nurse him, especially without a chaperon. Guillaume can—'

'No! Benn needs gentle care. Guillaume has too much else to do, and Berthe's hands are rough and clumsy. I am the only one able to dress his wounds properly when he is so weak. He is no danger to my virtue, Marguerite. Even you must be able to see that.'

'Even I?' Marguerite repeated, shocked.

'You really do not understand, do you? I love Benn, and I am sure he loves me in return. I know I am in no danger from him. But, even if I were, I would be prepared to take the risk. For love. For me, it is all that matters. But you, Marguerite, you have too much sense to allow yourself to fall in love. Once, I used to wish I was as sensible, and as clear-sighted, as you are. No longer.' She smiled a faraway and rather superior smile.

There was nothing Marguerite could say in response. She had always prided herself on her sound common sense, but where was it now? Suzanne might not see the change, but Marguerite knew her own failings. She had tried so hard to keep her feelings within sensible bounds, but in the end they had won through. It was as if Jacques had stolen away her ability to reason.

She was not about to parade her hidden love before her sister's critical gaze. It was a fragile thing, and private. It might never see the light of day, for Jacques might never be able to forgive the things she had done. If that was his verdict, she would learn to abide it. For as long as they remained together, she would be able to see him, to thrill to the sound of his voice, perhaps even to touch his skin. It was not much, the merest crumb to a beggar, but it would be something she could hoard against the cold, bleak future when she would be without him. This was for her alone. No one would learn of her feelings, not Jacques, not Suzanne, no one.

Her behaviour was the complete opposite of her vaunted common sense. She had agreed to be quite alone with Louis Jacques, a man she barely knew, but loved beyond reason. She had convinced herself that she was accompanying him out of duty, but it was only a pretext. If Jacques were lying here wounded, and Herr Benn were about to take post for Paris, would she have volunteered to go with him? Duty should have prevailed, but she rather suspected that, like Suzanne, she would have chosen to stay behind, to nurse the man she loved.

She reached out her hand and laid it over Suzanne's. Her sister was gazing into the fire, her thoughts far away, but she turned at Marguerite's touch and smiled lovingly at her. She was just about to speak when the door opened.

'Mama!' Suzanne jumped up and helped her mother into her own place, closest to the fire.

Out of the corner of her eye, Marguerite could see that Berthe was hovering by the door, ready to sweep Mama away if she became too agitated. 'Close the door and come to the fire, Berthe,' Marguerite said encouragingly. 'May I bring you a glass of wine, Mama?' At her mother's nod, Marguerite rose to fetch it. Now was the moment. Now she must tell Mama what she was about to do.

'Mama, I have to leave for Paris at first light tomorrow. You remember, do you not? The Duchess of Courland's silk has to be—'

At that moment, the door opened again to admit Jacques. He had not knocked. He was making free of their sitting room as if he owned it. And Guillaume was at his shoulder. Why? They had barely exchanged a civil word since Jacques had escaped. Marguerite began to fear that Guillaume was planning something. Why else would he have brought Jacques into this family gathering?

Both men bowed low to Marguerite's mother.

'I know you,' she said.

'Yes, Mama. This is Guillaume, who has served you faithfully since before I was born.'

'I will thank you not to patronise me, Marguerite. I know perfectly well who Guillaume is. I was referring to the other one. The duke's son.' She nodded towards Jacques.

Marguerite was aghast. Where on earth had Mama got such an idea? 'Mama, allow me to present Mr Louis Jacques. He came to my aid when Guillaume and I encountered some slight difficulties in Marseilles. When we were there to meet the new agent. You remember? Mr Jacques was kind enough to escort us home to Lyons. But he is leaving tomorrow.'

'And you are leaving tomorrow. For Paris, did you not say, Marguerite?'

'I— Yes, Mama, I am.'

'Are you proposing to travel with this gentleman? Without a chaperon?'

Oh dear. Unfortunately, Mama was awake on all suits today. What if she should forbid Marguerite to leave? 'Mr Jacques has kindly offered to escort me, yes. Guillaume cannot be spared, you see, and neither can Berthe.'

'Suzanne may go,' her mother said firmly. 'You may chaperon each other.'

'No!' Suzanne had jumped to her feet. 'No, Mama, that is not possible. I am needed here, to…er…to take charge of the business while Marguerite is away.'

'There is no cause for you to be concerned, Mama,' Marguerite said, improvising quickly. 'Mr Jacques and I shall travel as brother and sister. It will be quite innocuous. No one will pay us the least heed.'

Marguerite's mother rose to her feet and fixed a stern gaze on her errant child. 'The daughter of the Marquise de Jerbeaux does not travel alone with a man who is not a relative. No lady of breeding would do such a thing.' She turned to Jacques. 'Do you tell me, sir, that you have agreed to this outrage?'

Jacques stepped forward and bowed again. 'My lady, this

journey cannot be avoided. But if it will set your mind at rest, I will gladly give you my word of honour to treat your daughter throughout as though she truly were my sister.'

Guillaume snorted loudly. 'We know what *his* word of honour is worth.'

'That is enough,' Marguerite cried. 'Leave us, Guillaume.'

'Stay!'

Marguerite cringed. This was Mama at her most aristocratic, and her most unpredictable.

'Fetch the family bible, Guillaume.'

Guillaume smiled slyly. 'At once, my lady.'

No one said a word until he returned. He laid the huge bible on a small table and placed it at his mistress's hand before returning to stand by the door. Marguerite could see that Mama was beginning to look agitated, and anxious. Her fragile control might break at any moment.

'Step forward, young man,' she ordered. When Jacques obeyed, she said, in a slightly querulous voice, 'You offered me your word that you would treat my daughter honourably, as a sister. Now lay your hand on this bible, and swear it.' She reached out to grasp his hand, to pull it down and place it on the dark leather, but she misjudged the distance and began to topple. Berthe started forward with a cry. There was no need. Jacques caught Mama in his arms and set her safely on her chair before anyone else could reach her.

He turned for just a second towards the door where Guillaume stood. The look they exchanged explained much to Marguerite. In Guillaume's eyes, she saw gleeful triumph; in Jacques's, she saw stiff-necked pride and shrewd calculation. Guillaume had not won yet. Jacques turned back and placed his right hand flat upon the bible. In a clear voice, he declared, 'I swear that, so long as your daughter Marguerite is in my company, I will treat her with all honour. I will protect her from harm, if needs be with my life. And any dishonour to her shall be dishonour to me. On this holy book, I swear it.' He took his hand from the bible and raised Mama's fingers to his lips. 'On my honour, my lady,' he said softly.

Marguerite's mother had begun to shake in agitation. 'What is this bible doing here?' she cried. 'You know we never bring it into this room. Guillaume, take it away. Take it away!'

Berthe hurried forward and put an arm round her mistress's shoulders, urging her towards the door. 'Come back to your chamber, my dear lady. You will feel much more comfortable there, with your own things around you. I have built you a fine fire. And there are macaroons for you to dip in your tisane.'

'I like macaroons.' Nothing more was said. Berthe led her mistress gently towards the staircase.

Marguerite forced herself to appear icy calm. She did not so much as glance towards Jacques. Such an oath! Mama had asked him to treat Marguerite like a sister but, goaded by Guillaume, he had sworn to treat her like a queen, and to be her champion! No, on second thoughts, it was even worse than that. It was as if she were a goddess and he the worshipping high priest at her feet. And all to spite Guillaume. She never would understand men. If they were so much at odds, those two, why had they not simply brawled in the street until one of them could no longer stand? It would have done a great deal less harm, in Marguerite's view.

She had been so close. She had found the man she loved and learned that he was worthy. She had seen her one chance to win his love and she had determined to seize it. But it was now crushed under the weight of a petty male squabble over honour. Men! She would like to horsewhip them all!

'You did what?' Ben gasped.

'I had no choice, Ben. I had Guillaume on the one hand,

declaring that my word was worthless, and the mother on the other, daring me to put my hand on her bible. If I had refused, Marguerite would have believed the worst of me. And no doubt her mother would have forbidden her to travel. You did persuade me that I needed her, remember?' Jack tried to grin down into Ben's worried face, but he knew he was not being very convincing.

'So what exactly did you swear?' Ben was not to be diverted.

'Exactly?' Jack paused, trying to recall the scene. 'I'm not really sure. I was so determined to scotch Guillaume's confounded lies, and so furious, that I decided to make a grand, sweeping gesture, with an oath full of fine words about treating Marguerite with all honour, like a sister, and putting my life at her service. You can imagine the kind of thing, probably.'

Ben snorted. 'A little difficult to imagine, old man. Not the kind of gesture one encounters every day.'

Jack had to laugh then. After a moment, Ben began to laugh, too. Jack was glad. It was important for Ben not to be concerned about Jack. He must concentrate on getting well, and then on getting safely back to England. 'I've been thinking, Ben,' he said casually, not wishing to insult his friend, 'that once you're on your feet again, it might be best to go home by ship. Travelling across France on your own could be very dangerous, now that Bonaparte is back.'

Ben did not bridle, as Jack had feared he might. 'Suzanne said something very similar earlier. But we have agreed to wait and see. After all, by the time I'm able to leave, it may all be over. Bonaparte may be a prisoner of the King's army.'

Jack raised an eyebrow. 'You believe that the French army will remain loyal to fat Louis when they could have Bonaparte? And glory?'

Ben tried, unsuccessfully, to shrug his shoulders. It clearly hurt, for he was unable to prevent himself from groaning.

'Confound this blasted shoulder! I shall be mightily relieved when I'm back on my feet.'

'If you paid a little more attention to where you were putting your feet, my clumsy friend, you would be a great deal stronger than you are,' Jack said, trying to hide his concern. Then, looking round the tiny, gloomy room, he added, 'Not all your fault, I admit. This chamber is very cramped. The ones on the floor above are much bigger.'

'Suzanne said this was the only vacant chamber on this floor. She didn't want to be carrying bandages and hot water up two flights of stairs.'

'And she also wanted you to be conveniently close, I think.'

Ben coloured a little. 'I shall be closer after you've gone, as it happens. Miss Marguerite has said that I am to be moved into her bedchamber, after you have both left for Paris.'

'Does it happen to be next to Miss Suzanne's chamber, by any chance?' Jack asked with a wry grin.

'Certainly not! The silk store lies between Suzanne's bedchamber and her sister's. According to Suzanne, the silk is much too precious to be stored downstairs where it might get damp or be pilfered by strangers visiting the house. So it is kept up here.'

'I see. I had wondered where that door led. I'd assumed it was another bedchamber. I was more than a little insulted to be sent up to the top floor. I assumed they did not think it safe to allow me to be on the same floor as the Grolier young ladies.'

'They would probably have been right, too,' Ben said, giving his friend a knowing wink. 'But now that you've sworn on the bible to treat Miss Marguerite like a sister, you'll be no threat at all to her virtue, will you?'

Jack had to struggle hard to prevent the memory of their one searing kiss from invading his senses and making his rebellious body react like a schoolboy's. 'I swore an oath to the Mar—to Marguerite's mother that I would treat her daughter as honourably as a sister. And I shall, even if it kills me!'

Chapter Thirteen

Jack thrust the purse of silver down into the hidden pocket in the side of his valise. His gold coins, and the rest of the silver, were stitched into his clothing, as ever. A valise might be lost, or stolen, and he could not risk being without blunt, for they would be several days, perhaps as much as a week, on the road to Paris. The hire of post-chaises for such a distance was going to cost a great deal. However, once he had secured a safe refuge for Marguerite in Paris, he could always travel on to Calais on horseback, if he found himself getting short of funds. There was no need to make a decision on that now.

He took a last look around his bedchamber, bare now that most of his belongings were packed. Only his coat, hat and gloves remained, lying across the chair where he had sat as a frustrated captive, until freed by Marguerite's mother. He still did not understand why she had done it. Was it possible to understand her? She was the strangest combination of the apparently normal and the apparently demented. The poor lady was obviously subject to delusions, for why else would she claim to be a marquise? What was that name she had used? He could not quite remember, but it had been nothing like Grolier.

It occurred to Jack that, once he and Marguerite were alone together in the post-chaise, he might be able to probe a little into the circumstances of her family. She might rebuff him but, then again, she might welcome a chance to share her problems with someone she could trust to be discreet. Why was her father so seldom at home to look after his business and his sick wife? No responsible father would leave his daughters to shoulder such burdens alone. Yet neither of the daughters had uttered a word of complaint in Jack's hearing. They seemed to accept their huge responsibilities as the most normal thing in the world.

They were remarkable women, both of them. Remembering Marguerite with her candlestick, Jack smiled. Yes, she was certainly remarkable. At first, he had thought that Miss Suzanne was quite different, a meek, retiring girl. She had avoided his eye, and spoken barely a word when Jack and Ben first arrived. But things were different now, for Miss Suzanne was deep in love with Ben. She was prepared to face any danger, take on any responsibility, in order to defend him. Did love do that to all women? Jack had no idea. It was just another of the disadvantages of growing up in a family without sisters.

That pulled him up short. Confound it, he was going to have to pretend to be a brother to Marguerite. Or at least a half-brother. How did a brother and sister behave to each other? One thing he was sure of: a brother's behaviour did not include passionate kisses, or bodies pressed against each other and straining towards fulfilment. All thoughts of *that* description must be banished completely.

He had begun to realise that it was going to be a very trying journey, cooped up together for days in the narrow confines of a post-chaise. He would have to keep the maximum possible distance between them. There must be no touching, and only the most decorous of conversation. Marguerite would be of the same mind, Jack was sure. She was a clever, practical woman. She would be able to see all the risks, just as clearly as Jack did.

Marguerite finished tying the ribbons of her bonnet and began to pull on her gloves. Guillaume was just about to carry her valise downstairs.

'A moment, Guillaume.'

He turned back, a look of enquiry on his lined face. 'Yes, mistress?'

'While I am gone, I should like you to keep an eye on Herr Benn. None of the neighbours knows he is here. That is how it must stay. It is dangerous for him to remain here, but we dare not allow him to leave.'

'I understand, Miss Marguerite.'

Did he? Did he know what was going on between Suzanne and Herr Benn? Marguerite had intended to ask Guillaume to extract the same kind of oath from Herr Benn as her mother had extracted from Jacques. Her conscience was urging her to do so, for Suzanne's sake. Once Herr Benn was himself again, there would be nothing to stop him from taking advantage of Suzanne. Was it not Marguerite's duty to protect her younger sister's virtue?

Suzanne would not see it in that light. Marguerite grasped that in a trice. No, Suzanne would be incensed, just as Marguerite had been last evening, when Guillaume had interfered in that officious, mule-headed way. He had behaved as if Marguerite were a mere child, unfit to make decisions about her own life. Was Marguerite about to do the same to Suzanne?

'I shall rely on you, Guillaume, to ensure that no harm comes to him.' She nodded his dismissal.

Once he had gone, it was too late to change her mind. Had

she done right by her sister? Truly, she did not know. She hoped so. But in the back of her mind, she knew that Suzanne was not always sensible in her decisions. She was a quiet dreamer, and sometimes her dreams intruded into the real world. She believed that Herr Benn loved her. She probably saw him as a *preux chevalier*, a chivalrous knight who would carry her off on his saddle-bow. As well he might. But would his goal be a virtuous union? Or would this love destroy her?

Marguerite refused to let feelings of guilt overwhelm her. Suzanne was in love. She was old enough to decide about her own future, and she was wise enough to understand the consequences. Unlike Guillaume, Marguerite would not interfere.

She turned back to her glass for one last check of her appearance. The deep green bonnet with its grosgrain trim became her very well, with her fair curls gleaming against the dark silk. Her pelisse, in matching fine green wool, hung in beautifully draped folds to her ankles. She flattered herself that she looked her best. Jacques was not going to find it easy to keep to that stupid oath. On that she was determined!

She ran lightly down the stairs to the hallway. Suzanne was waiting by the door, and looking anxious. Marguerite embraced her sister warmly. 'Do not be concerned, my love. We shall take every care. I expect to return with the payment for the Duchess of Courland's silk, and some new orders, besides!'

Suzanne made a choking sound that could have been a sob and hugged Marguerite even more tightly. It was a long time before they parted.

Out of the corner of her eye, Marguerite saw Jacques appear through the street door. He looked her up and down assessingly. He did not smile, or speak, but she thought his eyes warmed. Then he stepped forward to take her valise from Guillaume. 'The silk is safely stowed. Have you made all your farewells?'

Marguerite nodded. It was one of her mother's bad days. She had not risen from her bed. She had seemed to understand when Marguerite kissed her goodbye, but it was impossible to be sure.

'Good. Then we had best be off at once. Miss Suzanne, I must thank you again for your care of my friend Benn.' He took her hand and kissed it gallantly. Suzanne blushed and murmured something inaudible. 'And I promise I will take equally good care of your sister.' With a distant nod to Guillaume, he strode out to the waiting chaise and stood by the door, ready to hand Marguerite up.

'God speed,' Suzanne whispered.

Marguerite reached out to give her sister's fingers a quick squeeze. 'May God protect you all,' she said, and hurried out.

He was standing by the step, his hand outstretched, waiting. She fancied there was a degree of impatience in his expression. So that was to be the way of it, was it? He clearly thought he was to be master here. Well, she would show him otherwise. Ignoring him completely, she climbed nimbly into the chaise and began to settle herself comfortably in the far corner.

A moment later, he had climbed in beside her and they were off.

Neither spoke while the chaise threaded its way slowly through the narrow, bustling streets of the city, but soon they were climbing away from the river, the horses pulling strongly. Marguerite could feel a child's excitement welling up inside her, for she had never thought to travel in a post-chaise, especially one drawn by a team rather than a pair. It must be costing a fortune. The Grolier family had not been able to afford such luxury since their arrival in Lyons.

Marguerite examined the chaise with interest. It looked and smelled almost new. The seats were deeply cushioned and the buttoned leather showed no signs of wear. The paintwork gleamed, inside and out. Their journey to Paris would be more than tolerable, especially if they found adequate horses at every change.

'This is a remarkably comfortable vehicle, Mr Jacques,' she said politely. 'I should even say sumptuous. Did you select it yourself?'

He had been sitting motionless, staring out of the window, but he half-turned towards her and said coolly, 'I did, ma'am. And the team also. I have found that a little attention at the start of a journey pays dividends by the end of it.'

How pompous he sounded! Was that intended as retribution for her having mounted without his assistance? Petty, then, as well as pompous.

She was taxing her brain to think of a suitably pithy response when he leant towards her a little and said, in something more like his normal deep voice, 'If you will allow me to advise you, ma'am, it would be safest if you did not address me as "Mr Jacques". We are travelling as brother and sister, remember? We do look very different, as you remarked once before, but I have a solution to that. You shall be the daughter of our father's second wife. We must use the Grolier name, of course, since it is Grolier silk we are trying to sell. So I shall be Jacques Grolier. Thus you can call me "Jacques", and I can call you "Marguerite", as we did on the journey north to Lyons. What say you?'

'I say it is remarkably convenient that you have a surname which can double as a given name. Do you not agree?'

He smiled rather smugly, Marguerite thought, but he did not reply, merely raising his eyebrows, and waiting for her to agree to his proposal.

'Obviously, we must use those names in company and when there is any risk of being overheard,' she began. 'But to use them when we are quite alone suggests of a degree of intimacy that could become…er…uncomfortable.' She sat up very primly and frowned across at him. She intended it to be a challenge.

'I had credited you with more sense, ma'am,' he retorted. 'You believe you can spend hours in this chaise addressing me as "Mr Jacques" and then remember, the moment you step out of it, to call me just "Jacques"? With never a slip?'

He was being truly superior now. She would have loved to give him a sharp set-down, but she could not. Unfortunately, he was right. 'I had not thought of that,' she admitted generously, with a rueful smile. She had expected him to unbend a little in response, but he did not. His eyes remained hard. 'I will call you "Jacques", even when we are alone. In return, *Jacques*, you will have to stop addressing me as "ma'am". I may have no direct experience of brothers, but I am quite sure no brother would address a younger sister with such courtesy.'

'I bow to your superior understanding, ma'am. Marguerite,' he added quickly, with just the tiniest twitch of his lips.

He was trying so hard not to unbend. Had he resolved to be cool and distant in order to make it easier to fulfil his vow? Marguerite smiled inwardly. She had the whole journey to make him repent of that ridiculous gesture. He and Guillaume had reminded her forcibly of a spitting contest she had once seen among the local urchins, with each little boy making strenuous efforts to prove himself able to spit further than his fellows. She had assumed that boys grew out of such childish rivalry when they became men. Perhaps they did not? She could not tell whether Jacques's behaviour was typical. She understood so little of men.

They drove on in almost total silence until the first change.

Jacques opened the door and jumped down. No doubt he wanted to ensure that the replacement team was up to his exalted standards. To her surprise, he did not immediately march off to consult the ostler. 'Would you like me to order some coffee to be brought out to you, sister?' he asked politely. 'It would not delay us too much if we waited while you drank it.'

That was definitely intended as a set-down, and Marguerite was not about to accept it. It was time she put her plan into action. It was time Jacques discovered that swearing such a stupid oath had consequences. Uncomfortable consequences.

She rose in her place. 'No, brother dear, there is no need. I prefer to drink my coffee in the comfort of the inn. I shall become intolerably stiff if I sit in this chaise all day. Be so good as to help me down.' She sounded, as she had intended, like a silly empty-headed chit who had been too much indulged by her family.

His brows contracted into a black frown, but there was nothing he could do. He reached up a hand. Smiling vacantly, Marguerite put her fingers into his and made to step down. It seemed as though she was not paying proper attention, for she missed her footing and had to grab his shoulder with her free hand. Even that was not enough to save her. Her whole body fell against his with so much force that he staggered back a pace. It was a wonder that he did not overbalance completely when Marguerite flung her arms around his neck.

'Oh, goodness. How clumsy of me!' she exclaimed. 'But for you, dear brother, I should have measured my length in the mud.' She smiled innocently up at him. There was considerable suspicion in his eyes, but what could he say? The postilions were watching, and listening to every word. 'Thank you for saving me,' Marguerite gushed. In a spirit of pure sisterly mischief, she tightened her arms into a hug and reached up to place a kiss on his cheek.

She might have gone just a mite too far there, Marguerite decided, on reflection, for his face was flushing a deep red.

Anger, was it? Or embarrassment? It was a very satisfying reaction, whatever the cause. She slowly unwound her arms and took a step back. He was looking daggers at her. And yet there was something more behind that furious gaze. She guessed that the touching of their bodies, and her lips on his skin, had produced a reaction he could not control. And he clearly wanted to be in control.

'You will find me in the coffee room when you have finished making your arrangements, Jacques,' she said airily. 'I shall order coffee for two.' Without allowing him a moment to reply, she started towards the inn, allowing her hips to sway provocatively as she walked. She did not once look back. She knew he was unable to take his eyes from her.

'A little more care this time, sister, if you please.'

It was difficult to resist the urge to smile, but she managed it. Just. It really would not do to give him any clues to her behaviour. He was puzzled and already a little frustrated. She intended that he should remain that way.

'Thank you, brother dear.' She took the hand he offered to help her back into the chaise. She wobbled a tiny fraction on the step, and gripped his fingers tightly. 'Goodness,' she said, glancing over her shoulder at him, 'I am not normally so unsteady. I declare that you must have put brandy in my coffee. Fie on you, brother, for playing me such a dastardly trick.' Behind his back, the postilions had begun to laugh. She sensed that, if Jacques had not been a true gentleman, he might have lifted her bodily and thrown her into the chaise.

'You try my patience, Marguerite,' he muttered grimly, pulling his fingers free. Then he spun round to glower at the grinning postboys. 'If you have quite finished, gentlemen, perhaps we might be on our way? I fear that we have lost a great deal of time.' He pulled out some coins and began to jingle them in his hand. 'Unless we can make it up, I fear I shall have to keep my silver in my pocket.'

The chaise was moving again almost before Marguerite had taken her seat.

Marguerite waited a full quarter of an hour. Then, without looking at Jacques, she slowly began to remove her gloves, finger by finger, smoothing the fine leather down her skin in long, sensuous movements. Next, she undid the ribbons of her bonnet and dropped it on to her lap. 'Ah, that is such a relief,' she said, as if to herself, before driving her fingers through her hair and shaking out her curls. 'Travelling in a bonnet gives me the headache.' She turned an enquiring look on Jacques. 'I hope you do not object to my disrobing?'

He made a sound that was something between a groan and a snort.

'I beg your pardon, sir? Oh, forgive me. I should treat you as a brother. Could you repeat what you said, brother dear? I did not quite catch it.'

He was staring straight ahead, refusing to look at her. She could see movement in the muscles of his jaw. 'I seem to recall, sister, that you wore your bonnet for the whole of our journey from Marseilles to Lyons.' His voice seemed to have risen by almost half an octave. She could hear the tension in it.

'Ah, but that was a much more comfortable bonnet than this one,' she replied brightly. 'This one is new, and a little tight. We poor females have to suffer to be fashionable, I fear.'

He did not reply, but his fist clenched against his thigh in the most satisfactory manner. He had begun to shift in his seat, too, as if he were unable to find a comfortable position. Unfortunately, those movements made Marguerite conscious of his body in a way she had, thus far, managed to avoid. She cursed silently. She wanted him to suffer, to lose control, but she could succeed there only if her own control was absolute. Until now, she had not allowed herself to think about how it felt to touch him. For that brazen kiss, she had told herself she was kissing her sister. It had worked at the time, but it was not working now, for she was starting to remember the feel of his skin, the beginnings of his dark stubble, rough against her lips, and the all too masculine scent of his body. Somewhere, deep in her belly, something began to quiver and melt.

She clasped her hands together and forced herself to concentrate on the passing landscape until her strange feelings had subsided. She had been trying him too far, she concluded. And herself too, perhaps. She would give them both a little respite. 'One thing I did not have a chance to ask you,' she began, keeping her eyes fixed on a distant stand of trees. 'How was it that you came to escape? Guillaume assured me that you had given him your word not to do so. I know nothing of that,' she added airily, 'but I will admit to being intrigued as to how you removed your bonds. Guillaume promised me they were as tight as could be.'

'I can assure you that they were exceedingly tight.'

She waited. He said nothing more. His jaw was working again. Was it the indignity of being a prisoner that roused his fury?

'I am sure Guillaume would be pleased to hear you say so,' she continued, almost without a pause. 'Though, to his mind, that was not the most important matter. I am afraid he felt he had been deceived, wronged even. You—'

'Guillaume was not deceived by me!' he thundered. 'He deceived himself.'

She turned to face him then, looking suitably incredulous. Wide-eyed surprise had the advantage of drawing attention to the colour of her eyes. 'Indeed? Might I ask how he did that?'

'Certainly, ma'am.' This time, he made no attempt to

correct his mode of address. 'Your man, Guillaume, hears what he wants to hear. I gave him my word of honour that I would not use my voice to draw attention to myself. In return, he did not replace the gag. I can tell you—though I hope, ma'am, that you have no need of such reassurance—that I did *not* use my voice. Not in any way.'

'No, of course you did not,' Marguerite said quietly. She understood everything now. 'You found another solution, did you not? A solution that you had already decided upon, well before you offered Guillaume your parole.'

She thought he looked guilty for a second or two, but he said only, 'I gave Guillaume my word. I did not break it.'

'No. You would not have done so. I have not the least doubt that you always keep your promises. To the letter.'

He bowed slightly. 'As you say, ma'am.'

What on earth had possessed him to agree to travel alone with Marguerite Grolier? And what a fool he had been to assume that she would understand the difficulties of their situation, and behave.

He risked a quick glance out of the corner of his eye. She was gazing calmly out of the window, as if she had not a care in the world, but her right hand was softly stroking the fingers of her left. He could almost sense the gentleness of that touch. He needed those fingers to be on his skin, stroking his—

He only just succeeded in swallowing the groan that rose in his throat. He shifted in his seat and adjusted his coat, trying to conceal the evidence of his arousal. Confound the woman, she must be doing it on purpose! She could not fail to be aware of the effect she was having on him, could she?

Of course she could. She was a complete innocent. He had known that, the moment he kissed her. But if she continued in this vein, he was going to find the journey very uncomfortable indeed.

She turned and smiled at him. With her fair curls dancing around her face, and the sparkle of excitement in her eyes, she looked good enough to devour. 'You were going to tell me how you escaped from your bonds,' she said calmly.

He had thought he had diverted her from that. 'No, Marguerite, I was not. The fact that you ask a question—twice in this case—does not mean that it will be answered.' Let her make what she would of that. He was not going to betray what her mother had done, at least partly because he felt guilty about having taken advantage of the lady's weaknesses. 'I did not break my word to Guillaume, but I did find a way of escaping from my prison. The prison, I should add, that you and he conspired to put me in.' Yes, that had turned the tables on her at last. She was blushing, conscious that she had done something outrageous.

'I…I apologise for drugging you, and for…for the rest. I thought you a staunch Bonapartist. I did what I believed was necessary to protect Herr Benn.' She was staring down at her bare hands. They were clasped together now, so tightly that the knuckles were turning white.

He felt truly ashamed then. What way was this to treat a woman who was risking her life for Jack's cause? It was not her fault that his body was responding so eagerly to her every movement. She was beautiful, and unconsciously seductive. But as a mature man, he should be able to control himself, and to behave as a gentleman should.

'Pray do not blame yourself, Marguerite,' he said, trying to appear much calmer than he felt. 'It would have been an excellent plan if I had been the enemy you thought me.'

'Sir, I think you seek to belittle me.' She sounded hurt.

He was tempted to reach across and put his hands over hers,

to ease that painful clasp, but he did not dare. Distance, he reminded himself, was the only defence he had. But he could not allow her to believe that he looked down on her. For all her strange starts during this journey together, she was still the most admirable, the most courageous woman he had ever met. 'No, Marguerite, I would never do that. I swore on your mother's bible that any dishonour to you would be dishonour to myself. I swore to treat you with all honour, as a sister.'

Her head whipped round to stare at him. 'But you di—' She stopped suddenly, in mid-word. Some of the tension seemed to leave her body. 'I take it that you will keep your oath, to the letter, as you did your promise to Guillaume?'

He sat a little taller in his seat and spoke proudly. 'Most certainly I shall,' he said. 'As long as we travel together, I will treat you as an honoured sister.'

Chapter Fourteen

Marguerite hugged her new-found secret to herself. She was hard put not to laugh at the absurdity of it all. Not only had he sworn a ridiculous oath in order to spite Guillaume, he could not even remember the way of it. Oh, it was delicious! And she had so nearly spoilt everything, by blurting out the truth.

She continued to gaze out of the window, with all sorts of madcap ideas racing through her mind. So far, she had been tempting him, punishing him, in order to make him regret that rash oath and view her as an object of desire. He had become uncomfortably aware, she was sure, that treating her with all honour was more than his body was prepared to do. But his position was even worse than she had imagined. He truly believed he had sworn to treat her as a sister. Ways might have been found to satisfy his urges while sticking to the letter of what he had actually sworn. But there was no leeway at all in an oath to treat her as a sister.

Louis Jacques would never, ever break his word. That was one of the many reasons why Marguerite loved him. He would suffer the torments of the damned before he would be forsworn. Poor, poor Jacques! How on earth was he going to survive the remaining days of their journey together?

Her conscience intruded then. Should she not tell him the truth, or at least stop her wicked teasing? She considered that carefully—for at least ten seconds—before rejecting it. No, her main purpose here was to make him burn for her, as she burned for him. Behaving demurely, like a sister, would certainly not achieve that. In this case, the demands of conscience must give way to the demands of Marguerite's heart.

They had stopped for the night in Mâcon, at a posting inn on the quay overlooking the River Saône. Jack assumed that Marguerite was very tired from the journey, for she spoke very little during the supper they shared, and took the first opportunity to retire to bed. Apart from her parting shot—she insisted on wishing him good night with a sisterly kiss on the cheek—she behaved with admirable decorum. Perhaps she had thought better of her actions earlier in the day? He hoped so. He doubted he could endure many more days of watching her from a distance of barely a couple of feet. After only one day, the chaise seemed to be filled with the scent of her—not an expensive French perfume, but the scent of fine soap plus the lavender she no doubt used in her clothes press to keep away the moth. It was, he decided, the scent of a very desirable woman.

Except that he had sworn to treat her as an honoured sister. Desire, in any form, was taboo.

He did not retire early. He knew that he would not be able to sleep, and he feared where his thoughts might turn. If he had travelled on horseback, instead of riding idly in a chaise, his body would have been tired enough to allow him to sleep. As it was, he must find something to occupy himself. Preferably something involving physical activity.

He could visit a brothel, of course. That would certainly

involve physical activity. Mâcon might be small, but it was bound to have at least one house to cater to the needs of travelling men. Jack glanced across at the landlord, standing behind the taproom bar. He was the sort of man who would be able to point a customer in the right direction. Provided he was properly greased in the fist.

Jack finished his brandy and started across to the bar. Travelling with Marguerite had shown him just how much he needed a woman. He could not have her—he had sworn it, had he not?—but he could find some relief elsewhere for his tormented body. He might even be able to sleep soundly afterwards.

He leant his elbow on the bar and raised an eyebrow to the landlord who came forward eagerly to serve him. 'Tell me, landlord,' Jack began, 'do you—?' He stopped dead. What was he thinking of? He couldn't do such a thing. Was he about to neglect his duty for a quick fumble that would probably bring him no more than momentary relief?

'Sir? You wanted something?'

Jack quickly turned his unfinished sentence into a request for a bottle of good red and carried it slowly back to his table. It was not simply that he had a mission to fulfil. It was Marguerite, and only Marguerite, he wanted to bed, not some small-town whore. Why hadn't he realised that before? She was eminently desirable. Each move she made, each tiny touch made her more so. If only she knew how much she was torturing him. When she had removed her gloves and bonnet, she had looked so alluring, so incredibly beddable, that he had begun to think he would soon explode. She, poor innocent Marguerite, the lady with no brothers, had not the least idea of what she was doing to him.

Or did she?

Jack took a large swig of his wine and concentrated on allowing its medley of flavours to fill his senses. He had never visited Mâcon before, but he knew its reputation for fine Burgundy. One day, if he survived long enough, he would have the estate that his brother Dominic had promised him, and a cellar full of wines as good as this. He took another mouthful and let the flavours tease and tempt his taste buds. Truly remarkable.

Marguerite Grolier was truly remarkable, too. He knew that. He had admired her courage and daring from the first time he had set eyes on her. She was strong, and quick-witted, and prepared to risk her life for the cause she believed in. But was she also a flirt? Could her teasing actions today have been deliberate?

He tried to remember exactly what she had done, and how. That was a mistake, for even the thought of her was enough to arouse him. Thankfully, he was sitting at a table, in a gloomy corner. No one could see. But Jack could feel. It was infuriating to think that she might have done it all on purpose, teasing him into agonies of frustration with the skill of a practised courtesan. And all the while knowing that he would never dream of touching her, for that would break his oath.

He finished his wine and stood up. That final surge of anger had doused his lust. There was nothing at all to be done about Marguerite tonight, but tomorrow, he would watch her much more carefully, and he would not be gullible enough to assume that her actions were innocent. If he became sure she was doing it deliberately, he would challenge her, and tell her precisely what he thought of her.

The one thing he would not do, tonight or ever, would be to allow her to best him. No matter whether her teasing was innocent or deliberate, he would not visit a brothel or give in to his frustrations in any way. If he did that, Marguerite Grolier would have beaten him. That he was not prepared to allow.

He would spend the rest of the night doing something

useful, he decided. This posting inn was frequented only by people of means. He needed to try some low taverns, the kind of places where old soldiers gathered. He would shell out some of his silver there and discover whether tongues could be loosened by a few bottles of the local red. His masters in London would expect him to report on the morale and disposition of the army, and on the level of loyalty to the King in the towns they passed through. He had garnered precious little of that since they left Lyons. It was high time he started.

'Did you sleep well, brother?' Marguerite was calmly spreading cherry preserve on a slice of bread.

'Well enough, thank you,' Jack lied. He had trawled the taverns for hours, but at least he had managed to resist the lure of the local gambling. Although the stakes were low, for Jack it was a point of honour not to play any more. He owed it to his brothers. He had relied on the local red to get men talking, but he had discovered only that in Mâcon there were both royalist factions and Bonapartist factions. The royalists were cowed, and truculent. Their victory had been short-lived and they now faced defeat all over again. One or two of the Bonapartists were cock-a-whoop, boasting of what they would do when their hero resumed the throne, as he surely would. Most were uncertain about the future, and were much more circumspect, even fearful. Jack supposed he would discover much the same shades of opinion wherever they went, as long as they stayed ahead of Bonaparte's advance. In Lyons, royalist sentiment had simply melted away once Bonaparte appeared. Jack imagined it would be the same almost everywhere.

Neither the wine nor the exercise had helped Jack to sleep. In spite of all his endeavours to concentrate on the information he had gleaned, he had spent too many hours debating whether Marguerite Grolier was a deliberate tease.

She glanced up at him and smiled innocently. Then she lifted the bread to her lips and took a dainty bite, her small white teeth cutting easily through the layers. Some of the preserve dripped on to her fingers. Instead of wiping them on a napkin, she put them to her lips, one by one, and slowly licked them clean. The look on Jack's face could not have escaped her, for she reddened noticeably. 'Forgive me, brother,' she said quickly, 'but these preserves are so good that it would be a crime to waste even a drop. Will you not try some?' She pushed the bowl across the table towards him.

'No,' he replied abruptly and rose to his feet. 'I shall check whether our chaise is ready to leave. I pray you, sister, do not delay us. We have a long way to travel today.' He marched out of the coffee room before his temper got the better of him. He could not berate her where others might overhear, but once they were alone in the chaise, with doors and windows closely fastened, he would make her sorry she was ever born. How dare she act so, running the tip of her tongue along the length of her finger, curling it back into her mouth with such obvious, sensual relish? And then doing the same thing all over again with the next finger? That was not the action of an innocent. He had been a fool to think so for a second.

Marguerite had fully intended to continue Jacques's torment today, but his reaction over breakfast give her pause. Her tactics could be working too well. She had not expected him to react with such passion so early in the morning. She had assumed that, at such an hour, a man was more intent on breaking his fast than on slaking his lust. Could she be mistaken there? Quite possibly. It might be unwise for an unschooled girl to make assumptions about what a man might do when desire was driving him. She resolved to behave as demurely as a sister, at least until she had the measure of him once more.

She hurried out to the chaise and allowed one of the postilions to help her in. Then she took her accustomed place, folded her gloved hands in her lap, and sat motionless, watching the bustle of the inn yard.

Jacques appeared by the door. 'Ah, there you are.' He sounded surprised to find her waiting in the chaise.

'I hope I have not delayed you, Jacques,' she said kindly.

'You know you have not,' he grunted. 'You have everything?'

'Of course.' She smiled sweetly down at him.

'Good. I must just pay the landlord, and then we can be off. I shall be five minutes, no more.'

Marguerite wriggled her bottom into the back of the seat until she was perfectly comfortable. She was more than content to wait. As a sister should.

In less than the promised five minutes, Jacques was back and the postboys were urging the new team out of the yard and on to the main road north to Tournus. For some distance, it followed the river, which was high and flowing fast through the town, its waters swollen by the first melt water from the distant mountains. The river was a strange, cloudy-grey colour. It seemed to absorb the spring sunlight totally, so that there was not a trace of sparkle, not even a passing shimmer, to be seen. Like the icy River Styx, the River of the Dead, Marguerite thought, with a shudder of foreboding. She preferred to look up at the bold, fierce blue of the sky. That, at least, seemed to offer no hint of shadow.

'How far do you mean to travel today, Jacques?' she asked, when the tense silence had become more than she could bear.

'To Autun, if the weather holds. But it will be a long journey. I doubt we shall arrive before nightfall.'

She risked a flirtatious sideways glance from under her lashes. He did not seem to be looking at her. 'Are you proposing that we should be alone together, in the dark?' Her voice was unusually low, and rather breathy. This time, it was not deliberate. She could not help it. It was the result of thinking about being so close to him, in a dark carriage, where not even the postilions could see what they did. He would do nothing indiscreet, of course, nothing at all, and yet she sorely wished he would. She would settle for a single kiss, if it would carry her back to paradise.

'I am proposing, Marguerite, that we should make our way to Paris with all possible speed, so that we may fulfil our mission,' he said brusquely.

Clearly, he did not share her longings. Her tactics seemed to be failing. She resolved to try a different tack. 'And what, pray, is our mission?' she asked coolly. She had discovered that Herr Benn was an English spy, and that Jacques was his French accomplice, but she had never been told what they planned to do. Since she might be risking her life, she believed she was entitled to share in the secret. Especially as he had called it 'our mission', not merely 'his'.

'I am not at liberty to tell you.' He turned to her then. His expression was quite blank, impossible to read.

'And if you should be injured, or killed, who would fulfil *our* mission then, may I ask?'

'Keep your voice down, Marguerite,' he urged, gesturing towards the bobbing postilions. 'There is only a single sheet of glass between us and them. We must not take any risks.'

'Say you so?' she hissed. 'And yet you risk your own life, and our mission, because you are not prepared to trust me.'

'No, I—'

'You swore to honour me as long as we were together. You, sir, have a very strange concept of honour.'

Jacques flushed to his hairline. His exaggerated sense of honour made him vulnerable, Marguerite realised. She must press home her advantage. 'We embarked on this mission together, Jacques. We both know the dangers we may encounter. I am more than prepared to face them, but you must not treat me like a…like a piece of troublesome baggage.' His bare hand lay along his thigh, his fist clenching and unclenching rhythmically. He seemed quite unaware of what he did. Marguerite laid her gloved fingers reassuringly on top of his and squeezed.

She might as well have sliced a dagger through his flesh.

He snatched his hand away as if it had touched a naked flame. 'No!' The word seemed to be torn from him. 'No,' he repeated in a low voice.

Marguerite raised her chin. 'That was uncalled for, Jacques. As your loving sister, I was only offering a little comfort. You appeared troubled.'

He narrowed his eyes, but said nothing.

'I imagine your conscience is troubling you. As it should be,' she added, with a touch of quiet venom. 'For we are partners in this enterprise, yet you would treat me like an underling.'

'I am trying to protect you, Marguerite. Can you not see that?'

'Your protection will follow me all the way to the guillotine, I dare say. I find it ironic that I might mount the steps to the scaffold, condemned, but still unaware of the true nature of my crime.' She reached out again and, with sudden daring, laid her fingers on his thigh. He could not pull away this time. The chaise was too cramped. But she felt his flesh contract, even through the fine leather of her glove. He would do almost anything to avoid her touch.

'Marguerite!' he hissed warningly.

'Do not concern yourself,' she answered blithely. 'The postilions are not looking in our direction. And, even if they were, they would not be able to see anything, for the panel obscures the lower part of our bodies.' It was only after the words were out that she understood what could be read into them. And into her rash move to touch him.

'You forget yourself, madam.' He lifted her fingers and dropped them back into her lap as if they were unclean. 'Remember, pray, that we are travelling as brother and sister and that I, at least, have sworn to behave with honour. Sadly, your actions lead me to believe that you are ready to forget your own. You have spent the last twenty-four hours trying to tease, and tempt, and tantalise me away from my sworn word. You will not succeed in that, I can assure you. Marguerite, your outrageous behaviour must cease. You will only succeed in making this journey intolerable, for both of us!'

'Sir, I must protest. I—'

'Let me remind you, Marguerite, that you agreed to obey my orders.'

'Only in times of danger,' she shot back, desperate to concede no advantage to him.

'You agreed to obey my orders when we were in danger. True. And I may tell you, my dear sister, that we are in danger every step of the way.'

Marguerite did not think so, not for a moment. It was his way of trying to exert his authority over her. She would not have it.

He gave her a long, meaningful look. There was exasperation in his face, and a hint of weariness in his eyes. Had he not slept at all?

'Marguerite, I think it is time you stopped arguing. It is dangerous. We may easily be overheard.' He dropped his voice a little more. 'Now, the last time I had to silence you, I kissed you.'

She felt herself blushing. And longing for it to happen again.

'Such a remedy is out of the question now, since I swore an oath to your mother. That means I might have to resort to other, more disreputable methods.'

'You would not dare!'

He smiled. He knew he had the upper hand at last. 'My dear girl, I would hazard much to protect the reputation of my innocent sister. I would not…er…chastise you in public, but I warn you, Marguerite, if you continue with these ridiculous starts, I will certainly take steps to put a stop to them.' He reached into his pocket for a handkerchief which he proceeded to spread out and then refold across the diagonal into a long band. 'I have some experience of gags. I have no doubt that this would be quite adequate.'

'You could not! The postilions would think you a monster!'

'I do not care what they think me, Marguerite, as long as they make good time along these infernal roads. Besides, I shall tell them that my sister is an insufferable gabblemonger and that, driven almost to distraction, I decided to gag her for a stage, in order to get a little peace. I'm sure each of them will be able to think of a chattering woman he would like to silence. They will sympathise with a fellow man, suffering from a woman's unstoppable tongue. Provided they see that I have done you no harm—no permanent harm—they will not intervene.'

Marguerite fancied that was all too likely. The more she came to understand about the ways of the male sex, the less she understood, and the less comfortable she felt.

'However, I think that must wait,' he said, with a quiver of excitement in his voice. 'Look!'

One of the postilions was waving his whip and pointing. Ahead of them, at the approach to Tournus, the road was barred.

'Soldiers!' Jacques exclaimed. 'They are guarding the road. We must be very, very careful here, Marguerite. This is real danger, for we do not know whose side they are on. Follow my lead, and say nothing more than you have to. You promised, remember?'

He smiled at her then, almost the first genuine smile since they had left Lyons, Marguerite thought. Her first impulse was to melt in response. But a sterner mood prevailed. She nodded at him, her face serious. She had promised to obey his orders in times of danger. She would fulfil it. Just like Jacques, she would keep her word. To the letter.

Chapter Fifteen

The chaise slowed as it approached the party of soldiers. A sergeant stepped forward to exchange a few words with the first postilion. Probably asking who we are and whither we are bound, Marguerite thought, but she said nothing. At her side, Jacques was idly playing with his shirt cuffs and looking extremely bored.

The sergeant marched up to the door and pulled it open. He nodded to Jacques but, on seeing Marguerite beside him, saluted with exaggerated courtesy. 'I must ask you your destination, sir, madam,' he said curtly.

'We are travelling to Paris, sergeant,' Jacques replied. 'On business.'

'Oh, and what business might that be?'

'The tiresome business of selling silk, I'm afraid.' Jacques stifled a yawn. 'Unfortunately, our father has a broken leg and remains in Lyons. He would normally have made the journey himself, with my sister here.' He waved a dismissive hand in Marguerite's direction. 'She has excellent skills when it comes to displaying our wares and encouraging the great ladies to buy, but of course she cannot possibly travel alone.

In any case, it needs a man's head to deal with financial matters. Sadly for me, I am the only son and obliged to take my father's place. Believe me, sergeant, I'd much rather be doing almost anything else.'

'Fie, brother,' Marguerite exclaimed. 'It is the first time you have been called upon to take our father's place. You are a good-for-nothing, I do declare. I wonder you could tear yourself away from the low taverns of Lyons to make such a journey. It may seem arduous to a man as idle as you, but Papa and I have made it together many times, and without complaint. We secured good business, too. I despair of your ability to do even half as well. And—'

'That is enough, sister,' Jacques hissed. He turned to the sergeant and shrugged his shoulders. 'You will appreciate, I think, why I find this journey tedious. Five days shut up alone with my sister is something of a trial. I have even had to threaten to gag her.' He lifted the folded handkerchief and waved it from side to side.

'You have my sympathies, sir. And such a pretty lady, too.'

'Well!' Marguerite judged it appropriate to look indignant and to turn her shoulder on the sergeant.

'Quite,' Jacques said with apparent fellow-feeling. 'I think you have the measure of her. Pretty, but with a venomous tongue. Now, was there anything else you needed to know, sergeant?'

The rapport had been established. The sergeant was already well disposed towards them. He listened very carefully, though, to Jacques's explanation of the kind of wares they carried and the customers they were seeking. 'M'father is right about one thing. He says he don't care whose money he takes for our cloth. If the money's good, he'll sell to anyone. How else are we to earn enough to keep body and soul together? Politics is a luxury we poor weavers cannot afford.'

The sergeant began to frown. He ran his eyes over the

opulent post-chaise and then over Marguerite's expensive clothes. 'Seems to me, sir, that you're not so poor as you'd have me believe. Perhaps you would be good enough to step down out of this 'ere vehicle?'

Marguerite spun round in her seat. Oh, heavens! Jacques had overdone it. Now they truly were in the suds. She held her breath and offered up a desperate prayer.

She would willingly sacrifice her own life, but Jacques, her beloved Jacques, must be saved.

Jack could hear the sound of Marguerite scrambling down from the chaise behind him. He did not dare to turn. He wished she had stayed safely inside the chaise, but of course she would not. His indomitable Amazon was going to try to save them, even though it was Jack who had made such a mull of everything so far. Why on earth had he let his tongue run on wheels?

'Sergeant. Sergeant!' She sounded increasingly like a termagant, bless her.

The sergeant turned back to face her. As he did so, he wiped the grimace off his face and replaced it with an expression of polite enquiry. 'Madam?'

'Sergeant, you will want to see what we are carrying. You wish to be assured that we are what we say we are. That is quite natural. You have your duty to do and we, as loyal citizens of France, would not for one moment try to impede you in carrying it out. Let me help you. My brother may think he is in charge of this expedition of ours—' she tossed Jacques a withering glance '—but I must tell you that he knows nothing at all of the silk business. He can neither weave our silk nor sell it. In fact, the only things he is good for are drinking and whor—'

'*Sister!*' Jack roared, judging it was time to intervene.

Marguerite waved him away. 'I am saying nothing less than

the truth, brother. The sergeant may judge for himself which of us knows more about this business of ours.' She took the sergeant by the arm and towed him round to look at the trunk of samples. She dug into her reticule for the key. 'My father does not trust him with this,' she said waspishly, waving it in Jacques's direction, 'which only goes to prove what I have been saying, does it not?' She flung open the lid to display her carefully stacked parcels. 'They are all wrapped in oiled paper, as you see, so that they will come to no harm if the journey should be wet. One cannot depend on this trunk to keep out every drop of water, you see, and I am most particular in the care of my silk. I wrapped every single parcel myself, you know.' She glared across at Jack. 'I certainly would not trust my brother to do it.'

By Jove, she was wonderful! The sergeant was clearly wilting under her barrage of words. Jack was even beginning to feel sorry for the man.

'Now, I take it you would like me to open some of these parcels, sergeant, so that you may check the contents. Pray choose.' When the sergeant did not move quickly enough for her, she urged him on by picking out one package after another. 'Shall it be this one? Or this? It is very much the same to me, you know. All contain precisely what I have said.'

The sergeant, unable to get a word in, pointed rather helplessly to a smallish parcel that still lay in the trunk. Marguerite seized it and carefully unwrapped it, talking nineteen to the dozen about the importance of slow careful wrapping so that the oiled paper could not tear or fail in its task of protecting the precious fabric. 'There!' she said at last, clearly triumphant. She lifted the silk and shook it out. It was patterned in rich reds and golds that glowed and shimmered as the light caught it. 'Is that not a work of art, sergeant? I may tell you that I wove it myself, and—'

'I do not need to see any more here, madam.' The man had had to raise his voice almost to parade-ground pitch in order to make himself heard. 'Pray take your time to wrap it up again.' He marched hastily back round to where Jack was standing and looked up at him with something like relief in his face. 'Now, sir, do you have any other luggage with you?'

'Why, yes, sergeant. We have a travelling valise each. In the chaise.' He pointed helpfully. 'If you wish to search them, please do. As my sister has said, we have nothing to hide.' That was not true, of course. Jack really did not want to have to explain the substantial store of silver concealed in his valise. He was beginning to concoct a story to use, when Marguerite appeared at his side once more. She still looked like a harridan, but a particularly bad-tempered one now.

'Are you proposing to search my valise, sergeant?' She sounded outraged. 'That is not the kind of treatment I should have expected from a man of your standing, I must say. Pawing over a lady's most intimate garments…' She put a hand to her throat as though the mere thought of such behaviour was giving her palpitations. Undeterred, the sergeant had opened her valise and was beginning, very gingerly, to move aside some of the clothing in order to search underneath. 'Why, I do believe your hands are not clean!' She rushed forward and snatched the valise from him. 'Let me do it!' She picked up one layer after another of her carefully packed clothing, allowing him barely time to squint underneath before replacing them. 'There! And there! Are you satisfied, sir?'

The sergeant admitted that he was and turned gratefully to Jack's valise. Marguerite was still repacking hers, so she could not see the look of exquisite anguish on the sergeant's face. In spite of their predicament, Jack found it very difficult not to laugh.

The man had just begun to poke his fingers into Jack's valise when Marguerite turned on him again. Jack could not imagine what she was going to do this time. If she went too far, they might both end up being arrested.

'Be careful of his clean linen, if you please, sergeant. I laundered and ironed it myself, you know, though he certainly does not deserve such devoted service, considering the abuse he hurls upon my head. Oh, no, please don't pull out that shirt! It will never—'

'Madam, I have seen enough,' the sergeant announced. 'There is nothing here to suggest you are anything other than silk merchants, as your brother said. This search has obviously delayed your journey, but it was a matter of duty, you understand. If you start again quickly, you will find that you have not lost too much time.' The poor man could not be more desperate to be rid of them.

'Thank you, sergeant, but before we drive on, I should like to say that—'

'No, sister, you will not,' Jack interrupted quickly. It was time for the foppish brother to reassert himself and start an argument with his impossible sister. That would be the last straw for the poor sergeant and would certainly dispel any lingering doubts. 'The sergeant is right. We have lost quite enough time already and neither he nor I wish to hear your opinions. On anything.'

'But I—'

Jack seized her arm and half-dragged her to the chaise door. 'Up with you now,' he said sharply, bundling her up the steps.

She almost fell into her seat. 'Well! Such appalling lack of manners.' She continued to rail at him while he replaced their valises and climbed in beside her.

Jack nodded to the sergeant. The soldier looked relieved that his own ordeal was over and more than a little sorry for

Jack, whose ordeal was about to continue. Jack shrugged and smiled wryly.

The chaise began to move forward quite slowly. Ahead of them, the line of soldiers parted in the middle at the sergeant's signal. There was just enough room for the chaise to pass between the two ranks. Marguerite, aware that danger was still all around them, continued to berate Jack energetically. The soldiers might not be able to make out her words, but they would certainly hear the angry tone and see her agitated, frowning face.

Jack was staring straight ahead, with an appropriately pained look on his face, as they drove through. He needed to thank her, now, and he could think of only one way. He laid his hand gently on top of Marguerite's and pressed her fingers lightly. She caught her breath for a split second, and then she continued ranting at him in the same colourful language.

But out of sight of the soldiers, she squeezed his hand and held it fast.

Marguerite clung to the memory of that magic moment throughout the rest of their journey to Paris. It took much longer than they had hoped, for the news of Bonaparte's advance seemed to have created turmoil everywhere. Posting houses were without sufficient horses or postilions, inns were full to overflowing with royalists fleeing north to escape the man they called 'the monster', and soldiers seemed to be everywhere, stopping, searching and questioning travellers, but rarely clear about the purpose of their actions. Their officers claimed they were serving King Louis, but the ill-concealed mutterings in the ranks suggested otherwise. Marguerite found herself becoming increasingly nervous. She did succeed in continuing to play the part of the harridan sister, whenever it proved necessary, but she felt her acting was becoming less and less convincing.

With each successive encounter with jumpy soldiers, she had become more afraid for Jacques, even though he showed no fear at all. Indeed, he seemed to be enjoying each brush with danger. Perhaps his buoyant good humour was because Marguerite had ceased to taunt him? That first search had taught her a frightening lesson—she and Jack were dependent on each other to get through this journey unscathed. They had to trust each other. Her wicked teasing had made him cross, and frustrated, both of which might lead him to say or do things that might betray them. The momentary satisfaction of punishing him for his stupid oath was of no moment compared with their survival.

She had even begun to think they were becoming friends. He still refused to disclose the details of his mission—she had asked just once more, and been rebuffed again—but on other subjects he was happy to talk, and his views were interesting and thoughtful. He seemed to have travelled all over Europe, in spite of his comparative youth. From a chance remark he had dropped, Marguerite deduced that he had even visited England. That seemed strange to her at first, but then she remembered that he was spying for England. No doubt his masters had insisted on a secret visit there, so that they could assess his reliability. It must have been something of the sort for, when she asked him what England was like, he turned the subject. He did not actually deny he had been there, but he did not admit it, either.

She did not attempt to pursue the issue. She contented herself with the knowledge that he had avoided lying to her. Perhaps that touch of their fingers had been more than just a sign of relief after all. It had certainly been so for her.

'You are looking pensive, Marguerite,' he said quietly when they were on the final approaches to Paris. 'There is no need to worry. We shall reach our goal soon now, largely thanks to your astonishing acting ability. I must say I do pity the poor idle brother of the termagant from Lyons,' he finished, with a broad grin.

She decided on the spot to share her concerns with him. After all, their mission must soon be over. He would make his report, she would deliver her silk to the Duchess of Courland and seek a few new customers, and then they would be able to start back south for Lyons. Suzanne, with her new-found confidence, might be coping perfectly well, but it did not stop Marguerite from worrying about her. 'I was wondering how long we are to remain in Paris and where we are to stay. I imagine you will wish to be close to the British embassy, so that you may make your report without being observed?'

'I...I...' Goodness, he was actually blushing. He ran a finger round the inside of his collar and swallowed hard. 'Marguerite, there are things I have not told you—things I may not tell you. For your own safety.'

He reached for her hand and held it for a moment. It was their first real touch for days, and it made her blood fizz like shaken champagne. One moment, she felt light-headed and unsteady, the next she was soaring up into the clouds.

'I must ask you a question, which you may find odd, but I beg you to answer it none the less. You told me, before we left Lyons, that your father is in the Low Countries, seeking orders. He is bound to return to Lyons to protect his family, as soon as he hears of Bonaparte's return. Any father would. His obvious route will take him through Paris. Where would you expect him to lodge in the city?'

Marguerite was so shocked that her jaw dropped. She had told Jacques the same practised lies that the whole family used, both in Lyons and elsewhere. Papa Grolier was travelling abroad on business, or Papa had been at home but he had

just left again and would not return for some months. No one
had ever called her bluff before. Why did Jacques have to do
so? To play for time, she said, 'I really don't know, Jacques.
Why do you ask?'

'I…I…' He was looking increasingly uncomfortable. At
last he said, rather hoarsely, 'I thought your father could
escort you home to Lyons.'

'But surely you will do that? What about Herr Benn? Do
you not have to return to collect him?'

'Er…no. I do not plan to return to Lyons.'

'But Herr Benn—?'

'Herr Benn is well aware of what I am planning.'

'I see,' Marguerite said crossly. 'So you and Herr Benn
have discussed everything, but I am not to be trusted with any
information at all. I take it you intend to deposit me in Paris,
like a parcel for collection?'

'Marguerite, I cannot remain in Paris with you. I have
to…er…go on. Alone.'

'Why? Surely you can deliver your information here, to the
embassy? Where else would you go?'

His jaw worked for a moment. Then, very softly, he said,
'I have to go to England.'

'What? And you would go alone? But that is madness! All
the roads and the ports will be watched. The journey from Paris
to the coast will be far more dangerous than anything we have
done so far.' She shook her head determinedly. 'No. If you
leave Paris, I shall go with you. You cannot safely travel alone.'

'Nonsense, Marguerite. Of course I can. It will be much
safer for you to stay here in Paris until your father arrives to
escort you home. I could not possibly leave you here otherwise. It would be a breach of my oath.'

Marguerite threw him a jaundiced look, but said nothing.
She was not sure that she could control her voice if she spoke.

He laid his fingers gently over hers. 'So, tell me, my brave Marguerite. How soon is your father likely to arrive in Paris?' He gave her hand a tiny squeeze.

That touch was the final straw. She began to laugh hysterically. She wanted to double over with the pain of it, but she eventually managed to suck in a breath and speak. 'My father? My father will not be arriving in Paris. My father is simply a convenient fiction to allow the silk business to continue to run.'

'What?' He jerked away from her.

She straightened her shoulders and stared at him. He did not understand what the Groliers were about. He was probably too rich to bother about mundane matters such as merchants' lives. She spoke slowly and clearly, as if to a simpleton. 'Our business cannot operate without a man to head it. I have no brothers. And no father, either. He died more than four years ago. We had no choice. As far as the world is concerned, my father is still alive.'

'Oh, God! Now what am I going to do?'

For a second or two, she felt sorry for him. His anguish was so real. But then she realised the import of his words. 'It is a question, sir, of what *we* are going to do, is it not?' She forced herself to smile confidently. 'If you are determined to travel on to England in spite of the risks—though I cannot see the point of it, I must say—we will continue to travel together, as brother and sister.'

He shook his head, not decisively, but as if he were trying to clear his thoughts. 'What a coil!' He had begun to run his fingers through his hair. It was almost standing on end. It made him look very young. 'How could I have been so stupid?' That was heartfelt.

'Perhaps it is time to rethink your plans?' She was trying to sound as calm and reasonable as she could. 'You could deliver your information to the embassy and then you could return to Herr Benn. With me.'

He was barely listening. 'I had intended to lodge you safely at a convent until your father arrived, but I dare not do so now. You might not be safe here, even with the nuns. Who knows what may happen once Bonaparte arrives in Paris?'

'Then let us complete our business as soon as we may, and return to Lyons.'

He groaned. 'Marguerite, it is impossible. I dare not go to the embassy, for I am too well known there. If my true identity were revealed now, my mission would be at an end. And you would be in real danger, too. I will not risk that.'

His concern warmed her heart. She knew she would never persuade him to abandon his mission—nor did she wish to, for she could not love a dishonourable man—but there must be another way. Yes, she had it. 'Trust me with your report, Jacques. I can take it to the embassy. There will be no risk then.'

'No!' He seized her hand again and held it firmly between both of his own. 'No, Marguerite. You do not understand. The embassy will be watched. You would be seen, and followed. Bonaparte's spies would have you arrested, the moment their master arrived in the city. No, I must find a place of safety for you, well away from Paris, and then I must make haste back to England.'

'*Back* to England? So you *have* been there before! But surely it is dangerous for a Frenchman to go there, especially now? Could you not—?'

He pulled her up short by squeezing her hand so hard it was almost painful. Her question expired on a gasp.

'Marguerite, I will trust you with my mission. And my life. I am an Englishman.'

Chapter Sixteen

The Pension Beauregard did not live up to its name. It was tucked away in a long, gloomy cul-de-sac near the rue St Honoré. The location was ideal for their purposes—close to the centre of Paris and yet too poor to tempt the people of wealth and fashion who might recognise Jacques.

Marguerite crossed to the parlour window yet again. She had done it so many times now that she had lost count. He had been gone for hours.

He was an English spy.

Those words kept going round and round in her head. She told herself she should be honoured that he had shared his dangerous secret with her. But she was not. She was tempted to weep, or to scream with frustration. She had done neither.

What a fool she had been. She had trusted him. She had believed they were almost friends. What kind of friendship could exist between a French weaver and an English gentleman?

A French royalist might have learned to return her love and to forgive her for what she had done to him. But a proud, stiff-necked Englishman would never do so, however worthy the cause. She had drugged him and imprisoned him in the most demeaning way. It was no wonder he was trying to get rid of her.

She was remembering exactly how she had behaved during their journey from Lyons, tempting, teasing, trying to make him lose control. A Frenchman might have found that amusing, but an English gentleman would be insulted. Jacques had lost control in the end, but not in the way she had hoped. There had been no passionate kisses. Rather a passionate outburst against her 'outrageous behaviour'. Exactly what she would have expected of an Englishman.

She sank back into her chair and closed her aching eyes. In spite of everything, she still loved him. There was no help for it. But she would never let him know it. Not now. No English gentleman could ever learn to love a woman like her. She was just a lowly weaver, and a failed temptress. But she still had her pride. Painful though it had been, she had not allowed herself even the tiniest touch since she had learned of his true identity. She would never allow him to despise her.

She straightened her back, rose and began to walk back and forth across the little parlour. He would return to her eventually, and she must be ready for him. She must concentrate on their mission. It was her duty to protect him, and there was only one way to do that now. She would have to behave as if they truly were brother and sister. It would require cool detachment. She would have to find a way to recover the common sense which her sister so admired. And to bury her feelings. She would have to learn to be calm and composed, no matter how much heartache it cost her.

She would begin to practise. Now. She forced herself to smile, and crossed to the window.

Down below, the quiet cul-de-sac was empty except for a one-legged soldier leaning on his crutches in a doorway opposite, playing a mournful melody on a tin whistle. It suited

Marguerite's melancholy mood too well. The man had been playing the same tune at odd intervals ever since their arrival.

It was beginning to rain. The old soldier ducked further back into his doorway. Down at the very far end of the alley, where it joined the bright, noisy bustle of the main road, a flicker of movement caught her eye. A man was hurrying down towards the pension, the skirts of his coat flapping awkwardly around his knees. With one hand, he was holding his hat against the rain and the swirling wind; the other was deep in his pocket. He did not look up, but Marguerite recognised his long-legged stride at once. Jacques was taking no chances. That pocket contained his money, and probably also a pistol.

Jacques was about to cross the alley to the pension when he stopped to exchange a few words with the old soldier. Marguerite was too far away to hear, but she saw the man's toothless grin and the nod of thanks. Then he stowed his whistle carefully inside his jacket and limped off towards the main street, his crutches slipping occasionally on the wet cobbles. In spite of the rain, Jacques stood watching the man until he disappeared round the corner.

Marguerite stepped back from the window before Jacques could see her. She did not want him to guess that she had been looking out for him. She certainly did not want him to suspect that she had been worrying about his safety.

She heard his quick, light step on the stair. By the time he reached the landing, she was sitting by the tiny fire with her hands folded demurely in her lap. She was determined to play the part of a sister, both in public and in private, at least until the terrible danger was past. It did not matter that she was having to suppress her own longings. They would never be fulfilled. Not now. What mattered now was to save Jacques from the risk of arrest.

The latch rattled. Marguerite resisted the temptation to go

to meet him at the door. It was best to remain where she was, calmly seated and suitably distant.

He flung the door wide and stepped inside, throwing his hat on to the small table alongside the fireplace. Some of the raindrops fell on the hearth with a sizzle. Marguerite risked a single enquiring glance and then looked quickly away. He frowned in response. That was clearly not the reaction he had been expecting from her. However, he made no comment. Instead, he quietly closed the door and shrugged off his heavy coat, before crossing to the fireplace to warm his hands.

Marguerite stared at the flickering flames. 'You have been a long time,' she said matter of factly.

He turned his head a fraction, but she refused to lift her head. It would be much more difficult to maintain the distance between them if she looked into his face. Besides, she was afraid of what he might see in her eyes.

'I apologise if I have worried you, Marguerite.'

She shook her head, hoping she looked impatient rather than concerned.

'I clearly don't know Paris as well as I thought I did, for it took longer than I had expected to find the Lyons coaching agent. He was delighted to have the chaise returned, of course. He has queues of customers wanting to journey south, in spite of Bonaparte's advance. Must say, that surprised me, but perhaps they are all sympathisers.'

'Will he provide us with a chaise for Calais?' Marguerite sat back in her chair and forced herself to appear calm. She let her gaze drift idly over Jacques's person, avoiding his eyes, and all the while reminding herself to think of him as a brother. Only a brother.

'No, he's on the wrong side of the river. He deals only with journeys to the south and east. I had to start all over again on this side of the Seine. Sadly, I had no luck at all, no matter how much money I offered them. It seems there is not a chaise to be had anywhere.'

'What are we to do?' To her annoyance, she detected a slight tremor in her voice as she spoke. He was bound to think she was afraid. She was, but for Jacques, not for herself. It was imperative that he leave Paris.

'The *diligence* for Boulogne and Calais leaves at noon each day from the rue Montmartre. It is fully booked today and tomorrow, but I have purchased the first two free places. We should reach Calais on Thursday.'

She clasped her hands more tightly together. Only a few more days and then he would be safe. But in the meantime—?

'Marguerite, what is the matter?' He pulled forward a rough wooden chair and sat down so close to her that their knees were almost touching. He tried to take her hands in his, but she snatched them away. 'Marguerite, I can understand your worries, and your fears, but I promise I will take every care of you until we leave here. We—'

She jumped to her feet, almost knocking him over in the process, and began to pace. She took refuge in anger. 'I am grateful for your concern, Jacques, but you misread the situation. I am not afraid.' He had risen, too, and was leaning casually against the fireplace with his eyes fixed on her face. She frowned at him. 'We are here as brother and sister. You acknowledge that it is safer for us to travel so, and yet you go off alone for hours, making a spectacle of yourself while you demand post-chaises and instant seats on the *diligence*. You even try to bribe the chaise owners. What sort of way is that to behave? The Bonapartists will mark you down for a royalist, trying to escape from Paris. No doubt they will bide their time, but if that monster does reach the city, you will be arrested.'

He smiled wryly at her. 'They would have to find me first,

my dear. And I can assure you I was not followed back here. I do have some basic skills as a spy, you know.'

'Oh!' She turned away before she could give in to the urge to stamp her foot like a child in a tantrum. She strode angrily across to the window, chewing at her lip. The more dangerous their situation, the more devil-may-care he became. Did he have no common sense at all? And how dare he address her as his 'dear'?

She stared down into the street, which was now totally deserted. The rain had stopped but, in places, the cobbles gleamed with a slick, metallic sheen. As Marguerite watched, a skinny cat emerged from a cellar and began to pick its way daintily around the puddles, making for the end of the alley. If she had been at home, she would have given it a saucer of milk. She—

His warm breath stroked the back of her neck like a fine velvet glove. She had not heard him move, but he was standing immediately behind her. She could feel the heat from his body, even through all the layers of their clothing. It felt as if she had her back to a blazing fire. If she turned, her face would be almost against his chest. And her lips would be only inches from his.

She did not move.

'Come back to the fire, Marguerite.' Each soft syllable of that rich voice was a caress on her naked skin. She shivered. 'You see?' There was a hint of masculine triumph in his voice, even though it was still barely audible. 'It is cold here by the window.'

She continued to focus on the distant cat. After a moment more, she felt the heat receding. She turned and saw that he was back by the fireplace, waiting for her to resume her seat. As if nothing at all had happened. She nodded coolly and returned to her chair so that he, too, might sit down.

He had put his chair back in its normal place, a respectable distance away from hers. It seemed that he had understood the rules she was trying to impose. When he began to speak, she was sure of it.

'We have gleaned a lot of information on our way here, information that will be useful to the Allies, I think. My wanderings today have shown me that Paris is much like Sens, where we stopped last night. Rumours everywhere, of course, and royalist sentiment almost invisible. I could understand that at Sens, but here, in Paris? I would have expected at least a pretence of loyalty while the King remains here, but I found none. The loudest voices belonged to Bonapartists plotting their revenge on their enemies. You have heard about the proclamation?'

Marguerite shook her head. It was all starting to sound very bad.

'Bonaparte issued a proclamation after we left Lyons. It stated that the Bourbons are unfit to reign and all troops are to join the "great Napoleon". By all accounts, they are already doing so.'

'Ney will arrest him. He has sworn an oath to the King.' Marguerite raised her eyes, hoping to see agreement in his face. There was none. His expression was a blank. It seemed he had no faith in Marshal Ney, and possibly none in the King, either.

'Let us hope you are right. No doubt we will learn soon enough.' He rose and reached for his coat. 'Since we are marooned here for at least two days, we might as well continue with our plan. Today being Sunday, you cannot wait upon the Duchess of Courland or any other potential customers. So I suggest we walk out calmly together, as brother and sister, to take the air after the rain and find ourselves a decent meal. I, for one, am starving.'

It had taken Jack some time to persuade her to accompany him, even though the Pension Beauregard did not serve food.

Jack knew that Marguerite had not eaten since their arrival, but she refused to admit that she was hungry. In the end, he resorted to underhand tactics, telling her that they were both needed out on the streets in order to find out what was really going on in Paris. That was untrue. The situation was already clear enough. Jack doubted whether anything else of use would turn up.

She would not be easily fooled, he knew. So he led her through the streets to the Palais Royal, where the cafés and gaming rooms were renowned as a hotbed of gossip and rebellion. The place would be full of Bonapartists, and therefore dangerous, but it was what she was bound to expect. She was as fearless as ever. She walked calmly by his side, looking about her, watching carefully. She did not speak. Occasionally, her heels clicked on the wet cobbles, but she showed no sign at all of losing her footing. And she flatly refused to take his arm, no matter how politely he offered.

Something had changed. Jack had been trying to tell himself that his imagination was playing tricks on him, but he could not swallow such a whisker any more. Marguerite had started their journey from Lyons by teasing and taunting him, to the point where he had thought his frustrations might boil over. He had been very tempted to turn her over his knee or, better, to kiss her senseless. But, after that first encounter with the soldiers, she had become very proper, almost like a true sister. He had been glad of it at first, since it gave him a chance to regain control of his unruly body. Unfortunately his control had not been as good as he would have wished. Not because of anything Marguerite had done—she had behaved impeccably—but because of his own memories of her seductive teasing. No matter how primly she looked at him, he kept seeing the sensual enchantress beneath. It had taken him two days of stern warnings to himself to put those pictures aside. And even then, they had returned at night in his dreams.

Playing the part of a sister had not stopped her from touching him in perfectly ordinary ways, or giving him a peck on the cheek when they retired for the night. After his initial surprise, Jack had come to expect her good-night kiss and to relish it in a strange sort of way. It was totally innocent, but the touch of her soft lips against his skin had been a glorious memory to carry to bed with him, even if it had tended to disturb his rest.

So why had she stopped?

What had he said? Or done? He understood now, too late, that he had enjoyed their time together, even when she was teasing him. It suggested that there might be some attraction between them, that Marguerite might— No! He must not allow himself to think such things. He had sworn an oath, to treat her honourably, as a sister. He could not break it.

But she was no longer allowing him to behave as a brother. Why?

The answer was obvious as soon as he began to consider it coolly and logically. He had confessed that he was an Englishman. Since then, she had not allowed him to lay a finger on her, even in the most innocuous way. And her good-night kiss was now only a memory. She was a royalist who would do her duty for her cause. That might include helping an English spy to escape from France, but it clearly did not include allowing such a man to touch her. If only he had not told her…

'Good gracious!' Marguerite had stopped in her tracks. Ahead of them, in a passage leading between one stall selling clocks and another selling toys, there was an apparently respectable young woman holding up a highly coloured print, which was anything but respectable. Jack cursed himself for forgetting. The booksellers in the arcades of the Palais Royal were renowned for the range of their erotic wares, and not in the least embarrassed about displaying them.

'Come away, sister.' He put an arm around her shoulder and forced her to move. For once, she did not attempt to shake him off, though he knew she would do so as soon as she regained her composure.

'That woman. Was she a…a prostitute?' Marguerite's voice was trembling a little. Her face was very white.

Jack gave her shoulders a tiny squeeze and then removed his arm. 'No, sister. She is just a Palais Royal bookseller. You may not believe it, but she considers herself highly respectable. They all do, in spite of what they sell.'

'Oh. I'm afraid I did not know. I have never visited the Palais Royal before.'

'You would have been unwise to do so, without an escort. But now that we are here together, you will allow me to show you, I hope, that we may eat as well here as anywhere in Paris.' He pointed to the row of restaurants, each with its bill of fare on display, and many with criers outside, encouraging potential customers to enter and sample the establishment's excellent cuisine. 'A restaurant of the middling sort for us, I fancy,' he added softly. 'One where we are unlikely to meet anyone we would prefer to avoid.'

The restaurant was almost full when they arrived, but they managed to secure a table in a corner from which they could study the whole room. As Jacques had predicted, the food was excellent and plentiful, and wine was included in the very modest price. Marguerite found her attention straying from her plate. Her mind was full of that extraordinary picture, of a man and a woman coupling on a sofa in a rose garden. She had never before seen such a thing. She had always assumed, perhaps naïvely, that sexual encounters took place in a bedchamber, in the dark. Such an outrageous print should have disgusted her, but in fact it had merely surprised her and started wild questions in her mind. The naked couple seemed to be enjoying each other very much. Was that what love-making was really like? Was it possible to delight in a lover's body? And in the open air?

She was sure she must be blushing. To divert her unruly thoughts, she focused on the mistress of the establishment, a stately woman with a resplendent bosom, dressed in a gown of deep purple trimmed with lace. Neither the silk of the gown nor the lace was of the first quality, but they did not need to be; the *patronne*'s manner was condescending enough for a duchess.

It was well after seven when they spilled out into the muggy darkness in the centre of the Palais Royal. The trees were almost invisible but, all around them, the cellars and shops and cafés rose in layers full of light, as if the dark centre were surrounded by a ring of fire. Marguerite tried un-successfully to swallow a giggle. She had had a sudden vision of the *patronne* cavorting within that fiery ring, her enormous bosom heaving.

'Do I detect that you have had one too many glasses of wine, sister?'

'Certainly not!' She straightened her face, with difficulty, and shot a glance back over her shoulder. *Madame* was nowhere to be seen. 'No, I'm afraid that the airs of *madame la patronne* were becoming too much for me. She oversees her empire like a bountiful deity.' She thought for a moment. 'No, perhaps not bountiful. I doubt she would be kind if her underlings failed to do her bidding.'

Or if her lover failed to come up to scratch.

Marguerite was at a loss to know where such a wicked thought had come from. Perhaps she really had drunk too much wine? She forced herself to remember their mission and her resolve. 'That was a splendid dinner, Jacques, but the customers were…er…rather subdued.' In truth, they had overheard nothing useful. 'Shall we return to the pension?'

He shook his head. 'I thought we might take coffee up there.' He pointed to the upper storey. 'But stay close by me. Some of the cafés here are full of prostitutes, and worse. I would not have you distressed in any way.'

He tucked her hand under his arm as he spoke and turned towards the stairs. Marguerite was too surprised to protest or pull away. Judging by the noise coming from some of the lighted windows, not all of these establishments were respectable. She could hear drunken laughter and all kinds of music—violins, and drums, and even what sounded like a tin whistle.

They had just reached the upper storey when an enormous shout came from the square below. A man had appeared in the middle of the darkness, carrying two pairs of huge lamps, which he proceeded to hang from the trees. 'Gentlemen!' he cried, twirling round on the spot so that he could be seen from all sides of the piazza. 'Gentlemen, I have great news!' He continued to yell at the top of his voice until crowds of people appeared from the cafés and gaming rooms.

Jack pulled Marguerite so close against his side that she could feel the shape of one of his pistols pressing against her hip bone. His breathing was shallow and uneven, and he had narrowed his eyes to watch the man below. Was he calculating how they might escape from here?

At last, the man in the square was satisfied with the size of his audience. 'Gentlemen! A great triumph! The Emperor Napoleon reached Auxerre last night. Marshall Ney was waiting for him and our beloved Emperor embraced him as a comrade. The fat Bourbon's threats have come to nothing, as we knew they would. Everyone flocks to the Emperor. Except fat Louis, of course, who has fled the country again, back to the arms of France's enemies. We are well rid of him and all the Bourbons. Let us rejoice, my friends. Our Emperor will be with us again, here in his capital, tomorrow!'

Chapter Seventeen

'How could he break his oath? It was an oath to France!' A night's sleep had made no difference to Marguerite's feelings. Her voice was still filled with loathing for the King she had supported so bravely. She had been prepared to die for him, while he, at the first sign of danger, had fled the country.

Jack did not know how to console her. There was no way he could defend King Louis. The man had made high-flown promises, but he was basically weak. Urged on by his cronies, he had turned the clock back towards repression rather than forward to reform, and now all France would be made to pay. Marguerite sounded totally disillusioned. Her royal hero had deceived her.

It was Marguerite herself who provided the solution. 'Whatever he has done, we cannot desert the cause we serve,' she announced proudly. 'We must continue our mission. We, at least, shall not break our oaths.'

Jack did not need that reminder. His vow to treat her as a sister was never far from his mind. He had told himself, throughout their journey from Lyons, that his oath must on no account be broken. He rather thought that, if he kissed her again, she would respond willingly, and perhaps eagerly—there had been enough hints in her unguarded reactions that she was not indifferent to him—but she would despise him once their passion was spent. He was not prepared to risk that, even for the pleasure of making love to her. He was a grown man. He could wait.

'Since we cannot leave Paris until tomorrow, I suggest we make the most of today to do as much business as possible,' she said brusquely. 'I have the Duchess of Courland's silk to deliver.'

'Do you think that is wise? Everyone knows that the Duchess is a fervent royalist. Her house will be watched now that Bonaparte's success is assured.'

'But she ordered this silk and—'

'She ordered it for a court dress. For King Louis's court, Marguerite. She will have no use for it now. And, to be frank, I would be surprised if she were prepared to pay you for it. Better to avoid the risk of going to her house.'

'Oh.' Marguerite sat down suddenly in her chair by the fireside. 'And the same will be true of all the other great ladies, I suppose.'

'I imagine so. The royalist ladies will not wish to buy, and the Bonapartist ladies have not yet returned to Paris. I am afraid that you are unlikely to find any buyers today.'

Marguerite rose and crossed to where her trunk of silk sat against the wall opposite the fireplace. By day she kept it here in the little parlour; at night, it sat safely next to her bed. She ran a hand lovingly across the worn leather. 'Can we take this with us in the *diligence*?'

'That is something we need to discuss, Marguerite. Thus far, we have pretended to be silk merchants, travelling to Paris to sell our wares. We cannot use that story on the road to Calais, for there are no great ladies there. I think we must leave your trunk behind.'

She spun round, hands on hips, to stand protectively in front of the trunk. 'No! There are months of work here. This silk is worth a small fortune to my family. I will not abandon it.'

This was going to be very difficult. 'Our luggage allowance on the *diligence* is only fifteen pounds each. Barely enough for our valises. The trunk would cost a great deal extra to transport, always assuming there was room for it.'

'But—'

'Be reasonable, Marguerite. You must see that we cannot take it.'

'I will not abandon it,' she said again, even more forcefully.

Jack took a deep breath and thought hard. He could not afford to argue with her over the trunk, which was relatively unimportant. He still had to persuade her about the convent. That might be much more difficult. 'Perhaps we can find a secure deposit for it here in Paris,' he suggested.

She was already shaking her head. 'Nothing will be secure once Bonaparte arrives here. It would be better to put it on a cart for home.'

'Now that gives me an idea,' Jack said, beaming with relief. 'You railed at me yesterday for spending so much time with the Lyons agent, but I begin to think it may have been worthwhile. I bought him a couple of glasses of red while he told me all about his business, and his troubles. It was good information. What's more, he owes me a favour now. He will be sending chaises and carriages south to Lyons. If I pay him well enough, he'll make sure your trunk is safely delivered back to Suzanne. What do you think?'

Marguerite smiled a little uncertainly. 'I suppose it could work. The chaise owner in Lyons is well known to our family, since we often hire carriages from him. He wouldn't want to lose our custom.'

'Excellent. I'll tell his Paris agent so. Then he'll take

doubly good care of your trunk.' He held out his hand. 'If you give me the key, I'll take it to him now and send it off.'

She shook her head. 'There is no need to send the key. Suzanne has a spare at home.' She paused for a moment. 'Since no one else will be able to open the trunk,' she mused, 'I could put a letter inside, telling Suzanne what has happened. She will worry when the trunk arrives back in Lyons and I do not.'

'You must not tell her about our mission, Marguerite!' he snapped.

She glowered at him. 'I thought you knew me better than that, Jacques.' She marched back to the fire and sat down, staring pensively into the flames. Eventually, her frown eased. 'I shall write things that she alone will understand. But I must also tell her where I am to be found.' She looked enquiringly up at Jack. There was uncertainty in her eyes, but no fear. 'Precisely where are we going? And where are we to part?'

She was very direct. And very brave. Jack owed her the truth. 'I have to travel back to England, but I can leave from any port. Calais is the easiest crossing, but it is also the furthest from Paris. And it will probably be crawling with Bonaparte's spies by now. Boulogne would do as well. Or even Dieppe. What matters is finding a safe haven for you. I had thought to find a convent, well away from the main roads. Or perhaps a school?'

She surprised him. He had expected her to object to the very idea of a convent, but she said only, 'I am too old to be left at a school, Jacques. Or had you not noticed?' She narrowed her eyes at him.

He felt himself reddening. She was a fully mature woman. He had most certainly noticed that.

She ignored his growing embarrassment. 'A convent would do, though. There is the Abbaye des Dames at Caen, for example, and at Rouen— Oh!' She grinned suddenly. 'I have a much better idea.' She waved him to the seat opposite her. She was suddenly feeling very pleased with herself. 'I have the perfect plan. We shall tell anyone who asks that we are travelling via Rouen to Caen, where I am to enter the abbey as a novice. It will be perfectly proper for my brother to escort me there.'

In spite of the urgency of their situation, he could not resist the chance to tease her. His sultry temptress would make a very unusual nun. 'Do you truly think you can play the part of a novice, Marguerite?'

She placed her palms together in an attitude of prayer and bowed her head meekly. 'We shall not go to Caen,' she continued solemnly, without lifting her head. 'There is a village near Barentin, on the road from Rouen to Dieppe. The curé there used to be—' She cleared her throat. 'The curé, Father Bertrand, knows my family well. He will shelter me until I am able to return to Lyons.'

'I cannot say how long it will be before I am able to return for you, Marguerite. Are you sure—?'

'You need have no concerns. You will be able to travel on to Dieppe and take ship from there.' She looked up at him with wide, sparkling eyes. Was she triumphant because she had found the solution they sought? Or was it—just perhaps— because he had promised to return for her?

Jack did not dare to ask. Nor could he question her about the mysterious curé, though he was sure she was hiding something. How would a cleric from Normandy come to know a family from Lyons? How could Marguerite be so very sure the curé would take her in?

'That seems a splendid plan,' he said heartily. His first priority had to be to get them both safely out of Paris. Their existing tickets to Calais would have to do. 'We can take the *diligence* as far as Beauvais. With luck, we'll be able to hire a chaise to Rouen from there. Now, if you will write your letter to your sister, I will take your trunk to the agent and send it safely on its way. And in the meantime,' he added with a grin, 'you can practise your role as a silent and submissive postulant nun.'

Marguerite was already in bed when the cheering began. She had been expecting it all day, but none the less it made her feel ill, as if she had swallowed something tainted.

She rose and dragged on her wrapper. From her tiny window, she could see nothing. She would have to go into the parlour.

Jacques was there before her. Unlike Marguerite, he had chosen not to retire early. He was still fully dressed. He turned at the sound of the latch and plastered a smile on to his features as soon as he saw her. But he had not been quick enough. She had seen the lines of worry on his face. She was worried, too. Paris was becoming ever more dangerous for royalists. Soon, it would be so all across France, and yet, in spite of the risks, Jacques had said he would return. For her. She could scarcely believe it. But it must be true. He would not fail to keep such a promise. Could it mean—?

Another burst of noise echoed in the distance. 'I suppose they are cheering for Bonaparte?' she asked quietly.

He shrugged. 'Who else could it be? To be honest, I had expected him to arrive before this. It's taken so long that I allowed myself to hope, for a moment, that the cavalry sent to arrest him had actually done their duty. Clearly they failed. Bonaparte will no doubt sleep soundly tonight, though some of the rest of us will not.' He shook his head in disgust. 'I had better go down to the Tuileries and see for myself how he is being received. London will wish to know if all Paris is cheering him.'

'London is very naïve if it believes otherwise. It would be foolhardy for anyone not to cheer.'

'Precisely so, but my masters will wish to have the testimony of their own eyewitness. So I shall go and cheer with the rest.' He crossed to the door. 'You had best return to your bedchamber while I am gone, Marguerite. And make sure you lock yourself in.'

'You will take care, Jacques?' She had not intended to say it aloud. The thought had been in her mind and, somehow, it had turned itself into words.

He smiled at her. 'Have no fear. I can play the Bonapartist with the best of them, as I think you may have noticed. Try to sleep. If it will reassure you, I will tap on your door when I return.' The smile turned into a wicked grin. 'I would not have you worrying all night, sister dear.'

She looked round for something to throw at him, but their spartan parlour boasted neither cushions nor books. When she turned back, he had gone. She tried the window, but she could see nothing. Was he down there in the alley, making his way towards the light and the cheering crowds? With no flambeaux outside the pension, it was impossible to tell.

For a split second, she thought she heard the sound of a tin whistle, but then it was gone. She told herself she had probably imagined it. After all, that silly little tune had been echoing round in her mind since the first time she heard it. The old soldier couldn't possibly be here again. Not in the dark.

Even though she knew she must be hearing things, she opened the window overlooking the alley. A rush of cold wind swirled round her, tugging at her wrapper and her hair. The dying fire coughed protesting smoke into the room. Shivering, Marguerite leaned out, straining her eyes to see. Nothing. And no sound either, nothing but the distant sounds of triumph as Paris acclaimed its returning hero.

Marguerite had been playing the part of the modest would-be nun for what seemed like hours now. She had the corner seat, facing forward, but there was barely room to move since all six inside seats were taken. The problem with being totally silent was that it gave her too much time to think. And to feel.

There was a very large woman in the other forward corner. She was dressed in so many layers of grubby skirts and petticoats that Jacques, in the middle, had barely room to breathe. Being a gentleman, he had not uttered a word of complaint. He had even made the appropriate noises in response to the large woman's almost ceaseless commentary on the towns they passed and the people she knew.

For Marguerite, it was a kind of glorious torture. Jacques was squeezed up against her so tightly that she could feel the heat of his body and the tiny movements of his thigh muscles every time he tried to shift to a slightly more comfortable position. She fancied he was trying not to push against her—did the constant contact start his temperature rising as it did hers?—but he really had no choice. For the first hour or so, she tried to shrink away, to give him room, to avoid the forbidden touch. But after a while, she had begun to lean into him, just a fraction. Why not, after all? There was nothing improper about what was happening between them. Travellers in a *diligence* were often forced to travel in just such close proximity.

But the touch of him almost took her breath away.

In less than a day, they would part. Jacques would travel on to Dieppe, and England, leaving Marguerite in the charge of Father Bertrand. She was not even sure the curé would recognise her, since he had fled from Lyons more than fifteen years before, condemned for his service to royalist, aristocratic families. But he would recognise her family name. His allegiances would not have changed. She was sure that her name would be enough to secure his help.

Father Bertrand would offer her shelter. But what if he was dead, or could not be found? What then? Would Jacques abandon her in some chilly convent? No, he would not. He had promised to return for her. He had promised.

She risked a tiny sideways glance up at his face. He was staring directly ahead, his gaze unfocused, as if his thoughts were elsewhere. But his jaw was clenched. He was finding this journey difficult, just as Marguerite was. On that satisfying discovery, she allowed herself to lean into him a fraction more. His throat worked as he swallowed hard, but otherwise he did not move. Marguerite bent her head once more and smiled down at her demurely clasped hands. She decided, in that moment, that she was not going to allow him to leave her without one more kiss. Not a sisterly peck on the cheek, but a real, passionate joining of man and woman. Since he would not take her with him, she would give him something momentous to remember, and to come back for.

It occurred to her then that she had never told him of his mistake about the oath. Would it make a difference if he knew he had not sworn to treat her as a sister? Possibly. But then again, possibly not. He *had* sworn to treat her with all honour as long as they travelled together. Did passionate kisses fall within his definition of honourable behaviour? She rather thought not. If there was to be passion between them, the initiative would have to come from Marguerite. What she was contemplating would be improper, even scandalous. Would that stop her? No.

The unremarkable young man sitting directly opposite Marguerite had just pulled a snuff box from the pocket of his threadbare coat. She noticed that his boots were cracked, too. He did not have the look of a man who could afford to pay the inside fare from Paris to Calais. Yet the snuff box was of the finest workmanship and probably worth more than all the clothes on his back. He opened it with a caressing hand and Marguerite saw, through her lashes, that the lid bore a beautifully enamelled portrait of Napoleon Bonaparte. Her heart missed a beat and then began to race. Jacques must take care!

'That is a very fine box, sir.' The fat woman leaned across Jacques to get a better view, pushing him even further against Marguerite.

She resisted the urge to reach out to Jacques. She had just enough sense left to realise she would protect him best by making no move at all.

'You are a supporter of our beloved Emperor, I take it?' the fat woman continued, smiling hopefully at the young man.

He took a delicate pinch of snuff and returned the box to his pocket with exaggerated care. 'I serve the Emperor as best I may, ma'am.' His tone was not encouraging. He clearly did not wish to converse with this gossipy stranger.

The woman sat back in her place, spread her arms to encourage the passengers to listen, and began to list all the enemies of the Empire who were fleeing Bonaparte's advance.

Marguerite closed her eyes and tried to shut out the sound. She needed to think. She should have wondered about that young man before now, but, besotted fool that she was, she had been totally focused on the man at her side, and on the feel of his body against hers. And as a result of her neglect, Jacques could be in real danger! The Bonapartist opposite had been the last passenger to climb into the *diligence*, only a moment before the off. He had been short of breath, as if he had been running. And, thinking back, Marguerite was almost sure the young man had brought no luggage.

Oh, heavens! Was he a Bonapartist agent set to follow Jacques? Perhaps to arrest him?

'And fat Louis's women have no courage, either,' the fat woman said, warming to her theme. 'Why, one of them fled the city in such haste that she left her grandchildren behind.

She was gone even before fat Louis.' She chortled. 'It's quite a feat to be more of a coward than him, don't you think?'

No one replied.

'Of course, she's not a Frenchwoman, which might explain it. Courland is in Germany somewhere, is it not?'

Marguerite gasped and jerked upright.

'Know her, do you, dearie?' The fat woman leaned forward to smirk at Marguerite.

'I—'

'My sister is about to enter a convent, ma'am,' Jacques said gravely, reaching out to lay his hand over Marguerite's tightly clasped ones. 'She knows nothing of court ladies, whatever their allegiances. In the convent, everyone is equal in the sight of God.'

Marguerite closed her eyes again and allowed Jacques's strength to flow into her. She heard the fat woman mutter something and then silence fell in the coach, like a blessing.

Jacques gave her fingers a final tiny squeeze of encouragement and removed his hand. He had no choice, of course. They were travelling as brother and sister. But the loss of his touch left Marguerite feeling bereft, and alone.

She raised her head. Opposite her, the young Bonapartist was scrutinising her with narrowed, piercing eyes. And his left hand was abstractedly fingering the Bonaparte snuff box in his pocket.

Chapter Eighteen

Jack pushed the bread basket towards Marguerite. 'You must eat,' he said, trying to sound encouraging rather than worried. 'You have not had even half your bowl of soup.' He took another spoonful of his own. 'It is excellent, you know, and warming for the journey ahead.'

He watched as she made a half-hearted attempt to eat. He thought he knew precisely why her appetite had vanished. That episode in the *diligence* had terrified her. And no wonder. It was supremely unlucky that that fat gossip should have mentioned the Duchess of Courland. Marguerite had betrayed herself there, though only for an instant. He did not blame her. He had been shocked, too.

He reached across the table to take her hand. Although he knew he should not, for the merest touch of her silken skin was enough to arouse him, he felt he had to do something to reassure her. And what else was there? He did not dare to talk openly about what had happened, not until the *diligence* and its passengers had left Beauvais and were safely on the way to Calais. It should have left already, since the stop was supposed to be only an hour. Why the delay? It might seem that he and Marguerite were safe here alone in the coffee room, but there was no knowing who might be listening outside the door, or who might walk in on them.

They dare not take any more risks. That gossiping woman would certainly repeat whatever she overheard. And then there was the man with the snuff box. Jack was far from sure about him. He might be simply a young man who hero-worshipped Bonaparte. Many did. On the other hand, he might be something much more dangerous.

Marguerite put down her spoon. At first, she simply gazed at his hand, where it lay over hers. Then she looked up into his face. There was hope in her eyes now, he decided, and determination had replaced her understandable fear. He smiled slightly and squeezed her hand. The glow was returning to her face and her eyes had softened. He had thought her pretty before, but now, with the low, flickering light of fire and candles catching the pale mass of her hair, she was radiantly beautiful. He caught his breath and allowed all his senses to fill with the look, the touch, and the scent of her.

'Jacques, that man—'

Her words jerked him out of his dangerous reverie. He tightened his grip on her hand and put an urgent finger to his lips. He managed to resist the urge to shake his head in warning, in case someone was watching them from the shadows.

She was quick to catch his meaning. She did not say another word, but she lifted her chin in that resolute way he had noticed before. It was one of the many things he so admired about her. She had understood the danger and would act on it.

'I wonder whether the *diligence* has left yet,' Jack said nonchalantly, in a voice that would carry to any eavesdropper. 'Must say, I do not envy them the rest of the journey. It was exceedingly cramped.'

'There will be much more space now,' Marguerite answered,

taking her cue from him. 'After all, there will be only four persons inside, instead of six.'

'True, sister, true. But I had much rather travel post, where we can take care of our own comfort. The chaise should be ready soon, the landlord said.'

Marguerite's response was drowned by the noise of the *diligence* outside the coffee room window. Relieved, Jack rose and went to look out. He was just in time to see it turn out of the inn yard and disappear into the gathering gloom. The next stage of its journey to Calais would be in the dark.

'It has gone,' he said, in something more like his normal voice. 'You need not worry any more, Marguerite.'

'Thank God,' she breathed. Some of the tension seemed to leave her body as she spoke. She even began to eat her soup.

Jack returned to the table. This time, he resisted the lure of her fingers, though he could not avoid inhaling her subtle scent. It was part of what she was—delicate, beautiful, and immensely desirable. Did she add lavender to the water she used to rinse her curls? He rather fancied she must. During all their time in the *diligence*, her hair had been only inches from his face. He had been itching to reach out to wind one of those silken ringlets around his fingers, to touch it to his cheek, to test it against his tongue. Being so close to her, for hour after hour, had been almost more than his body could stand.

'That man, Jacques, the one in the *diligence*. He seemed to be watching us. And he had no luggage. Did you notice?'

Jack nodded. He had wondered about the man from the beginning. Showing that portrait of Bonaparte had been no accident. It had been intended to provoke a reaction. And it had.

'I think that someone must have suspected us as soon as we reached Paris. That man outside the pension. He was a spy, I think.'

'What man?' Jack said sharply.

'You saw him. You spoke to him. The one-legged soldier with the tin whistle. I'm sure he was at the pension again last night, when you went to the Tuileries.'

'Oh, *that* man.' Jack laughed and relaxed back into his chair. 'Yes, you are right. He was there. I paid him to keep watch when I was not with you. I did not think you would notice him. Obviously I underestimated you.'

Marguerite glowered at him.

'Poor Marguerite. If he frightened you, I apologise.'

'I am not your "poor Marguerite" and I was not frightened,' she snapped. 'Except for you, you idiotish man. Oh, Jacques, why will you not trust me?'

'I have told you everything I can. I need to keep you safe.' His protestations were making no impact on her. She still looked mutinous. He shrugged his shoulders. Perhaps she had earned the right. 'What more do you want to know?'

She bit her lip. And she had started to twist her fingers together. 'I know you are a royalist. And I know you are taking information about Bonaparte back to England. But who are you really, Jacques? I don't believe—'

Her question was cut off by the sound of the door opening. Jack leapt to his feet, putting his own body between Marguerite and the newcomer. He strained his eyes. In the gloom beyond the candlelight, it was impossible to make out more than a shadowy figure. 'Is that you, landlord? Is our chaise ready?'

'It is, sir.'

Jack tensed. The voice was too young to be the landlord's. 'Who is there?' he said sharply. 'Come forward. Let me see you.'

The man took a single pace forward. Jack recognised the young face and the threadbare clothes. There was a tiny pistol in the man's right hand. The metal on the barrel caught the candlelight as he levelled it.

And then he fired.

* * *

Marguerite screamed and flung herself on top of Jacques's body. It was ominously still. She could feel blood, warm and sticky, on his face and in his hair. There was a great deal of blood. 'Jacques! No! Oh, Jacques, please don't die!' She must do something, bandage him, stop the bleeding. She jumped to her feet and grabbed the napkins from the table, balling them into pads.

'I should save yourself the trouble, ma'am,' the young man said coolly. 'Head wounds are generally fatal. Especially when they are intended to be so.'

Stunned, she stared at the little pistol in his hand. How could such a tiny pop have done so much harm? Yet Jacques's body lay lifeless in front of the hearth. Lifeless! 'You have killed him!' Her voice was part-gasp, part-scream. She seized the carving knife from the table and launched herself at him. He had killed the man she loved, and she would make him pay the price.

He caught her easily. He was slight, but he was strong, and quick on his feet. He grasped her wrist and twisted it up her back until she cried out in pain and dropped the knife. He kicked it casually aside. Then he pushed her roughly into her chair. It rocked back with the sudden impact, but then righted itself.

Marguerite's body was frozen. Her limbs refused to move. She cursed him.

He paused in the act of stowing the pistol in his pocket. 'Yes, I thought as much. You, madam, would make a very inadequate nun.' Very deliberately, he walked across to where Jacques's body was lying and stared down at it. 'So perish all the Emperor's enemies,' he said quietly.

His icy certainty roused her to boiling fury. 'Who gave you the power to act as judge and executioner?' she spat.

'You did. When you proclaimed him an English spy in this

very room. Did it not occur to you that someone might be listening?'

His words pummelled her like blows. Marguerite crumpled into her chair, wrapping her arms round her body and burying her head to shut out the pain. She gulped for breath, but she had no tears. She had no right to weep. It was her fault. Jacques was dead and it was her fault!

The man turned to leave. He did not seem to care that he was turning his back on Marguerite, that she would kill him if she could. 'Do not try for the knife,' he said coldly over his shoulder. 'I prefer not to kill women, even when they are enemies.'

His words stung her out of her stupor. She cursed him again, even more foully.

He turned back to face her. He was smiling. 'Perhaps it will help your peace of mind, ma'am, if I tell you that the fault was not all yours. Your friend brought suspicion upon himself, by asking far too many questions at the Tuileries last night. Your role was simply to confirm what I already knew.' He paused. 'It is a pity that a proper trial was not possible, but these are difficult times. I'm sure you will understand.' He spoke as coldly as if he were apologising for arriving late at a very inferior dinner party.

He dug into his pocket. Had he changed his mind? Was he going to shoot her? Marguerite knew, in that instant, that she did not care whether she lived or died.

'The Emperor is a man of honour. He would wish even his enemies to have a decent funeral. Here.' He held up a single coin so that it gleamed in the firelight. It was a twenty-franc piece. A gold Napoleon.

Without another word, he tossed the coin on to the floor by the body and stalked out of the room. He was gone.

And her beloved Jacques was dead.

She threw herself to the floor and crawled across to the

body, putting her hands to his poor lifeless cheeks and her lips to his forehead. She had so longed to kiss him. Now she could, but he would never be able to return her love. It was too late. He was gone. The River of Death now flowed between them. She could not reach across its icy waters to the warm, vibrant man he had been. All she could do was to cradle his body. And mourn.

Vaguely, she heard the sound of horses in the yard. She touched her lips to his mouth and began to weep.

'Apologies for the delay, sir. Your chaise is ready. It—' The landlord's mouth dropped open. 'Good God! Madam, what has happened?'

Marguerite raised her head. She felt totally exhausted, too drained to attempt any real explanations. 'He is dead,' she said simply.

The landlord flung himself to his knees by the body. 'But he is bleeding, ma'am. Why did you not call for help?'

'He is beyond mortal help. Apart from prayers.'

The landlord frowned crossly. 'He is bleeding, ma'am. He is alive.'

'Alive? But it's impossible. He—' It was probably the landlord's snort of disbelief that brought Marguerite to her senses. Dear God, she had been stroking his cheek and kissing his mouth when she should have been looking to his hurts. If he died now, it truly would be her fault. 'Be so good as to fetch me some clean cloth for bandages. And a basin of hot water,' she ordered crisply. She pulled Jacques's coat from the back of the chair and began to roll it into a pillow. 'And I shall need more light. Bring candles. And send someone to build up the fire.'

The landlord leapt to his feet surprisingly quickly for a man of his bulk. 'At once, ma'am. Shall I have a bedchamber prepared? Your husband would be better in a proper bed than lying here on the floor.'

'My hus—? Oh, yes. Yes, of course. Pray do.'

'And I will send for the surgeon immediately.'

There was no help for it. Marguerite nodded her agreement. Only a surgeon could remove the ball. Only a surgeon could say whether Jacques would live or die. His confounded mission was of no consequence compared with his life.

'Your husband, ma'am, has a very hard head.' The surgeon accepted the towel Marguerite held out to him and began to dry his hands. He was a much cleaner man than the surgeon who had removed the ball from Herr Benn's shoulder. This man inspired confidence, in ways that the other had not. Or was it that Marguerite herself was more confident, having already dealt once with a wounded man? She was not sure. No injured man had ever mattered as much to her as this one did.

She looked yet again at the motionless figure on the bed. 'Will he recover?' She had to know the truth.

'I think so, yes. There was very little damage from the bullet itself. It merely grazed his temple. The real harm was done when he fell against the edge of the hearth. There was a lot of blood, of course, but that is only to be expected with head wounds. I cannot find that he has damaged his skull. It will probably take him some time, perhaps even days, to come to himself, but with rest, and your devoted nursing, ma'am, I dare say he will be as right as ninepence. Eventually.'

'Are you sure, sir?'

'Sure, ma'am? It is impossible to be absolutely sure in such cases. But I have seen men recover well from much worse falls. Their heads ache, of course, and their tempers flare, but you are probably well used to dealing with that. Most wives are, in my experience.'

'As you say, sir,' Marguerite replied automatically. Her thoughts were in turmoil. Questions and ideas were crowding in on her, elbowing aside the heartache and the guilt. What was she to do? If they remained here at Beauvais, that young killer might return. She must protect Jacques. So far, only the surgeon knew that a shot had been fired. The landlord must continue to believe Jacques's injuries were accidental, the result of a fall. Any mention of a gunshot would be bound to arouse suspicions. And to increase the danger to Jacques.

'I shall call again tomorrow, ma'am, if you permit, to see how our patient does.'

Marguerite did not think she dare stay in Beauvais another day, even to secure the services of a first-class surgeon. 'Pray do, sir.' She was managing to sound like a competent but anxious wife. And now she had to spin a story he could believe. 'However, I should perhaps warn you that we may not be here tomorrow. We have already been much delayed on our journey. If my husband should be well enough in the morning, we must leave. It is a matter of urgency, you understand. My husband's father is dying. In Caen.'

'I quite understand, ma'am. My sympathies.' He hesitated. 'Perhaps it would be convenient, in the circumstances, for me to tender my bill now?'

Marguerite agreed that it would be very satisfactory. The surgeon named his fee. Marguerite crossed to the chair to delve into Jacques's coat for money. 'You will understand, I am sure, sir, that this incident has been most disturbing. It would be particularly distressing if any word of it were to reach my husband's family, especially while his father is so ill.' Encouraged by the surgeon's murmur of sympathy, she continued, 'The young man who fired the shot was obviously deranged. He accused my husband of having debauched his sister.' The surgeon exclaimed in horror. 'Quite so. I can assure you that he was mistaken. My husband has never even met his sister.'

'You will have this man arrested, ma'am?'

'No, for that would simply increase the scandal and the gossip. He will not threaten anyone else, I am sure. Besides, he has fled. The landlord told me he had hired a horse and set off back to Paris.' She returned to stand beside the man. 'Sir, these are troubled times and I would do much to keep my family safe. May I rely on your discretion?' She was counting out twice his fee as she spoke. She pressed the money into his hand.

'You may depend on me, ma'am.' He pocketed the money with a satisfied smile. 'And I shall return tomorrow, as I said.'

Marguerite escorted him to the door. For the moment, they were safe. But she had made up her mind. If Jacques should be well enough in the morning, she would hire a carriage and have them driven to Rouen. From there, she could take him to Father Bertrand's house. Jacques would be much safer there than at any posting inn on the Paris road.

And if Jacques were not well enough to travel, she would have to find a way of defending him here in Beauvais. This time she would not be reduced to wielding a carving knife. Jacques had two pistols. And Marguerite was more than prepared to use them against anyone who threatened the man she loved.

Someone had split his head with an axe.

There was no other possible explanation for the stabbing pains. His body was heavy as lead. Every limb ached. His eyes would not open, either.

'Jacques.'

Someone was calling his name. A woman's voice, with a foreign accent. He thought he ought to recognise it, but somehow he could not quite place it. Perhaps if he turned towards her?

Pain shot through him like a bolt of lightning. He swore.

'If you must swear, Jacques,' said that gentle voice in immaculate French, 'perhaps you would be good enough to do so in French?'

That was when he remembered where he was.

Chapter Nineteen

She was bathing Jack's forehead, ever so gently, with warm water. It smelled, very subtly, of lavender.

'Don't try to move yet,' the voice said. It was Marguerite's voice. His incredible Marguerite. 'It will simply cause you pain if you do. And I would prefer to learn no more new oaths, if you don't mind.'

He heard the sound of the cloth being soaked again, and wrung out. Then she was stroking his forehead once more. His body relaxed under her hand. The motion was very soothing. It must be magic, for it seemed to lessen the pain.

'Where am I?' he croaked. Mindful of her words, he was lying very still.

The bed sagged as she leant across to put her lips against his ear. He could feel the tiny tickle of her curls against his cheek. The scent of pure lavender filled his senses and conjured up pictures of purple fields, their flowers swaying together in the breeze like the skirts of a ball gown moving in time to the music.

'We are still in Beauvais, Jacques,' she whispered in French. 'It is dangerous to speak English here. If your brain will not function well enough to speak French, you must not speak at all.'

He was finding it very difficult to concentrate on what she was saying. His brain did not want to respond to such mundane things. The tiny puffs of her honeyed breath against his ear were much too distracting. She was so close to his skin that she was almost kissing him. And he wished she would. Somehow, he knew that a kiss from her would cure all his pain.

'French, Jacques,' she said a little more forcefully. 'French, or nothing.'

He understood then. 'What happened?' he croaked, but in French this time.

'Let me bring you something to drink first.'

He heard her moving away from the bed, followed by the sound of liquid being poured. Why could he not open his eyes?

She slid an arm under his shoulders and raised him slightly so that he could drink. The pain was excruciating, even from that tiny movement. He tried to swallow his groan, but he was only partly successful.

'Drink,' she said, putting a cup to his mouth. 'Slowly now.'

He sipped and swallowed. It was barley water. It tasted of lemon, and fresh air, and made him think of summer pastures. It was nectar to his parched throat. When he had drunk as much as he could, she let him relax back on to the pillows. This time, by a supreme effort of will, he managed not to groan.

'You are a stubborn man, Jacques.' There was a thread of amusement in her voice. 'It really does not matter if you admit to being in pain. No one else will hear, you know.'

He groaned theatrically.

'Very good,' she said, laughing. It was a glorious sound. He could imagine her sitting there beside him, her beautiful hair catching the light, her sea-green eyes wide and gleaming with good humour. His mind might be confused about how he came to be in this state, but it was absolutely clear about the woman who was tending him. She was radiant. And she was a heroine.

He heard her walk across the room and open the door, then close it again gently. Why had she done that? He tried to work it out, but it was too taxing.

'We were together in the coffee room downstairs, eating supper while we waited for our chaise to Rouen. Do you remember that?'

Jack grunted assent. The memory was dull, but it was there.

'Good. The surgeon did say you might have no memory at all of what happened. That young man from the *diligence*, the one with the Bonaparte snuff box, heard us talking.' She cleared her throat. 'Or rather, he heard *me* admitting you were a spy for England. So he shot you. He meant to kill you.'

Jack grunted again. The stark picture came back to him. He had stood there, defenceless, facing a man with a pistol in his hand. It was the sort of tiny pistol that a lady might carry in her reticule, but it could still be lethal. And that was why—'Oh, God! I'm blind. He blinded me!'

Marguerite seized his hand and held it fast. 'No, Jacques. You are not blind. The surgeon assured me that your eyes were undamaged. It was simply that the wounds on your head were so extensive that he had to wrap the bandages round your face as well.' She stroked his hand slowly, caressingly. 'Later, I shall change the dressings and you will be able to see. I am certain of it.'

He wanted very much to believe her. She would not lie to him, would she? No, what she said must be the truth. He sighed out a long breath.

She stroked his hand again. 'I see that you believe me. I am glad. We have quite enough to worry about, without that.'

'How long have I been lying here?'

'Since yesterday. The assassin's bullet only grazed your temple, but you fell back and struck your head on the hearth. There was a great deal of blood. Perhaps that was why that man was so sure he had killed you. You were certainly lying there like a corpse.'

He had failed to protect her. He should have protected her! 'Marguerite! What did he do to you? You—'

'I managed well enough,' she said curtly, reminding him that she was a very resolute woman and capable of defending herself. 'He informed me that he did not kill women, even enemy women. He tossed me a gold Napoleon to pay for your funeral.'

An icy shiver ran through him. What kind of a man would do such a thing? It was so cold-blooded. 'And what happened then?' He could not bring himself to voice his fears. Such a man could have done anything to Marguerite.

'It appears he mounted a hired horse and rode off back towards Paris. At least, that is what the landlord told me.'

'The landlord?' In his swirling thoughts, Jack could not quite remember why the landlord mattered, but he was sure it was something to do with danger. 'Don't trust him, Marguerite. He—'

'Oh, have no fears on that score. The landlord was out in the stables and did not hear the pistol shot. As far as he knows, you simply fell and cracked your head, probably as a result of too much wine. A lot of blood, but no real harm done. He won't gossip about it, since it does nothing for the reputation of his house. Only the surgeon knows the truth. Nothing will be said about mad young men waving pistols about. And before you ask, I did buy the surgeon's silence.'

Jack digested that information for a while. His memories were beginning to put themselves into some kind of order, thank goodness, though he had clearly been totally useless for hours. Marguerite appeared to have been very busy in the meantime, and very efficient at covering their tracks. Then Jack realised the flaw. 'But the gunman—'

'He's gone, Jacques. If he was an agent of Bonaparte, he will no doubt have returned to Paris to report his success. And yet, surely a real agent would have made certain you were actually dead? I think he may have been simply a young hothead who had taken it upon himself to defend his hero. He suspected you at the Tuileries, and followed you here. If I'm right, he has probably drunk himself insensible, somewhere between here and Paris. Whatever he is, I doubt he will return here.'

'That sounds like the sort of speech I might have made to you, Marguerite.'

'Yes, it does, doesn't it?' There was a smile in her voice. 'But it also has the advantage of being logical, and probably correct.'

His brain was too confused to cope with logic. 'So what do we do now?' He was in her hands. He could not see and he could barely move. He was in no fit state to make decisions, even if he knew what was going on, which he did not. He would have to rely on Marguerite. It would be the first time that he had ever entrusted his mission, his very life, to a woman, but he found that he had total confidence in her. She was extraordinary.

If anyone could bring them safely out of this coil, it was Marguerite Grolier.

The hired carriage was proving to be much more comfortable than Marguerite had expected. Thankfully, the road to Rouen was not too rough, either. Jacques had been carefully installed, sitting back in one corner with his legs stretched along the seat, and his poor head cushioned with every scrap of padding she had managed to buy from the landlord. Jacques had barely moved, and had not spoken, since they left

Beauvais. He might even be asleep under those bandages, though she doubted it. She fancied he was concentrating on not allowing her to see how much he was suffering from the rocking and lurching of the carriage.

It made her feel guilty, but what else could she have done? His wounds had healed enough to allow him to travel. She had the surgeon's word for that. One extra day's delay was as much as she had dared to risk. In spite of what she had said to Jacques, she was quite sure in her own mind that the would-be assassin was a Bonapartist agent. It had been their good fortune that the man was incompetent and had fled. But he, or his accomplices, could well return. Marguerite had to take Jacques away from the scene of the shooting. She had to get him to the coast, and on to a ship for England. Until then, he would not be safe.

Those two nights at Beauvais had changed much. After the surgeon had assumed she was Jacques's wife, she had deliberately chosen to act as if it were so. That first night, she had lain on the bed beside him, wide awake and watchful, waiting for the slightest sign of fever or distress. In the silent hours of darkness, it had felt normal to behave so, and absolutely necessary; but now, in the broad light of day, she understood that Jacques might view her actions as scandalous. If he learned the truth, what would he do?

She prayed that it would not happen. He appeared to remember nothing after the shot, which gave her a little reassurance. She would not want him to remember how she had held his hand and stroked his poor, bandaged face, or the quiet words of love she had dared to whisper in his ear. He had been deeply unconscious, but he had murmured softly in response, as if his body was happy to ignore the oath he had sworn. He would not remember any of that. But for Marguerite, being able to touch him, and to say the words, had been enough to bind her to him, for ever. She loved this man. No matter what happened between them, she would never love anyone but Jacques.

The carriage hit a pothole and swayed dangerously. Marguerite gasped and automatically grabbed for the strap. Opposite her, Jacques did the same, but he missed and began to fall. Marguerite threw herself forward, putting all her weight against him to keep his body on the seat. By the time she succeeded in pushing him back into his corner, he was moaning with pain. He swore vehemently. She tried not to listen. At least he was not swearing in English.

'Marguerite, I need to be able to see,' he groaned, clawing at his face.

He was right. If he had had the use of his eyes, he would not have missed the strap. He would not have been further hurt.

'Very well. I will try to redo the bandages so that they do not cover your eyes.' It would take a long time, since she was hampered by the lack of space and the rolling of the carriage.

Jacques bore it stoically with hardly a murmur. 'I'm surprised you have not dosed me with that laudanum you always carry,' he said quietly, when she was just about to uncover his eyes.

'I would have, but the surgeon warned me it was dangerous to use it with head wounds. I'm sure you would have been a much less troublesome patient if I had kept you insensible,' she added mischievously, slowly unwinding the last bandage.

He blinked and then opened his eyes wide in the gathering gloom. 'Have I been so very troublesome, Marguerite?' he asked, his voice very soft and deep.

She caught her breath.

He turned his head to look into her face, but the movement was too sudden. He gasped with pain.

'Yes, very troublesome,' she said firmly, avoiding his eyes.

'In that case, you had better give me something instead of

the laudanum. If you put your hand down the side of my valise, you will find a flask of brandy. I dare say the surgeon did not forbid me that.'

Jack let his battered body relax into the soft bed and closed his eyes. The journey from Beauvais had seemed never-ending. He felt bruised all over. Without the brandy to help him doze, it would have been unbearable. Now all he wanted was to rest on a bed that did not lurch and sway.

Bells began to toll. They were very close and very loud. He tried to sink deeper into his pillows to muffle the noise, but it did not help. He groaned in frustration.

'May I help you, sir?' That sounded like the voice of the inn servant who had helped him to undress and get into bed.

'Those bells. Don't they ever stop?'

'Them's the cathedral bells, sir. From just over the way. You'll get used to them. Never hears 'em, meself.'

Jack muttered an oath. He was beginning to feel rather bad-tempered, which probably meant he was mending. Alternatively, it was the result of the brandy he had drunk. If his head still hurt in the morning, it might be the fault of the brandy rather than his wounds. Just at present, he did not care. He simply wanted to sleep.

Marguerite watched from the shadow by the door where Jacques could not see her. When she was sure he was asleep, she nodded to the servant to leave, dropping a few small coins into his hand as he made his way out of the room. For two nights, she had tended Jacques almost unaided but, now that he was recovering, she could not do so without embarrassing him, and herself. Let him think that servants had seen to all his needs while he was insensible.

She crept across to the bed and gazed down at him for a long time. He was sound asleep now, and breathing easily. He was certainly improving. There was no sign of the spasms of pain that had twisted his limbs on the two previous nights. At Beauvais, she had lain on top of the covers, fully clothed, waiting to stroke away his pain with soft hands and soothing words. Here, in Rouen, it seemed that her touch would not be needed.

She took a deep breath and sighed it out. Surely he would never know if she lay down beside him one last time? He was bound to sleep soundly, for he was still very weak. And he had drunk rather a lot of brandy during their hours on the road.

Her conscience told her it was wrong, but her body was already melting at the thought of lying next to his warmth, and breathing in the scent of him. It was the last chance she would have. Tomorrow, they would travel the short distance to Father Bertrand's house, where Jacques would be able to regain his strength for the journey to Dieppe and a ship for England. The good father would certainly not permit an unmarried girl like Marguerite to be alone with a man in his bedchamber, no matter how ill he might be.

Jacques moaned softly. He was trying to roll over and finding it difficult. Marguerite decided it was a sign. She reached across and gently helped him to move into a more comfortable position. Then, with slow deliberate movements, she stripped off her gown, her petticoats, her stays and her stockings, snuffed the last candle, and slipped between the sheets to lie beside him, dressed only in her shift.

'Mmm.' It was not a groan of pain this time. He was welcoming her, even though he was too deeply asleep to know she was there.

She took a long, slow breath and slid closer, not quite touching, but near enough to feel his warmth radiating out to caress her skin. Although she could see nothing in the dark, she closed her eyes. When she was not straining to see, her other senses were so much more alive. She could inhale his scent and listen to his slow breathing. If she wished, she could even put her lips to his skin and taste him on the tip of her tongue. In the light, she would be much too shy to do such outrageous things, but in the dark, blossoming in their shared warmth, she could dare anything. Just for this one night.

'Mmm,' he said again. The sound was deeper than before. But he was trying to move his head again. Marguerite stiffened, worrying that his wounds might give him renewed pain. Apparently they did not. His head turned easily on the pillow and came to rest against Marguerite's neck, with his lips on her skin. He gave a low grunt of satisfaction and began to nuzzle the side of her throat.

She should stop him. She knew she should, for he was breaking his oath. Unwittingly, perhaps, but breaking it none the less.

His lips reached her earlobe, sending a spasm of wicked pleasure lancing through her. All her misgivings melted away, along with her defences. This was the man she loved, the man who had been avoiding even her slightest touch, and now he was avidly kissing her, giving and receiving delight. She had not thought that such feelings were possible. Even that picture of the lovers in the rose garden had not prepared her for this. She had to have more.

He nipped gently at her earlobe and then returned to kissing her neck. It was too much. Murmuring his name, she moved so that her mouth was on a level with his. Very gently, she touched her lips to his.

His response sent a thrill of desire through her. He groaned, deep in his chest, and began to kiss her in earnest, so fiercely that she wanted to swoon with the passion of it. She yielded her mouth gladly. Soon she was returning his kisses with increasing ardour, entwining her tongue with his in a dance of desire. She could feel her breasts swelling and straining against the silk of her shift as if they were begging for his touch.

He waited a long time. Then, at last, he was stroking her through the fine silk, and weighing her breast gently in his cupped hand like a precious gift. All the while he continued to kiss her mouth as if he could not get enough of her. She knew in her heart that she was truly desired, and she rejoiced in it.

He lifted his hand from her breast for a second and then began to touch her again, so lightly that she could not be sure it was happening. He seemed to be running the tip of a fingernail around the outside of her nipple, very slowly and deliberately. It was the most delicious torture. Her nipple was swelling in anticipation of the touch that did not come. She groaned into his mouth.

The sound seemed to urge him on. He circled his finger closer and closer until he reached her nipple and began to roll it between finger and thumb. The chemise which had seemed so fine now felt like a harsh barrier between them. She wanted him to touch her, skin to skin.

He must have sensed her need, for he skimmed his fingers over her ribcage and across her flat belly to lay the heel of his hand over the core of her. He cupped her and pressed hard. Heat flared and centred, until she ached with longing. When he removed his hand, she whimpered at the loss. But in a moment, his touch returned, this time without the chemise which had been lifted away.

She was kissing him in pure frenzy now, unable to get enough of him. She wanted him. So very much. When he touched a finger to the inside of her thigh, she opened to him like a flower to the sunshine. He was her sun, and her love would die without his light.

He stroked his fingers gently along the tender skin of her thigh, advancing and retreating, never quite reaching the longing core of her, until she was almost mindless with need. Desperate, she put a hand over his and guided him to touch her hot, molten centre. She did not know why she wanted this so much. She did not understand anything that was happening to her. But she knew that she had to have his touch on her flesh. 'Please, Jacques,' she moaned into his mouth.

And then she understood, for he touched her and her world exploded.

It was a remarkably vivid dream. He had been kissing and caressing a beautiful woman who had come willingly into his arms. His dream was filled with light, but somehow he could not see her face. Her scent was strangely familiar, but elusive. A voice in his head was telling him he ought to recognise it, but he could not. The more he struggled to remember, the more fragile the thought became, like a cobweb ready to collapse at a touch. But he did understand one thing: she was an innocent in the ways of lovers. He must go slowly if she were not to dissolve into mist. He must feed her desire until the flames were white hot.

He was succeeding. His vision clung to him, and kissed him, and guided his hands to touch the secrets of her body. Yet he knew he was only dreaming, that he would wake soon and find himself alone. He did not want to wake. He did not want this glorious dream to end. He wanted to hold her, and caress her, and join his tormented body to hers so that they could both find release.

She was pleading with him, kissing his mouth, nipping at his lower lip with her teeth. She was whispering his name. And then he touched her, and she climaxed against him, with a long gasp of ecstasy.

That voice. Even in the throes of passion, he recognised the danger in that voice. It belonged to a woman who was forbidden.

Who was she? Was she real?

He did not know. The lights of his dream were fading and his vision was melting in the gathering darkness. She was forbidden. He could not reach her any more. She was forbidden.

Chapter Twenty

Jack awoke lying on his back, feeling much refreshed and almost free of pain. To his surprise, he found he was suffering no after-effects from all the brandy he had drunk. It must be a sovereign remedy after all.

The bells were tolling again. He listened a moment and then laughed up at the canopy of his bed. What else did he expect in the Pension de la Cathédrale? The bells of Rouen's cathedral were reminding him to rejoice; he was alive, and almost whole, and would soon be on his way back to England with his precious cargo of information. Life was very good, especially when spiced with a little adventure.

There was a tap at the door. Jack pushed himself up on to his elbows, marvelling that his head did not protest, and looked around the room. He was alone. Marguerite would have taken a separate bedchamber, of course. Perhaps that had been her knock? She would be delighted to see how well her devoted nursing had succeeded. He cleared his throat and bade her enter.

'Morning, sir.' It was the servant from the previous night, carrying a jug of steaming water. Jack felt a prick of disappointment that he could not share his amazing recovery with Marguerite. He owed her so much.

'Your wife bade me come to help you dress, sir.'

Wife? Marguerite had claimed they were *man and wife*, rather than brother and sister?

Jack did not pause to wonder why. She would have had good reason for anything she did. She had dealt very cleverly with the aftermath of the shooting in Beauvais, had she not? He knew that he had been no help at all there. He remembered being unable to move without pain. He remembered lying in the dark, listening to that voice touched with laughter and calm reassurance. Unless he had dreamt it all? There was a strange muddle of memories jostling for position in his brain: images of pain, and danger, and of Marguerite, strong and resolute. There was another image, too, hiding in the shadows. He sensed it was a good memory, a memory to set in the scales against all the others, but he could not quite grasp it. When he tried to seize it, it dissolved.

He would speak to Marguerite as soon as he was presentable again. She would be able to tell him all that had happened. She would help him to separate truth from mirage.

'Now, sir, let me help you up. I'm sure you will feel much better for a wash and a shave.'

Jack put a hand to his head. The bandage was gone. Had he dreamt that, too? No, it was lying on the pillow. It must have come loose in the night. Very gingerly, he touched his fingers to his temple and then to the back of his head. Under his hair, he had a number of blood-encrusted swellings which were still very tender, but there was no sign of fresh bleeding. He had certainly not imagined those egg-shaped lumps. It might be some time before he would be able to put a comb through his hair, or wear a hat, but at least he would not need the bandages any more. And he would no longer be courting even more danger by advertising that he had been wounded. For himself, that was of little account. But he had to take every precaution in order to protect Marguerite.

He owed her his life. If his mission finally succeeded, he would owe her that, too. Yet he was planning to leave her behind in France. Alone. Until now, he had been preoccupied with their day-to-day survival, but that was not good enough any longer. There must be something more he could do. Marguerite, his astonishing accomplice, must be kept safe. Far too many of the jumbled images in his brain were of Marguerite in danger.

Marguerite appeared just as the servant left with the bowl of dirty water and the wet towels. She stood in the doorway, rather shyly, he thought. She was wearing the same dark green travelling gown that she had worn under her elegant pelisse for most of their journey from Lyons. But today, she had added a lace fichu to the neckline, so that it covered every last inch of her throat.

He grinned at her, but he waited until she had closed the door before saying, 'Good morning, wife.'

She blushed scarlet to the roots of her hair and turned to leave.

'Don't go, Marguerite! I need to talk to you.'

She stopped, but she did not turn back.

'Look how much good your careful nursing has done. I declare, I am almost human again. Would you not agree?'

She turned then, and gave him a long, appraising look.

'No more bandages,' he said, with a fleeting grin, touching the front of his hair, the only part he had been able to comb.

She ignored that. 'I take it you slept well? You seem wonderfully recovered since yesterday.' For some reason, she was unwilling to meet his gaze.

'Indeed. I swear it must all be thanks to the ministrations of my darling wife.'

She blushed again, almost as much as before. But this time, he caught sight of a spark of anger in her eyes. 'You choose to mock me, sir, but what else would you have had me do? You seemed to be at death's door. Only a wife could be expected to give you the constant care you needed.'

He frowned, trying to think. Surely that was not true? Surely a sister—? And then he remembered his oath. Marguerite had changed their story without thought for his oath! What had he done these last two days? It would have been so easy to break that solemn oath, even unawares. He felt an icy knot settle in his gut and start to grow. It was the fear that he might be dishonoured.

Only she would know precisely what he had done. But he must not blame Marguerite for his own failings. They were his alone.

'You puzzle me a little, Marguerite. I thought we had agreed that we must travel as brother and sister, that it was the only safe and sensible course.'

She shook her head. 'Circumstances change. I had to do what I thought was best.' She was beginning to look guilty. Was she hiding something?

'But surely a sister could have nursed a brother with quite as much propriety as a wife her husband?' he asked in the voice of sweet reason.

'What do you know of sisters, pray? You do not care a fig that I had to deal with the assumptions of the landlord and the surgeon. You care only for that stupid oath you think you swore.' She stopped short. Her eyes widened. Then she stared down at her feet.

Jack took a long deep breath. He had not misheard. He strode across to the door and leaned against it, effectively blocking her escape. 'Now, Marguerite,' he began, crossing his arms and frowning down at her, 'perhaps you would be so good as to tell me precisely what you are implying? I swore on your mother's bible that I would treat you as an honoured sister, as long as we travelled together. I have done my utmost to keep my vow, though not always with a great deal of help from you.' He let his voice drop until it was almost a whisper. 'Are you suggesting that I am dishonoured?'

She raised her chin and started towards him. When he showed no sign of moving, she glared at him with narrowed eyes. There were spots of high colour on her cheeks, but her bearing was erect and proud. 'You are obsessed with the idea of treating me as a sister.'

'I swore—' he began, taking a step towards her.

'You swore to treat me with all honour while we travelled together. You did *not* swear to treat me as a sister. You imagined you had, simply because you were so intent on besting Guillaume. He behaved like a silly schoolboy. And so did you!'

She caught hold of his shirt sleeve and pulled hard. Jack was so astonished by what she had said that he did not try to resist. He staggered a couple of steps.

'Now, sir, if you will excuse me, *someone* has to make the arrangements for the next part of our journey.' With an angry toss of her head, she threw the door wide and strode out on to the landing.

Jack could not believe it. He had been so sure. She must be lying, or else mistaken. If he had been wrong about the oath, surely Marguerite would have told him the truth before now?

He had always known that he did not understand women. A man would have told him of his mistake, and laughed about it. But a woman's ways were unfathomable. Even a woman as apparently strong and logical as Marguerite Grolier.

What if it were true? What if he had been trying to hold to an oath he had not sworn, while neglecting the one he had?

She said he had sworn to treat her with all honour. Surely he could not have failed in that?

Those jumbled memories were worrying at him again. And now a new one had forced its way to centre stage. When Ben had asked, Jack had been unable to relate the precise terms of his oath. He had said that it did not really matter. But it clearly did, for there was a dark shadow lurking at the back of his mind, eating away at his conscience. He was beginning to fear that, somewhere along the way, with his mind fuddled by pain and brandy, he might have forfeited his honour.

The bells began again, in great cascading peals.

'Your pardon, sir, I did knock.' It was the servant. 'Your wife bade me fetch down your valises.' He crossed the room to retrieve them.

Jack ignored the luggage. Those bells were beginning to drive him mad. 'What on earth are all those bells for now, my good man? Do they never stop ringing in Rouen?'

The man grinned. 'Today's is a special peal. There's about to be a grand wedding in the cathedral. Two of the greatest houses of Normandy are joining their honours this morning.'

Honours? The ominous weight in Jack's gut grew another heavy layer of ice. His head had begun to pound all over again.

Marguerite had not relished the prospect of being cooped up in a chaise with Jacques, but she consoled herself with the thought that it was less than fifteen miles to Father Bertrand's house. She would pass the journey in dignified silence, she decided.

Jacques appeared to have reached the same decision, for he spent the first part of the journey staring straight ahead, with an unreadable look on his face. Was he angry, or embarrassed, or concerned? Marguerite had no way of knowing. She had thought, these last few days, that she understood him, because she loved him. But love and understanding were miles apart. He blamed her, unfairly, for his own muddle over that stupid oath. She would not be able to stop loving him— she knew that—but that did not mean she had to approve of everything he did. Most certainly not.

To her surprise, he turned to her and smiled. 'I presume that is Barentin?' He pointed to the small town just ahead of them. 'Then our destination cannot be far,' he added. 'Let us hope that the good Father Bertrand is at home to receive us.'

It seemed he was able to change his mood from moment to moment, like the sun appearing from behind a thunder cloud. And he had just done it again! Oh, he could be very charming when he tried. She supposed that was part of the reason she loved him. But his charm could be exasperating, too. Especially that smile. That smile was haunting her. Her moment of ecstasy last night had been too glorious for words. But for him, it had been some kind of threat, for only moments later he was moaning and thrashing around, as if he were trying to fend off an attacker. She had been too frightened to remain. She had slipped out of the bed, dressed herself once more, and curled up in the chair in the far corner. This morning, he had still been fast asleep when she awoke. And when she crossed to the bed to check on him, she had found him lying peacefully on his back, smiling up at nothing at all.

No, she would never understand men.

'Marguerite?'

'I beg your pardon,' she said automatically. 'I'm afraid I was wool-gathering.'

He repeated his question without a hint of impatience. He had impeccable manners. Most of the time.

'I am sure there will be someone to receive us. His housekeeper will be there, even if he is not.' She put her hands to her throat and began to rearrange the fichu. The lace was starting to scratch at her nape, but she did not dare to remove it. Jacques's enthusiastic kisses had left a small but very obvious bruise at the base of her neck.

The horses were beginning to slow. Ahead of them was a sizeable village, built around a church with a tall spire. Jacques would be safe soon! A few moments later, the chaise drew up outside the church. The curé's house was just alongside, modest but welcoming. Jacques reached for the door handle.

'Pray allow me to alight alone,' Marguerite said quickly. 'The good father is not expecting us, and he has not seen me for some years. It would be best, I believe, if I spoke to him by myself.'

'Are you afraid that he might not welcome you?'

She hesitated. 'No. But there are things—private things— that I must explain to him.'

Jacques's face was expressionless. 'You will allow me to help you down, Marguerite, even if I may not escort you to the door?'

She was afraid of the effects of touching him again, but she had no choice. She let him hand her down, but immediately hurried across to the curé's door to pull the bell.

It was the priest himself who opened it. He was much shorter, and rounder, than Marguerite remembered. He seemed surprised, but he smiled at her. 'Yes, my child? How may I help you?'

'Father Bertrand, you may not remember me. I have travelled from Lyons to seek refuge in your house. My name is Marguerite Grolier de Jer—'

'Marguerite! My dear, dear child!' He embraced her warmly. 'Come in, come in. You are most welcome!' He glanced over her shoulder to the waiting chaise. Jacques was standing motionless by the open door. 'But what of your escort? Should we not invite him also?'

Marguerite tucked her arm through the curé's and urged him into the hallway. 'My escort, Father, is the reason I am here.'

Jack watched the door close and turned back to the chaise. He could not dismiss the post boys until he was sure that the curé was prepared to accept both of his unexpected guests. It was more than possible that Marguerite would remain, while Jack would be forced to return to Rouen alone.

He glanced at the sparse interior of the chaise. He would not wait there. He had spent far too much time doing nothing, these last two days. He needed exercise, to recover his strength. He began to pace.

The postilion touched his hat. 'Shall I bring the valises out of the chaise, sir?'

Why not? Marguerite's valise was bound to be needed, even if Jack's had to be carried back to Rouen. 'Yes. Pray do so.' He continued to pace up and down, trying to fathom what Marguerite might be about. What was she telling the curé that she refused to share with Jack? Something about her family perhaps? If the curé had left Lyons so many years before, he would not know of her father's death, and might not be aware of Madame Grolier's illness, either. But that made no sense. Jack already knew about those. There must be something more.

He turned again. He had to move a little to one side to avoid the two valises which the post boy had placed at some distance from the chaise. *Two* valises? The icy knot tightened once more in Jack's gut. Why had Marguerite's valise been in Jack's bedchamber?

The curé bustled about in his small study. There was barely room to sit down, for there were books and papers everywhere. The chair alongside Marguerite's was stacked with papers that he swept on to the floor, before waving Jack to take the seat. 'You will join me in a glass of wine, my son?'

Jack accepted politely. His head had not suffered from the brandy he had drunk; an extra glass of wine would do no harm.

The curé poured two large measures and one smaller one, which he placed in front of Marguerite. He raised his own glass. 'To the restoration.'

Jack glanced sideways at Marguerite, but she was showing no concern about the priest's ambiguous words. All three drank the toast. 'Father Bertrand, I have to speak to—'

'My son, there is no need to worry. Marguerite has explained everything. You will remain here, as my guests, until you are well enough to travel. Tomorrow, I myself shall drive to Dieppe to discover what I can about a passage to England.'

The little curé was no spy. What if he drew suspicion on to himself by his well-intentioned questions? 'You must not take any risks for me, Father,' Jack said firmly. 'The longer I remain here, the greater the dangers to you and Marguerite. My wounds have healed well enough. I shall travel to Dieppe tomorrow. Alone.'

'No!' Marguerite exclaimed. Jack began to explain his reasoning, but she would not listen. She appealed to the curé. 'Father, he is in much more danger travelling alone. Bonaparte's agents will always suspect a lone man, especially one who has recently been wounded. And there are bound to be many agents at Dieppe. If I go with him, as his sister, no one will look at us twice.'

'That is all very well, Marguerite, but what will you do once you get there?' The priest shook his head. 'Jacques will be taking one berth for England, not two. Unless you were planning to continue this charade all the way to England?'

'No, Father. I planned to see him safely out of Dieppe harbour and then return to you.'

'Unescorted?' The curé sounded horrified. 'I could not permit that.'

'And neither will I,' Jack said grimly. 'Let that be an end of the matter.'

She was not so easily routed. 'Say you so, Jacques? And by what right do you presume to direct me? You—'

'There is a simpler solution,' the priest said, raising a hand to calm her angry words. 'All three of us shall go together. And then I can escort Marguerite back here.'

Marguerite beamed at having won her point. For Jack, however, the curé's intervention was doubly unwelcome. Jack had been hoping to say his farewells to Marguerite in private, where he could at last confess how much he valued her and repeat his promise to return. He could not possibly say such things in front of the priest. And it would be purgatory to travel all those miles with the good father looking on and judging every word he spoke to her.

He turned to look her full in the face. She was no longer beaming. Perhaps she, too, had realised the drawbacks of travelling with the curé as chaperon? He reached for her hand, but she snatched it away, frowning at him. He was not prepared to be denied, however. He rose to his feet and offered his arm. 'Marguerite, there are things that must be said between us, in private. We both know that there may not be another opportunity. Let us take a stroll in the garden.' He nodded towards the window. 'Father Bertrand will be able to watch us from here if he has any concerns, though I can promise him that there will be no impropriety. My oath still stands.'

'But I—'

'Go along, my child. I think, in the circumstances, that you ought to give him a hearing. You have endured much together, from all you said. And we none of us know what dangers we may face tomorrow.'

High colour had flared in her cheeks, but she nodded

meekly. Then she walked straight past Jack and out of the room, leaving him to follow in her wake.

The curé chuckled. 'If you'll take my advice, my son,' he said genially, 'you will tell her the truth. It is what she is waiting for.'

Chapter Twenty-One

'You, Marguerite Grolier, are a very stubborn woman.'

She looked blankly at him, but said nothing.

He made the most of his opportunity, seizing her hand and drawing it firmly through his arm. 'You agreed to a stroll in the garden. So that is what we shall do.' She began to struggle to free her arm. 'Marguerite, the good father is watching us. What on earth will he think of such appalling manners?'

She snorted angrily. But she did stop struggling.

'Thank you,' Jack said calmly. 'Shall we walk?' They began to walk slowly along the path that led through the small vegetable garden and towards the orchard, where the cherries were coming into bloom. 'Marguerite, there are many things I have to say to you, beyond thanks for the risks you have taken to help me in my mission. You have done more than I could have expected from any man.'

She was starting to blush a delicate rose. She murmured some words that Jack could not hear.

'But I am concerned that—' He swallowed. There was no polite way of asking this. 'Marguerite, where did you sleep last night?'

She stopped dead. 'What?'

'Your valise was in my bedchamber this morning. Where did you sleep?'

She was now bright scarlet. She tried to speak, but no words came out.

It was as bad as he had feared. 'I take it you spent the night in my bedchamber? After you told the landlord that we were man and wife?'

She nodded dumbly, staring at the gravel beneath her feet.

'Dear God, woman, have you no thought for your reputation? Rouen is not even fifteen miles away. Do you think that tale will not follow you here?'

'I did what was necessary for the sake of the cause. My behaviour is no concern of yours, Louis Jacques,' she protested, pulling away from him.

He was not prepared to let her go. Not over this. He reached out to grab her by the shoulders, to hold her still. But his fingers tangled with the fichu around her neck. It came undone and sagged off her shoulders. 'Good God!' That bruise on her neck looked like— He stared and stared, trying to think of an acceptable explanation for it. He could find none. The fichu drifted lazily to the ground.

Marguerite bent to retrieve her lace and calmly retied it. She was no longer trying to escape him. She lifted her chin proudly.

'That bruise,' he said, trying to control the self-loathing that was threatening to overwhelm him, 'is a lover's mark. You admitted you shared my bedchamber last night. I take it I attacked you?' He had broken his oath. He was dishonoured. Worse, he had defiled the woman he desired more than anything in the world, the woman he loved. What he had done was unspeakably foul. No woman could ever forgive such a betrayal. 'I quite understand why you have recoiled from me,' he went on hurriedly, 'but I will make amends. Marguerite, will you do me the honour of becoming my wife?'

Her eyes widened. The colour had turned to almost pure green. She put a slightly nervous hand to her throat, clutching at the lace. 'I am very conscious of the honour you do me, Jacques, but I cannot accept your offer.'

He seized both her hands and held them fast. He loved her. He would spend his whole life making amends for what he had done, but he must not lose her now! 'I can understand that I have given you a disgust of me, but I will do everything in my power to be a good husband. Marguerite, you cannot refuse me. What if there should be a child?'

She smiled rather tightly. 'There will be no child. You did not rape me.'

He groaned at the sound of that terrible word. Then he realised what she had said. 'But I did attack you, did I not? That bruise is the proof of it. By God, I swear I shall never touch brandy again. Marguerite, I—'

Marguerite swallowed hard. She was going to have to tell him the truth. If she did not, he would believe the worst of himself. She could not bear that. His honour meant so very much to him. She must be ready to sacrifice her own honour, her own self-respect, for his. It was only fitting, for it was all her fault.

'Jacques, listen to me,' she began earnestly. She squeezed his fingers to gain his full attention. 'You did not attack me. You did not. I— You—' She could feel the tears of shame welling up into her eyes. She blinked hard. She refused to weep. 'Everything that happened between us was with my consent.'

'But—'

'You were three-parts insensible. You kissed me. That was all.' It was not all, but he need not learn the rest. 'I was a virgin yesterday. I remain a virgin today.'

He frowned down at her, trying to make sense of her words.

She thought she saw a flash of relief in his eyes. He would not feel obliged to offer marriage now. He would not offer for a woman without honour.

'I think perhaps we should return to the house,' she said quietly. She tried to release her hands, but he would not let her move.

'Wait. Please, Marguerite.'

She let her shoulders slump. She could not fight him any more. Her hands lay limp in his and she stared at the ground.

'Whatever I did, I dishonoured you and broke my oath. I must—'

'No, Jacques,' she whispered, 'you did not.' She hesitated, but it had to be said. 'You did nothing dishonourable. I came to you of my own free will.' She wrenched her hands free and started to run back to the house.

He caught her before she had gone more than a few steps and pulled her into his arms. She could not escape this time. It felt so warm, so wonderful, to be in his embrace that she did not try. It would be the last time.

He held her close with one arm and used the other to tip up her chin so that she could not avoid his gaze. 'You came to me of your own free will,' he said, very softly, caressing each word. 'Why, Marguerite?'

She tried to shake her head. The tears had begun to spill over. 'Because I—because I—' She could not say the words.

Jacques bent his head and kissed her. It was a gentle kiss at first, as if he were uncertain of how she might respond, as if he were afraid that she might reject him. But she could not. The moment his lips touched hers, her whole body went up in flames. She wrapped her arms around his neck and clung to him, returning kiss for kiss. She had not been able to say the words, but she could show him the passion she felt. And then she would let him go.

'Harrumph.' It was the little curé. He was standing on the path watching them, with a very smug look on his face. 'Perhaps you would like to continue your…er…discussion indoors?'

Jack was jubilant. Marguerite loved him! There was no other possible explanation for what she had done. Or for the way she had returned his kiss. He had found the woman of his dreams.

The woman of his dreams? Was that what had happened? Had it been real? Had Marguerite—?

That was something for later, when they were quite alone. He would tease her unmercifully for this. Once he had the right.

'We will travel together to England,' he announced.

'No,' Marguerite said firmly. 'We will travel as far as Dieppe only. Once you are safely on the boat for England, you will have no more need of me. I shall stay here. If I were to leave with you, I should become an outcast. I would never be able to go home. No, I shall remain here with Father Bertrand.'

Jack could not believe his ears. She was rejecting him. How could she, if she loved him?

The curé shook his head sadly and rose. 'I will leave you alone. I…er…I have things to do in the church.' He picked up some papers from the desk and scuttled out. He even closed the door.

Jack took that as an encouraging sign. He had Marguerite to himself, but probably not for long. He must make his case, and persuade her to marry him. He must weigh every word before he spoke. It would be so easy to frighten her away.

He thought hard. Why might she be unwilling to marry him? Because he was the son of a duke and she was only a weaver's daughter? No, it could not be that. Their stations were unequal, but only he knew that. He did not care that she was only a weaver's daughter. His family would not care, either. Dominic held the title, after all, and he was marrying a woman who had served in the Russian cavalry. Jack's marriage would be commonplace compared with Dominic's. Marguerite might be a *bourgeoise* by birth, but she had the bearing and manners of a lady. And the courage of a lion. His Amazon was more than fit to be the wife of Lord Jack Aikenhead.

It was a great deal to ask of her, even if she did love him. She would have to leave France, and her family, and everything she knew in order to join him in England. She knew no one there; she understood nothing of English ways; she probably did not even speak a word of the language. Perhaps she felt she had already made enough sacrifices for the sake of Jack's mission? Perhaps she did not love him enough to make so many more?

The single church bell began to toll.

Marguerite raised her head and looked solemnly at Jack. She did not smile. 'That bell reminds me how I have sinned, in thought and in deed. I will not go with you, Jacques, though I freely admit I will suffer once you are no longer by my side. There is a remedy, however. I shall go to the Abbaye des Dames.'

Jack rocked back in his chair. Then, at last, he understood. The bell was telling him what he should do. He must join honour to honour, and truth to truth. 'Marguerite, my darling girl, I think you would make a much better wife than a nun.' For a second, her eyes widened in shock. 'I love you with all my heart. Please say you will marry me.'

'Marriage? You want marriage? Truly?'

He smiled. His suspicions had been proved right. How could she have thought, even for a moment, that he would offer her anything less honourable than marriage? 'I love you, Marguerite, and I think you love me.' He paused. She blushed, but then she nodded, smiling shyly across at him. 'Precisely so. For two people so grievously afflicted, is not marriage the obvious and only solution?'

'Jacques, that is the most pompous marriage proposal I have ever received.'

He grinned. 'I hope, my love, that it is the *only* proposal you have ever received. And that you will never entertain another.'

He rose to his feet and drew her, unresisting, into his arms for the kiss that would bind them together always.

Marguerite sank into the corner of their carriage with a sigh of relief. It had been a long and very painful crossing. She was extremely glad to be back on dry land, even if it was not in her own country.

Jack leant his head back against the deeply cushioned seat and closed his eyes. In the feeble light from the inn yard, Marguerite could see that his face was returning to something like a normal colour. It had been a sickly green throughout their voyage, for he had suffered very much.

He recovered remarkably quickly. The carriage had barely reached the high road for London when he spoke. 'England.' He gestured vaguely in the direction of the countryside through which they were passing, ignoring the fact that there was not enough light to see any of it. 'This, my lady wife, will be your home from now on. I hope you do not dislike it?'

She laid her hand over his. 'Since I took a solemn vow, less than twenty-four hours ago, to love and honour my husband, how should I dare to dislike the home to which he brings me?'

'Very true. Very true.' He was trying to sound superior, but he failed to maintain his pose. After a moment, he began to laugh.

Marguerite smiled broadly. 'I can see that you are very much better. I can admit to you now that there were times, on board that filthy little boat, when I thought that we would never reach land. I worried for you, my love.' She squeezed his hand.

He responded by pulling her into the crook of his arm. 'My

seasickness looks dreadful, I admit. And it feels dreadful at the time, too. But it passes almost as soon as I step on to dry land. Brother Dominic used to accuse me of feigning illness in order to avoid duties on board his yacht.'

'Surely not?'

'Well, I exaggerate perhaps. A little. And Dominic does have a tisane than really helps. If I'd had it on the crossing, I probably wouldn't have frightened you quite so much.'

'What is in it?'

'Ginger, mostly, and some other herbs and spices. You can ask Dominic, if he ever returns from Russia. He's been gone for months now. Didn't even return to England after his marriage, which seemed rather strange. But I suppose he had his reasons. He usually does.'

Marguerite was not really paying attention. She was making a mental note to discover the receipt for Dominic's tisane and then to ensure that she always had the necessary ingredients by her. She was not prepared to admit it to Jack, but towards the end of their crossing she had been afraid that he might die.

She snuggled into his side and rearranged the fur rug so that it covered Jack's knees as well as her own. She sighed with pleasure. Jack was safe at last.

He began to play with her hair, picking up curls and rolling them round his fingers. 'You have beautiful hair, my Lady Jack.' His voice was a sensuous and seductive murmur.

Marguerite was tempted to respond in kind, but a carriage—even a closed carriage like this one—was not where she wished to give herself to her husband for the first time. She longed for him, but she wanted their first joining to be perfect. Everything in France had been done in too much of a hurry. The curé had insisted on marrying them on the spot. She had had to plead for time to don her favourite blue silk gown. And then to remove it again, before their mad dash to Dieppe to slip on to the first available boat. They had found one that claimed to be sailing to Brest. Its shifty captain had been more than willing to take a bribe to cross the Channel instead, and he had even provided a tiny, smelly cabin for his only passengers. It was no place for passion. In any case, Jack was much too ill to leave the open deck.

'Lady Jack.' She tried the title. 'Is that how I am to be called?'

'As my wife, you are Lady Jack Aikenhead. But, if you prefer, you could be Lady Marguerite. Your father was a marquis, after all, so you have the title in your own right.'

She was not sure which she preferred. She would consider it. Later.

'I'm sorry I didn't believe your mama when she said you were the daughter of the Marquise de Jerbeaux. At the time, it just seemed so very strange.'

'For a weaver's daughter, you mean?'

'Well, yes. In England, the aristocracy may make money from trade, very quietly, but none of us ever sullies our hands with actually making things.' He laughed in a slightly embarrassed way.

'In England, you have not had a revolution, followed by terror. Necessity changes much. For us, it was work, or starve.'

'Father Bertrand knew the truth, I collect? He did not seem surprised when he was noting down your parents' names.'

'The good father served my family for many years. He had to flee Lyons because of it. But I do think he was very surprised to learn that Mr Jacques was the son of a duke. As was I.'

'Now that, my love, is because you did not listen to your mama. She did tell you, you know.' He bent his head and began to kiss the side of her neck below her curls.

She could not prevent the tiny moan that rose in her throat. His touch conjured up memories of that night in Beauvais, when he had done precisely this, but remembered none of it next morning. One day, she would tell him what she had done. But not yet. Not now.

He was dropping a line of tiny kisses down her neck and throat. When he reached her bosom, he did not stop.

'Jacques! Jack! Someone will see!'

He did not raise his head. 'I doubt it, my love. Why do you think I insisted on a closed carriage rather than a chaise for this journey? I wanted you to myself for once.' He nuzzled the top of her breast. 'A husband has duties, you know, and so far I have signally failed to fulfil them.' He turned his head on one side for just long enough to leer up into her face. Then he spoiled the effect by laughing.

She put a hand to his hair and ran it carefully down the back of his head, mindful of his wounds. He did not wince away from her touch. He was definitely mending. There was no reason now why they should not be lovers, fully and sweetly.

That thought was too much for her fragile composure. Jack was her husband. She had the right to want him. 'Might we not rack up for the night, Jack?' she asked shyly. His tantalising kisses were beginning to drive her wild.

He stopped abruptly and lifted his head. With his free hand, he pulled her bodice back to its proper position. 'It was unfair of me to do that. I apologise.' When she began to protest, he touched a finger to her lips. 'Believe me, I should like nothing better than to find a comfortable inn and make you my true wife. But my mission—our mission—comes first. We have risked our lives to bring this information home. We must deliver it with all speed. Only then will we be free to take our pleasure of each other.'

'Oh. You are right, of course. I should have thought of—' That wicked memory surfaced again in her brain, beckoning seductively. There were other pleasures, too. With her free hand, she undid the buttons at the waistline of his coat and slid her hand inside, so that there was only his fine linen shirt between her fingers and his skin. He drew in his breath in a quick gasp. And then he sighed, relaxing against her touch. She put her lips to his ear and whispered. 'We may not stop for the night, but since we are confined together in this dark, private carriage, might there not be other ways of—?' She stopped short, shocked by her own daring, and buried her face in his shoulder.

He put a hand to her hair and caressed it. 'My love, I do believe I have married the most seductive woman in France. Yes, there are other ways. And since you require it of me, it shall be my pleasure to show you what they are.' He tipped up her face to bring his mouth down on hers. 'Starting now.'

Epilogue

ﾟ~~~~~~

Aikenhead Park, England—July 1815

'Poor Father Bertrand. He was adamant that he had to marry us before we left for Dieppe, but it came as rather a shock when he found out who I was.' Jack grinned at the company assembled round the dinner table.

'I am not surprised,' his mother said. 'It came as a shock to me that you should have proposed to Marguerite without first telling her the truth about yourself, Jack.'

Jack shrugged and reached out to take Marguerite's hand. 'She was prepared to marry Louis Jacques, a simple English gentleman travelling under an assumed name. I took that as a great compliment, especially when I discovered that she was the daughter of a French marquis.'

'I suppose that was another shock for the poor priest,' the Dowager said with an indulgent smile for Marguerite.

'Oh, no, ma'am.' Marguerite had begun to feel quite at home with the Aikenhead banter, after more than three months at the Park. With the help of the Dowager, Marguerite's rather shaky English was improving by the day. 'Father Bertrand has always known the truth. It was because of his loyalty to the Jerbeaux family that he had to flee to Normandy. In the years after the Terror, it was very dangerous to have the wrong allegiances.'

'And it will be dangerous now,' Leo said seriously, 'both for the curé and for your family, Marguerite.' Leo, the second Aikenhead brother, was presiding over the table. 'France is in turmoil since Bonaparte's defeat at Waterloo. There are reprisals everywhere. From all sides. Wellington has curbed the worst of the excesses in Paris, but in other cities—' He stopped short and looked round in surprise at his wife.

Sophie ignored him and said innocently, 'Leo exaggerates, I am sure, Marguerite.'

'No doubt,' Cousin Harriet Penworthy said, raising her lorgnette to her eyes. 'By the way, Sophie, did you kick Leo's ankle then, or was it sufficient just to step on his foot?'

'I—'

'Cousin Harriet, I swear you go out of your way to prove to these poor ladies that you are the most outrageous woman alive.' Leo smiled encouragingly at Marguerite and then at Sophie. 'But since you ask, I will cheerfully admit that my dear wife kicked me. Hard. If it were not for the fact that she is wearing evening slippers, I should no doubt have a broken ankle.'

'Nothing more than you deserve,' Cousin Harriet retorted, but she could not conceal her smile. She was a very outspoken old lady, as Marguerite had soon discovered, but she loved the Aikenhead family very much. She had quickly taken the two new members to her heart. It was enough for her that Sophie and Marguerite were loved by Leo and Jack, and that they loved her boys in return.

Within a week of her arrival, Marguerite had become fair game for Cousin Harriet's sharp tongue. That, she was solemnly assured by her laughing husband, was a singular mark of distinction. At first, Marguerite had not known how to respond, but, with Jack's encouragement, she had learned to reply in kind. And to enjoy the challenge. Sophie, more recently arrived with Leo from their own estate, was just beginning to learn that same lesson.

The butler entered, with a bevy of footmen at his back. 'Shall I remove the cloth, your Grace?'

The Dowager glanced round at her guests. 'Thank you, Withering.' In next to no time, the table had been cleared and all the servants had withdrawn, leaving the family alone. The Dowager smiled down the table at Leo and then across as Jack. She rose elegantly to her feet. 'I suppose, ladies, that we had best withdraw and leave these two…um…gentlemen to their port.'

'I'd much rather you remained, Mama,' said a voice from the doorway behind her.

'Dominic!' The Dowager spun round in her place. Leo and Jack sprang to their feet, exclaiming in unison, and then rushed to welcome the new arrival.

Marguerite had risen with the Dowager, but now she felt more than a little awkward. This new arrival was clearly Dominic, Duke of Calder, Jack's oldest brother. The resemblance was uncanny. Dominic was taller, and a little broader than Jack, but otherwise they could have been twins. Yet there was something more than a little daunting about Dominic. He had an air. She was sure he could be intimidating in a way that her beloved Jack would always fail to achieve. For Jack was always too ready to laugh.

Marguerite glanced across at Sophie, standing in her place on the opposite side of the table. She looked as uncertain as Marguerite felt. Marguerite smiled tentatively and received a broader smile in return. They understood each other. They were not yet truly members of this extraordinary family. Their turn would come, once the initial uproar was over. There was no doubt that the three Aikenhead brothers could make a great deal of noise.

Dominic called for quiet. The hubbub and questions quickly subsided. 'Mama, Harriet, you will allow me to present my wife, Alex, Duchess of Calder.' He held out his hand to a dainty little lady with reddish-brown curls threaded with ribbon. She came forward a little hesitantly and curtsied elegantly to the Dowager. 'Alex,' Dominic continued, 'this is my mother, the Dowager Duchess, and my cousin, Miss Harriet Penworthy.' The new Duchess curtsied again. 'And these two so-called gentlemen,' he continued, with a soft laugh, 'are my brothers, Leo and Jack.'

Jack caught up Alex's hand and carried it to his lips. 'No need to introduce me, Dominic, for we—'

'Jack Aikenhead!' Cousin Harriet was outraged. She stormed down to the end of the table and put herself between Jack and Dominic's wife. 'I clearly did not tan your hide well enough when I had the chance. Where are your manners, pray? This lady is the wife of the head of the family. Since you are now meeting her *for the first time*, it is your duty to allow yourself to be properly introduced.'

Jack started, and coloured. Marguerite thought he looked deliciously confused. He was being his usual self, generous and direct. He was forgetting that, while the whole family might know that Alex had visited them before in her guise as a Russian army officer, it could never be spoken of, even at private gatherings such as this. No one must so much as hint that Alex was anything other than what she appeared, a beautiful, elegant, aristocratic lady.

'Oh.' Jack swallowed and then bowed low over Alex's hand. 'I ask you to forgive my impertinence, sister,' he said apologetically. 'I am delighted to meet you at last. Dominic is a very lucky man.'

Alex dipped him a tiny curtsy. There was a very mischievous smile on her lips. It remained and widened while Dominic introduced her, rather more sedately, to Leo.

'Well,' said the Dowager with satisfaction, looking round the table once all the introductions had been made, 'that is splendid.' Dominic sat at the head, as was his right, with Alex at the opposite end. The Dowager had happily yielded up her place and moved alongside Alex. 'Would you wish me to ring for some refreshments, my dear? You and Dominic must be hungry after your journey.'

Withering appeared in answer to her summons. He stood impassively while Alex instructed him, in English with a slight Scottish burr, to bring a light supper for the Duke and herself. 'At once, your Grace,' Withering said, bowing.

'Well done, my dear.' The Dowager patted Alex's hand.

Alex was trying not to laugh. 'Dominic has had me practising for the last six months, ma'am,' she said softly. 'He tells me I am improving,' she added wryly.

'He is an impudent puppy,' the Duchess said behind her hand. 'I hope you intend to cure him of that?'

Alex's only answer was an enigmatic smile.

Withering had not withdrawn. He was still standing in the doorway, looking uncertain. He cleared his throat and took a pace forward. 'Might I be so bold as to ask your Grace what I am to do with Lord Dexter?'

At the far end of the table, Dominic burst out laughing. 'Oh, Lord, I forgot all about Ben. We've towed him all the way from London, and now I've left him cooling his heels in the hall. Send him in, Withering, and make that supper for three!'

It took a considerable time for all the questions to be asked and answered, for Dominic had been away from England for almost a year. 'I am most curious to discover,' he said wryly, 'how a couple of ne'er-do-wells like Leo and Jack managed to persuade these beautiful ladies to marry them. It's more than an old greybeard like me can fathom.'

That produced considerable protest, followed by a colourful recital of Leo's adventures in Vienna and Jack's in France. The account of the two courtships was rather more restrained.

Marguerite could not wait any longer. 'Herr Benn,' she began, but stopped to correct herself. 'Lord Dexter, have you news of my mother and sister? The rumours from France have been so worrying. I am afraid—'

'They were well, and safe, when I left Lyons, ma'am. And I am sure that will still be the case.'

'How long ago did you leave Lyons?'

'I had only just arrived in London when Dominic found me.' He paused. 'I left Lyons a little over a month ago, I suppose. I had to come out through Spain, I'm afraid. Unlike the Aikenheads, my French isn't good enough to allow me to pass for a Frenchman. If it were, I should have travelled through France, and brought your sister out with me. Your mother, too, of course.'

Marguerite looked closely at the man she had always thought of as Herr Benn. He too, it transpired, was an English aristocrat. And he seemed to be more than a little self-conscious when he spoke about Suzanne. 'Travelling with my mother can be very difficult,' she admitted. 'The things she says are sometimes unwise.'

Lord Dexter seemed relieved by her words. 'We discussed what to do and we decided, Suzanne and I, that it would be safest if I went alone. Suzanne promised that she would keep the family close until I am able to return.'

'You are going back, sir?' Marguerite was surprised for a moment, but then she remembered the hours that Suzanne had spent tending Herr Benn. They clearly had a deep understanding, those two. If only—

Lord Dexter drew himself up proudly. 'It is my duty. I cannot leave my wife, and my mother-in-law, unprotected.'

'Oh! Oh, that is wonderful!' Marguerite exclaimed. He had married Suzanne. Marguerite felt a great surge of joy for her sister's happiness. Suzanne had been in love with Herr Benn from the first moment she set eyes on him. And now all her instincts had been proved right. It was perfect.

The rest of the family seemed to agree, for they all offered hearty congratulations.

'When do you plan to leave, Ben?' Dominic asked.

'As soon as I've collected together enough blunt to pay for the journey. I'll need to take a few stout lads with me as well. There's no knowing what ruffians we might encounter between Lyons and the coast. I prefer to be prepared.'

Dominic leaned back in his chair and smiled lazily, first at Leo and then at Jack. Leo responded with a tiny nod. Jack winked. And then he grinned. Dominic sighed theatrically. 'And to think that I believed you had grown up, Jack.' He shook his head. 'Perhaps we should leave you behind?'

Marguerite could see that Dominic was waiting for Jack to rise to the bait. But Jack did not. He shrugged his shoulders and said, simply, 'So be it, Ace. You are the leader.'

'Well, well, well!' Dominic was shaking his head. 'I never expected that.'

Jack grinned back. Then he turned to Ben. 'I understand, sir,' he began in an atrocious country accent, 'that you be looking for stout fellows to take to France with ye. I be pretty good with these 'ere fists. 'Ow much was you planning to pay?'

Everyone round the table began to laugh, even Cousin Harriet.

'I think, Ben, that the decision is made,' Dominic said. 'The wars may be over, but there is one last mission for the Aiken-head Honours. We shall travel to Lyons together—Ace, King, Knave and Ten—and bring home your wife, and the Marquise.

She may live in comfort here at the Park, with her own servants around her, for as long as she desires.'

Marguerite tried to thank him, but he brushed her aside with a warm smile. 'No need, my dear. They are family. As are you.'

Dominic rose to his feet and raised his glass. 'A toast, ladies and gentlemen. To the Aikenhead Honours and the fair ladies they have married. And to the success of our final mission!'

Chairs scraped on the polished wooden floor. Everyone rose. 'The Aikenhead Honours!' they cried in chorus. 'And success!'

Author's Note

Napoleon Bonaparte sailed from Elba to land in France at 5 p.m. on Wednesday, 1 March 1815, fulfilling the promise he had made a year earlier to return *with the violets*. He was careful to avoid the well-defended port of Toulon. Instead, he landed at Golfe-Juan, between Cannes and Antibes, with about 1,000 men, more than half of them from the Imperial Guard. They spent the next two days scrambling over the mountains, en route for Gap and the road to Grenoble and Lyons. Napoleon had judged, correctly, that the King's forces would not look for him away from the main routes. By the time news of his escape reached Paris, three days after he landed, Napoleon was already nearly 100 miles inland. Thus began the Hundred Days.

The historical events I have shown in *His Forbidden Liaison* happened much as I have described. When Napoleon met his first opposing royalist troops, south of Grenoble, he did challenge them to shoot him, though the sources differ on precisely what he said. The soldiers rallied to him, as did the regiment that was waiting for him in Grenoble. In Lyons, the troops changed sides even before Napoleon arrived; the

King's brother, who was supposed to lead them against Napoleon, decamped for Paris instead. Napoleon remained some days in Lyons, issuing decrees and summoning the parliament to Paris. He also summoned his wife and son back from Vienna though, if you have read Leo's story, *His Reluctant Mistress*, you will know that that did not go quite according to plan.

By the time Napoleon reached Paris, on Monday, 20 March 1815, his journey had become a triumphal royal progress. Not a shot had been fired. The regiments sent to oppose him along the route from Fontainebleau to Paris presented arms instead. At 10.30 p.m. he was carried shoulder-high into the Tuileries palace. His eyes were shut, and he was smiling.

The news took a long time to reach other European capitals, since they did not have the French telegraph system. In London, Jack's eyewitness testimony would have been vital. In Paris, the Duchess of Courland set out on the same day that the King fled the country. It took her more than five days to reach Vienna with the news. That was on Good Friday. By Easter Sunday, 25 March, 1815, a new Allied coalition had been formed and the Duke of Wellington had been appointed commander-in-chief. Barely a week later, on 4 April 1815, Wellington was back in Brussels to take command of the army.

By the end of June, it was over. Napoleon had lost the battle of Waterloo—on 18 June 1815—though, as Wellington admitted, it had been a *damned close-run thing.* By the middle of July, Napoleon was on a British ship bound for England, and later, for exile in St Helena; King Louis XVIII had been restored and Paris was an occupied city, filled with foreign troops. The situation was dangerous, and volatile. The Parisians were ready to rise against the occupiers, and royalists were clamouring for blood. No one was safe. Even royalists were attacked for failing to oppose Napoleon with sufficient vigour. Republicans and Bonapartists were also ready to fight, since they felt they had nothing to lose. Many people died in revenge attacks as gangs went on the rampage in cities across France. But down in Lyons, Ben Dexter managed to protect the woman he loved. His story, and Suzanne's, will be available as a Harlequin e-book in the *Undone!* series.

* * * * *

In honor of our 60th anniversary,
Harlequin® American Romance® is celebrating
by featuring an all-American male each month,
all year long with
MEN MADE IN AMERICA!
This June, we'll be featuring American men
living in the West.

Here's a sneak preview of
THE CHIEF RANGER by Rebecca Winters.

Chief Ranger Vance Rossiter has to confront the sister of a
man who died while under Vance's watch...and also
confront his attraction to her.

"Chief Ranger Rossiter?" The sight of the woman who'd stepped inside Vance's office brought him to his feet. "I'm Rachel Darrow. Your secretary said I should come right in."

"Please," he said, walking around his desk to shake her hand. At a glance he estimated she was in her midtwenties. Her feminine curves did wonders for the pale blue T-shirt and jeans she was wearing. "Ranger Jarvis informed me there's a young boy with you."

The unfriendly expression in her beautiful green eyes caught him off guard. "Yes," was her clipped reply. "When we arrived in Yosemite the ranger told me I couldn't go anywhere in the park until I talked to you first."

"That's right."

"Knowing you wanted this meeting to be private, he offered to show my nephew around Headquarters."

So this woman was the victim's sister.... "What's his name?"

"Nicky."

The boy who haunted Vance's dreams now had a name. "How old is he?"

"He turned six three weeks ago. Were you the man in charge when my brother and sister-in-law were killed?"

"Yes. To tell you I'm sorry for what happened couldn't begin to convey my feelings."

The woman's gaze didn't flicker. "I won't even try to describe mine. Just tell me one thing. Was their accident preventable?"

"Yes," he answered without hesitation.

"In other words, the people working under you fell asleep on your watch and two lives were snuffed out as a result."

Hearing it put like that, he had to set the record straight. "My staff had nothing to do with it. I, myself, could have prevented the loss of life."

Ms. Darrow's expression hardened. "So you admit culpability."

"Yes. I take full blame."

A look of pain crossed over her features. "You can just stand there and admit it?" Her cry echoed that of his own tortured soul.

"Yes." He sucked in his breath.

"I work for a cruise line. Aboard ship, it's the captain's responsibility to maintain rigid safety regulations. If a disaster like that had happened while he was in charge he would have been relieved of his command and never given another ship again."

Rachel Darrow couldn't know she was preaching to the converted. "If you've come to the park with the intention of bringing a lawsuit against me for negligence, maybe you should." It would only be what he deserved.

"Maybe I will."

In the next instant, she wheeled around and hurried out of his office. Vance could have gone after her, but it would cause a scene, something he was loath to do for a variety of reasons. In the first place, he needed to cool down before he approached her again.

The discovery of the Darrows' frozen bodies had affected every ranger in the park. A little boy had been orphaned—a boy whose aunt was all he had left.

* * * * *

Will Rachel allow Vance to explain—
and will she let him into her heart?
Find out in
THE CHIEF RANGER
Available June 2009
from Harlequin® American Romance®.

We'll be spotlighting a different series every month
throughout 2009 to celebrate our 60th anniversary.

Look for Harlequin®
American Romance® in June!

Join us for a year-long celebration of the rugged
American male! From cops to cowboys—
Men Made in America has the hero
you've been dreaming about!

Look for

The Chief Ranger

by Rebecca Winters, on sale in June!

You're invited to join our Tell Harlequin Reader Panel!

By joining our new reader panel you will:

- Receive Harlequin® books—they are FREE and yours to keep with no obligation to purchase anything!
- Participate in fun online surveys
- Exchange opinions and ideas with women just like you
- Have a say in our new book ideas and help us publish the best in women's fiction

In addition, you will have a chance to win great prizes and receive special gifts! See Web site for details. Some conditions apply. Space is limited.

To join, visit us at
www.TellHarlequin.com.

Escape Around the World

Dream destinations, whirlwind weddings!

Honeymoon with the Boss
by
JESSICA HART

Top tycoon Tom Maddison is used to calling the
shots—until his convenient marriage falls through.
But rather than waste his honeymoon, he'll take
his boardroom to the beach and bring his oh-so-
sensible secretary Imogen on a tropical business
trip! But will Tom finally see the sexy woman
that prudent Imogen truly is?

Available in June wherever books are sold.

Silhouette Desire

MAN of the MONTH

USA TODAY bestselling author

ANN MAJOR

THE BRIDE HUNTER

Former marine turned P.I. Connor Storm is hired to find the long-lost Golden Spurs heiress, Rebecca Collins, aka Anna Barton. Once Connor finds her, desire takes over and he marries her within two weeks! On their wedding night he reveals he knows her true identity and she flees. When he finds her again, can he convince her that the love they share is worth fighting for?

**Available June
wherever books are sold.**

REQUEST YOUR FREE BOOKS!

Harlequin® Historical
Historical Romantic Adventure!

™

2 FREE NOVELS PLUS 2 FREE GIFTS!

HH09R

nocturne™

New York Times Bestselling Author

REBECCA BRANDEWYNE

FROM THE MISTS OF WOLF CREEK

Hallie Muldoon suspects that her grandmother
has special abilities, but her sudden death
forces Hallie to return to Wolf Creek, where
details emerge of a spell cast. Local farmer
Trace Coltrane and the wolf that prowls around
the farmhouse both appear out of nowhere, and
a killer has Hallie in his sights. With no other
choice, Hallie relies on Trace for help,
not knowing if the mysterious Trace is a
mesmerizing friend or a deadly foe....

Available June wherever books are sold.

COMING NEXT MONTH FROM

HARLEQUIN®
HISTORICAL

Available May 26, 2009

- **STETSONS, SPRING AND WEDDING RINGS**
  by **Jillian Hart, Judith Stacy and Stacey Kayne**
  (Western)
  Meet Clara, Brynn and Constance as they go west. They are looking fo
  new lives, and three forceful men are determined to be their new loves!
  They want to keep these courageous women where they belong—in
  their towns, in their hearts and, most of all, in their beds....

- **LORD BRAYBROOK'S PENNILESS BRIDE**
  by **Elizabeth Rolls**
  (Regency)
  Viscount Braybrook is paying Christiana Daventry to keep her wayward
  brother far away from his stepsister. But when he realizes he wants to
  keep Christy *intimately* close, suddenly his heart is at risk from the one
  thing money can't buy—love!

- **THE SURGEON'S LADY**
  by **Carla Kelly**
  (Regency)
  Lady Laura Taunton seeks solace from her unhappy past by nursing the
  wounded, but naval surgeon Philemon Brittle would rather she sought
  pleasure in his arms! Can he convince her that marriage is the truest
  path to happiness...and passion?

- **BEDDED BY THE WARRIOR**
  by **Denise Lynn**
  (Medieval)
  Newly wedded, Lady Sarah of Remy has a hidden purpose—one that
  shouldn't involve being passionately bedded by her warrior husband!
  William of Bronwyn also has his own reasons for the marriage, but his
  secretive wife is too alluring to resist....